T0198858

# INSTINCTS:
# RISE OF THE
# INSTINCTSION

STEFAN G. JOHNSON

authorHOUSE®

AuthorHouse™
1663 Liberty Drive
Bloomington, IN 47403
www.authorhouse.com
Phone: 1 (800) 839-8640

Published by AuthorHouse 05/10/2018

ISBN: 978-1-5462-4142-3 (sc)
ISBN: 978-1-5462-4141-6 (e)

Library of Congress Control Number: 2018905552

Print information available on the last page.

This book is printed on acid-free paper.

INSTINCTS: RISE OF THE INSTINCTSION
TO MY SISTER, COUSINS, AND FRIENDS

# CHAPTER 1

"All I'm asking for is a quarter."

"Yeah, a quarter of a trillion dollars?" he chuckled. "You're funny Charles."

"Listen, Jonothan, if it works then it could replace all armies and we could make a fortune." Charles excitedly leaned forward in the short office chair.

"You mean that *you* could make a fortune!" Jonothan said irritably. He put his fingers to his temples and hoped that his headache of a brother would just leave and disappear for another few years.

Jonothan stood up and turned around to look out of the giant window that took up the entire wall. He watched the cars with his company's labels and logos. He gazed and marveled at how his skyscrapers held up the sky and how the entire city held his technology wherever they went. In every pocket and in every step.

"No," said Charles. "We do this one together. And there's more to it this time." Charles leaned back in the chair.

Jonothan stayed at the window. "This isn't like when we were kids, Charles. Times have changed. I'm the head of the world's biggest technology company. I've put every day and every minute of my life into this. I can't just walk away from this. Besides, what do you know about fortune? I'm literally the richest man on the planet. And you...you, Charles..."

"Jonothan-" Charles started but was interrupted.

"You're still trying to play these *childish* games. It doesn't work anyway, Charles. Just...get out of my office," Jonothan said as he finally looked away from the window and at Charles.

"Jon, you're on the council. All you have to do is-"

"GET OUT OF MY OFFICE!" Jonothan spun around and flew to his desk. His fist pounded the desk with a loud slam that echoed through the entire building.

Charles stood up and walked out of the annoyingly clean white office clutching papers in his hand. Papers that, in his mind, could change the world. "If he won't help me," said Charles to himself. "Then I'll do it myself." He ran out of the building and into his car. He drove to his small apartment and sat at his desk.

He stared at his phone and at the pile of papers. "With a little help, of course." He said.

He picked up the phone and called several people. To all of whom he said, "activate" and hung up.

The activation had everyone take what little money they had and put it together. They figured it out when they were all just kids; the leaders of the group being Charles and Jonothan.

<T1 A2 S3 K4 S5>

Two months later a building, the size of Charles' 200 square foot apartment building was built. It was just the beginning, but it would be the main room in the end. Much like a maze, the inside of the full building would be designed to confuse. The building, in general, was difficult to locate due to the fact that it was located in the most remote area in Alaska.

"Well, boss," said one of Charles' new employees, Lance. "How do we get started?"

Charles sat back in his black leather office chair and thought. Then he leaned forward and said, "First, I'm President now. If we are creating a new world, a *safe haven*, then I am President. Gardo, you take the van and pick up the first specimen. *Only* the first. Lance, go to the first door on the right and mark it: MANDS-T1. Joan, make some clothes. We need hospital gowns and regular clothes. Yellow is the first one's color. And Harry...."

"Yes, Sir?" Harry said.

"Stay out of the way. You are to have no contact with them until I say so. And when that time comes you will tell them *exactly* what I tell you and do *exactly* as I say." Charles pointed his finger at Harry to show how serious he was. It was just a finger, but it showed that there would be much worse if he didn't listen.

"Yes, sir," Harry said with his head down.

Charles/President swiveled his chair around and faced the window. The building was at the bottom of a mountain and rested in a saddle between two hills and a giant dirt mountain. Through the window, the entire mountain was visible.

"Tomorrow, history begins." And they all left to start their missions.

&lt;T1 A2 S3 K4 S5&gt;

The next day everyone came back with their jobs done. Gardo met President in his office. "Did you get her?" Asked President.

"I got her," said Gardo. "She is on her way to her room as we speak. She's asleep and dressed in the attire you requested. The first door from the right."

They walked down to the room marked: MANDS-T1. President excitedly followed. He tried his best to contain his excitement. He was finally doing it.

They opened the door. Inside was a blonde girl in a white hospital gown with yellow trim laying on a gurney. Her blonde hair reached well beyond her waist and hung lifelessly hung over the sides of the table. She was hooked up to a machine. The machine was going through her DNA strands. Strands flew around and occasionally one would freeze, enhance and label sequences in its helix. They looked like Watson and Crick models.

Lance, the head scientists got his clipboard and his bag of equipment. "What do we do with this one, Sir?" President stood and watched the DNA strands on the monitor screen swim and dance around. An idea came to him for her ability.

A machine with a robotic arm was wheeled next to the girl. The arm reached out and grabbed her left forearm. A metal table constructed itself just below her arm and her arm was held to the table. Another arm came out of the table. It had two 'fingers' on it. One was an oddly shaped needle and the other was a tattoo needle.

The oddly shaped needle inserted itself into the girls' arm and formed a letter under the skin. The other finger of the robotic arm jabbed at the

3

other needle through the skin and left ink as the other heated up. The arm was burning the skin inside of her am and tattooing it on the outside. The girl unconsciously grimaced and pulled on her arm as the machine finished the first letter.

M.

The machine did it again next to the M on her arm. Insert, shape, burn, tattoo. A. Insert, shape, burn, tattoo. N. Insert, shape, burn, tattoo. D. Insert, shape, burn, tattoo. S. The machine gave the girl her entire mark, MANDS-T1, and then released her. The machine collapsed into a metal pole and hid in the corner until it was needed again.

Lance noted a few things before President made his decision on her enhancement. "Blood is O positive, age is 17 and sir...she is blind. Something that can allow two enhancements. Might I suggest-"

President turned to walk back down the hall to his office but before he left he said, "Make her a changeling. A shapeshifter, if you will. I'll be in my office. I need to make a call."

President chose to make her a shapeshifter because with her being blind, the DNA from different animals will agree more and change her mind easier, starting with the eyes. If she wants to see, she will be forced to use her ability for the ability to see, at least. Being forced to use her ability every day will increase her ability and make her stronger.

President went to his office and called Jonothan.

"Join me and you get double of what I wanted two months ago."

"Why would I do that? Did you not hear a word I said? Especially the 'richest man on the planet' part? I don't have time for this, Charles," said Jonothan.

There was silence over the phone for a while. "All you have to do is combine your company with mine, bring some of your people, and make things...techy."

Jonothan sighed, "Anything else, Charles?"

"I know your secret. I am not an idiot," Said President. They both hung up without another word.

Jonothan always wanted to do what Charles was doing but never had much faith in it. Now that it was actually happening, he wanted a piece of their old childhood dream. Charles knew that. He kept in mind that Jonothan may have turned it down because he was too busy worrying about his own specimens. If Jonothan wanted in, all he would have to do is add better technology to his brother's company. If Jonathan already started, the question came to light:

*How far ahead was Jonothan?*

Three months later the two companies were merged. The building that Jonothan was in charge of, Jonothan Industries, was just a few hundred yards away from MANDS on the other side of a mountain. A tunnel was put through the mountain for easier access between the two building. The buildings may not have been attached but the two companies were working together.

Jonothan designed every bit of technology that everyone used and helped the varies branches of the military. President/Charles used to have the company that did research on everything. He was the fifth evolution of Google and studied everything Especially science. He was a member of the world's smartest scientists. Their latest success was developing a cure for the newest kind of cancer. The cancer destroyed every white blood cell in its host and fought back against antibodies. It was highly contagious and basically turned its hosts into the walking dead.

Now the two could work together and research their projects to make a better military with better equipment in a better, safer, world.

The next day an inspector came into Charles' building to check on how everything was working out. He walked tall down the confusing hallway and ignored the eyes of every scientist he passed. He walked right up to President's office.

"How can I help you?" President asked. The inspector took his shoes off outside of the office as a sign of respect and found a seat in the blinding white-tiled office and got straight to business. He didn't want to muddy President's office but showed no concern for the scientist's paths.

"No, No. Make yourself comfortable" President said sarcastically. The inspector took out a stack of papers and threw them onto the desk. President shifted his eyes onto them, so it looked like he had no interest in them. The top page was about the condition of the building.

"How many?" the inspector asked as he sat in the available seat.

"I have one to start out with," said President. "One for now and after the tests are done we will see what she is capable-"

"*She?*" The inspector interrupted.

"Yes," President continued. "We will see what she is capable of and how much we can control her."

The inspector put a disapproving look on his face threw another stack of papers on the desk, but President still didn't pick up a single paper. Instead, he opened his desk and pulled out a small silver chest. He opened it and reached inside.

Afraid of what could be inside, the inspector sat straight up; ready to jump up and run.

Instead of a gun or a knife President pulled out a glowing white orb. He threw it over the inspector's head and it froze in mid-air. He swiped his hand and it opened into digital documents from wall to wall.

"Here is my plan, with every intention made perfectly clear. Read, leave, and keep to yourself." President said with a smile growing from ear to ear from his new-found power. If the inspector approved of what Charles was doing, Charles would have unlimited power to do whatever he wanted, how he wanted. Charles was more than confident that he would get approved.

<T1 A2 S3 K4 S5>

It took a while to read all of the documents, but the inspector was impressed. "You were right Char-" the inspector was interrupted.

"I'm President now. It's got a nice ring to it and because of the project, it fits. You see-"

The inspector continued, "Well whoever you are, you were right. Intentions *were* clear. I've assessed all information and I think the government will be very interested to see how this plays out." The inspector went through the notes he took on the documents. "Your first specimen will be the girl; her brand will be MANDS-T1. And-"

"Not trying to be rude Mr. Inspector but, I am very aware of my own intentions. And I also recall telling you to read, leave and keep to yourself. You've done your reading." President smiled and looked at the door. "Have a nice day, Sir."

The inspector got up and walked through the digital documents that covered the doorway and through the door; grabbing his muddy shoes on the way out. He smacked them on the doorway as he left. Pieces of mud and dirt littered the threshold of the office.

President leaned back in his chair and looked at his own documents. He held his hand up and the hologram returned to ball-form and back to his hand. He put it back in the chest but didn't put the chest back. The blinding white light emitted from the chest and cast a square beam towards the ceiling and lit up the already bright office.

He laced his fingers on his white desk that matched everything else in the entire building perfectly. The desk was designed to make it seem to emerge from the floor. He couldn't help but look at the papers again. He picked them up and began to read. The first few sentences, and diagrams did not make him happy.

They consisted of information about how the government would control all of President's work and he would be a part of a large council. One of five hundred and fifty in charge. He would have very little control over the program and there would be only two specimens. President could tell that Jonothan had something to do with this plan.

Just then the new person President planned on hiring, arrived. President spoke his mind.

"Damn government. You give 'em an idea and they make it their own. Not to mention all the waiting I would have to do," He looked at the young man standing in the doorway. "Please. Take a seat." He leaned to the right side of his desk and dropped the inspector's papers in a hole in the floor. The Incinerator.

The young man stepped in and sat in the lone chair in front of the desk. "I've read the files and there is one thing I want to add."

President's friendly smile disappeared. "And what is *that*?" He asked

The young man leaned forward, pushed his glasses to the bridge of his nose and said, "Four more." He leaned back, laced his fingers behind his head and smiled.

"Why four?" President asks. "If you truly *did* read the files, you would know that we call for six to get things going. That is *five* more."

The young man chuckled and said, "That is why we clone the most successful specimen. Or at least split the power of a dangerous one. If one is *really* bad, make a clone of it and manipulate their traits to balance out the other."

President nodded curiously and thought about it a little more. "We could capture four more, turn one into a complete clone of another, and make *that one* our eyes and ears while the others are doing their final test. Possibly keep switching them out during the final test."

The young man leaned forward and waited for President's final say.

"And I know just the man to do it," President said. He reached into his desk and pulled out a tablet. The young man lifted his finger and was ready to sign. President stared at him until he put his finger down. When the young man put his finger down, President slid the tablet across the desk. "It's a new hand signature. A contract really." President explained. The man put his right hand on the tablet and a white scanning light, from his fingers to the ball of his palm and from his thumb to his pinkie, went off under his hand.

The tablet spoke his name in a computer monotoned voice and flashed a blinding white as it spoke. "Thank-you-Ja-son," it said. The young man who was Jason stood up and prepared to walk out. President stopped him before he did.

"Did you really read the files?" President asked. Jason nodded in reply. "Then tell me, Jackson," "Jason" he corrected.

"Whatever. Tell me. What power do we give her and how do we do it?" President asked curiously.

"Well, Sir, she is getting the power of shapeshifting. A changeling I believe it is. I will be accessing her DNA strands and weaving in DNA of different animals. And we will go into her brain so that, when she is ready, she can turn into objects and other people as well. Even things that shouldn't exist. If she can think it, she can be it."

President sat back and smiled. "I'm impressed. Here's what we are going to do. I'm going to promote you to a very high position. Hire more scientists to put under yourself and then seek out the second specimen. I'll start you out with a challenge."

President reached into the chest and swirled his hand around like he was scooping something from the bottom. The white light dimmed and turned yellow. A little more swirling and the yellow light turned blue. President cuffed the light and pulled his hand out of the box. The blue light turned into particles that hovered in President's hands. It then semi-solidified into an orb similar to the white one that was previously in the chest.

"And take this." He threw the blue orb at Jason. Jason ducked. He turned around and wondered where the crashing and shattering glass was. Then he faced President and saw the blue orb floating just a few inches from his face.

Jason rolled his eyes and snatched the orb from the air. He put it in his lab coat pocket and left. His pocket glowed blue as he walked down the hall. He stopped before he got too far and turned around.

"There's also a Lisa or Liza or whatever her name is waiting outside too. The guards won't let her in. I had difficulty getting in as well," Jason said.

"Send her in," President said with his arms open. Jason left.

President spun around in his chair and faced the giant window in his office. The sun was just rising over the mountain that he made. He built the mountain as the final test for the specimens. Not a single blade of grass or sapling was growing yet. He still had plenty of time.

After the mountain is grown, and the specimens are ready, they will be tested on the mountain. If they survive the elements and each other, they will be brought down and cloned. The originals will have figured everything out, so they will be killed. With the army of enhanced created with the instinct of their abilities, Charles can ensure world peace until they can get to a planet that isn't dying.

"This is going to be brilliant," said President with an evil smirk.

# Chapter 2

# PRESIDENT

Today the girl marked: MANDS-T1 gets her power. The process will take a little over a month. We will access her DNA strands and weave in animal DNA. It will all be connected to her mind so that she will be able to think of an animal and turn into *that* animal when she is ready.

I'm still waiting for the scientists that Jason hired to get back to me with the second specimen. He is having great difficulty finding her.

I am starting to regret all that I did with him. I made him head of most of what Jonothan and I have so far. That means he is a general of our very small private army and manager of the new technology that we are working on. It's a lot to do for a new guy who doesn't fully understand what we are doing but I think it's the best way to build trust.

In the future, he will still be in charge of a section of our army and run our technology but not nearly as much. That is if he makes it that long.

<T1 A2 S3 K4 S5>

A month later the surgery on MANDS-T1 was complete and she was resting. I was still waiting for the next specimen. I was in my still and silent office when the door burst open. It was MANDS-T1.

"Do you want help?" She said. Her voice cracked quietly due to being asleep for over a month. She walked in and stumbled to the chair in my office. The legs of the chair screeched as it was pushed across the floor.

Her white hospital gown swayed side to side and the yellow collar part of the gown rubbed against her neck.

Each step her bare feet took, slapped against the tiled floor. "I can help you" she quietly cracked again.

I leaned forward and found myself unable to speak. She was supposed to be asleep. She had only just gotten out of surgery.

*How could she help me? What would she help me with?*

Two guards that were trying to find her finally found her in my office. They ran to the door and were preparing to drag her out. They slowed as they got to the doorway and looked at me as if asking permission. Without taking my eyes off of this strange creation that sat in my office, I slightly waved away the guards.

She continued in her scratchy voice. "Jason's men won't find anyone unless I tell them how and where to find her. Right about now the girl is dodging every place your men look and is literally having Jason run in circles. You *are* looking for the girl, right?"

I was in awe. How did she know?

"Yes" I replied. "We *are* looking for the girl." She swayed and kept going. Struggling to keep herself up.

"I don't know what you did to me. My head is swirling with sights and smells and sounds and-" I cut her off. "You can't know that yet," I said.

"And visions" she finished.

"Visions?" I asked. "That counts as sight," I said with great confusion.

She leaned forward and struggled even more to hold herself. Her pale blue eyes looked around me as if she was studying me. "Not if they are of the future." She smiled and passed out on my desk. Her golden hair sprawled out around her head and her face was hidden in her golden hair.

I looked at her wondering if she was breathing. I just stared at the motionless body of the one who could change MANDS. If she could see the future (which wasn't an ability we gave her), MANDS would be untouchable. I would know every little variable and be able to prepare for it.

The girl snarled like a lion and slid off the desk and onto the floor.

I looked up at the two guards still in the doorway. They walked in and one picked her up like she was dead. I stopped him before he got too far. "Tell Jason to cancel it!" I screamed down the long hallway.

The one walking behind the nodded and kept moving.

I sat down and pulled out a special tablet. I logged in and went to two pages. Promotion and Chamber Remodeling Blueprints or CRB. Maybe if she trusts us, she can help us. She will be one of us. But one of *them* as well. Our eyes and ears in the test.

I pulled out a knife and cut my index finger. These kinds of transactions require a special signature. Once the smell of blood hit the tablet's sensors, a tray popped out.

I tilted my finger and watched the drop of blood fall onto the tray. She is one of us now. We need her on our side.

<T1 A2 S3 K4 S5>

The days have been a bit confusing for the girl. Maybe more than a bit. As she was still passed out, I had some men do some remodeling and decorating in her chamber. Just a few rocks and mats to help her enter a state where she could see into the future from the comfort of her room.

When she woke up, she was in awe. She stood up and slowly spun around and took in all of her new life. She closed her eyes and when she opened them, they were like any other person's eyes. Except the irises were gray. She looked at the floor first. All white with three mats in the middle. All placed so there was a triangle of the white floor.

The right side of the room had a window with metal shades horizontally set. Below it along the wall was a bench with candles perfectly spaced out with stones in-between them. The left corner had a stone stream.

The left side was identical but without a window. She turned around from the small triangle of white to face the men in gray and white armor.

I tried to make the guards as adaptable as the specimens. Given that these men are all cowards and the specimens would be very powerful, the guards have a gray bulletproof vest on the outside. To avoid broken arms and/or legs, the limbs of the suit have a white steel armor that protects the wearer from dangers on the outside. If something on the outside *does* manage to break bones, the suit will recognize it and activate splints. The steel compresses on the limb and supports it until the wearer can seek medical attention.

Under the bulletproof vest is a material that not even knives can get through. The entire thing is fireproof and if water goes above the waist, a system inside locks down the helmet and activates a breathing apparatus around the neck.

The helmet has a chip in it that picks up brain waves. There are several settings based on the scenario: Heat signature, night vision and x-Ray.

Since we don't want to *kill* the specimens, each guard is equipped with special grenades that have a five second delay for a knock-out gas along with two magazines of tranquillizing darts for their weapons that are full of a serum that takes away 5% of the dosage from the serums that gives them thier abilities and puts them to sleep for several days. It's only 5% because we don't want to risk taking away too much. There is a serum to reverse what was taken away, but we just try to stay away from shooting them at all.

The two guards stepped aside, and I walked between them.

"You help me, and I will help you." I said. I stepped beyond the threshold of the newly decorated chamber. For some reason I couldn't find trust in her. I could see the anger growing in her. Her stomach twisting, urging to take form.

A growl came through her gritted teeth. I backed off a little. Her eyes turned a glowing yellow. She changed her eyes into those of an animal, so she could see more than just the room, which I had no problem with. The more she uses her abilities, the better.

But she was looking right at me. That was a problem. I put my hands up in surrender but continued to walk forward.

"I am *not* going to play boss's favorite lab rat." She said through gritted teeth. "I will do nothing you ask me to do."

"I won't ask you to do anything. You offered to help me, MANDS-T1." I said to her. You can see the future. You would be a very valuable addition to my team. An extremely important person. This is my way of showing that I am grateful for your offer and that I would appreciate your help."

I watched her eyes glow. The glowing yellow in her eyes swam around her pale blue pupils.

Her eyes went to my right hand. I could tell that she saw even the smallest detail. The smallest movement.

"I was still disoriented after the surgery, so it wasn't fair to agree with anything I said." She said. I tried to do a small signal to tell the guards behind me to shoot a tranquilizer at her if things got out of control.

"Don't!" She growled. She put her hands into fists and tried to shake off the claws that were trying to replace her nails.

The emotions of the animals in her blood were swirling and she fought everything her anger was letting show. I saw her trying to shake away the claws and trying to divert their paths from her fingers.

Shaking off the fur that was attempting to take over her hands. I put my hands at my sides and stepped in even further and bent down to her height.

"Remarkable," I let slip out with great curiosity. I was studying her irises. They were ample blue but bolts of gold shot around inside them. "Do you know what I was going to do?"

"Yes," She replied while trying to hide her fangs. I could tell she still wanted to bite out my throat.

"And do you know what are in those guns?" I asked only getting closer. I pointed behind me to the two guards with guns.

Her fangs shrunk back into incisors, but she clearly wanted her claws to remain seen. She made sure everyone could see them. Especially the guards.

They saw the claws grow a little longer and they raised their guns and did exactly as she wanted. They took the safety off their weapons and cocked their guns.

Her ears twitched and her eyes, after racing over the guns and guards, returned to mine. "The guns don't have bullets in them. You converted them from bullets to darts and added things like the built-in laser sights and shoulder-fitted padding on the buttstock. Each gun has a magazine capacity of 50 darts. This skinny one to my right forgot to reload his so he has 4 darts. This 'big guy' to my left has a full mag but I can see that his barrel is hotter than this guys' so he got a little trigger happy recently. Given the barrels' temperature, I would say he last fired it at about 3 am."

The guards were so surprised that I could see their astonishment through their tinted helmets. They dropped their guns down to their sides.

"Fantastic!" I said as I stood up straight. I reached into my suit pocket and pulled out a tablet. "We document everything here and I would like to document your addition to my team. Put your hand on this," I said. "Please."

She put her hand on it, but she still had wolf pads on her palm and claws for nails. "Without those please," I said with a smile.

I tried my best to hide how annoyed I was getting with her. She glared at me and put her claws away. Slowly.

I stared at the tablet and impatiently said, "still can't read you."

She put the wolf pads away and glanced down at the tablet. Yellow streams shot from the screen and wrapped around her hand and help it down. Then it all collected below her hand and lifted her hand off the tablet.

An orb rested in her palm as she turned her hand over. She looked at me and back at her hand.

She looked straight at the far wall in the chamber and threw it between the two stone fountains.

She couldn't help but be amazed at what she saw.

Wall-to-wall documents. CRB's, mountain layout, test aversion, and all the information that I had wiped from her mind. I had her old school, her old address, her parents' names, blood type, weight, height, age, and every other thing she had forgotten. It also included all of her new information; which wasn't much.

Along with the documents, came a holographic incinerator. She closed her past history information into an orb and watched the information swirl around in her hand.

"I won't tell you everything just yet, but I will tell you this: a long time ago, you once trusted me. Disoriented, your first instinct is to continue that trust. I advise you to keep up the trust." I said.

"Who are you?" She asked me.

"I am President. This is my White House. I chose a name and a new life. Now it's your turn." She slowly placed the small yellow orb into the holographic incinerator. We all watched as her past was being burned in digital flames and then she spoke,

"I am...Tressa."

## <T1 A2 S3 K4 S5>

"So how are you going to help me find the girl?" I asked.

Tressa sighed heavily and finished trying her left shoe before starting on the other. "I still don't like that you're putting me to my disoriented words. That's like letting your reckless drunk friend who knows too much give a speech at your wedding. But there are a lot of things you could do. As long as Jason's men don't go, we will find her." Tressa said; zipping up her yellow hoodie and tying her white tennis shoes.

"Why's that?"

"Because they're sloppy and new and the girl is too smart for them."

"You're just as new," I said. She ignored my comment and looked passed me and out the giant window in my office that over-looked the mountain. "Have you got a plan? "I asked.

"I will fly above where she is and you will drive directly under me."

I didn't know if I was expecting more or not. She finished tying her shoes and walked back to her room. I closed the door and found my black leather chair. I sat and thought. I spun to face my window.

Grass was growing on the mountain and I could see a small caribou step out of the woods next to the mountain. A bigger caribou stepped out and stood in front of the little one. It looked at me and then headed up the mountain. The little caribou followed. Not long after they left, a wolf stepped out and followed the caribou's exact path.

"Sir! Sir! We think we know where to find her!"

I looked up at Jason and his two higher officials who stood with him in the doorway. "How many men do you have, Jason?"

"Sir?"

"How many men?" "Uhm...500 men, sir."

I stood up and went to the front of my desk and leaned on it. "500 men," I began. "and you can't find one person in the smallest city in this state. If I send that Tressa girl out there and she finds her in one day, you will be cloned and then killed! We will start all over with you! Do you understand me?!"

Jason didn't even flinch at the tone of my voice. He only nodded and went to his office. He didn't look as defeated as I expected him to be.

I would have guessed he went to pack his stuff and run. Something about him gave the impression that he would give up so easily. It told me that he tied too much to this already.

I walked out of my office and went to the garage. There, Tressa was waiting in front of my car. She didn't say a word. She waited for me to get into my most hated vehicle; a silver 2066

Galaxy Prius VI. A vehicle released a year early to the richest. It was slow with terrible gas mileage and its only function was to help me blend in while I visit the city. It had a nice color, was compatible with my phone and included autopilot so it worked for me.

When I put my seat belt on, Tressa crouched down and her legs shorten to match the length of her arms which quickly became front legs.

Fur, blonde with black spots, covered her body. Her tailbone now held a tail. The spots on her blonde tail were close enough to be stripes. She was a cheetah. She turned around and through her fangs I thought I could make out a smile. She looked forward and when she did, within a blink of an eye, she was speeding down the dirt road towards the city roads.

I was excited. Not because I was going to personally capture the second specimen, but because Tressa was faster than a normal cheetah.

I put the pedal to the metal and found her on the highway. Tressa went even faster. She dodged cars left and right. She started to take bigger turns and eventually went down smaller streets. Left then right then left again. She knew exactly where she was going.

Then she jumped up and feathers covered her body. Her head was now covered in white feathers. Her body in black and brown feathers. She was an eagle. She flew so high I couldn't see her. I slowed to a stop and sat back in my seat. I punched the steering wheel. The horn honked. This was the perfect opportunity for her to escape. She played me, and I fell for it.

I looked up again and saw an eagle spiraling down to one specific spot.

"I knew it!" I screamed with a smile and sped to that spot only three blocks away.

I got to the spot and found a blonde wolf growling at a girl in an alley. She trapped her. I got out of my car and walked towards the two.

"Brilliant!" I exclaimed. I walked in front of Tressa, who was still growling, and tried to talk to the scared girl.

The girl backed up further into a brick wall. She put her hands to it and sunk down. Her breathing was accelerating, and she wore a panicked expression.

"Do you know who I am?" I asked the panicking girl against the brick wall.

She hysterically shook her head and continued to watch the wolf that slowly crept towards her. I turned around and waved my hand. Tressa saw this and turned back into a girl.

I looked back at the girl and saw how amazed, yet terrified, she was. "She was chosen," I said. "And so are you."

She looked at me instead of Tressa. "Chosen for what?" She asked.

"I will explain a little now, and the rest later. But only if you come with me." I tried to negotiate. She nodded and straightened up. I could still see fear in her eyes. "You and the others all have two things that make you very special. It's in your blood-" I paused and looked to Tressa and then back to the girl. "and it's in your head."

"What's in my head?!" She asked out of fear.

"You will have to wait to find out," I said and gestured to my car. She shook her head and backed against the wall again.

"Would you rather talk to the wolf?" I looked to Tressa and she gave a growl that showed fangs.

The girl realized she was trapped and that there was no way out. She put her head down and walked to the car without a word. Once she got closer to my car, she started to swing her arms in circles.

She kept swinging them faster and faster. She got even closer and ducked down a little. Then she swung as hard as she could.

Tressa and I dove in opposite directions as two tiny disk that looked like nothing more than distortion in the air flew towards my car. They flew through both of my back tires and kept going. The girl slid across the hood of my car and ran out of the alley and suddenly vanished like she turned invisible. I could hear car horns honking and cars crashing.

I looked to Tressa who turned into a giant grey wolf with a blonde stripe from her head to her tail. She jumped over my disabled car and chased after the girl. Scratching the roof as she pushed herself forward.

"This won't take long," I said to myself as I climbed into my car. I pressed a round button under my steering wheel and felt my rear wheels mend themselves and reinflate. I sped off.

<T1 A2 S3 K4 S5>

We brought the new girl in and hooked her up to the same machines that Tressa was hooked up to. DNA strands sped around the monitor. We made sure that we could monitor her brain flow and activity as well.

According to her brain flow, she shouldn't have been able to throw disks yet. But if that was low activity, we needed to find a way to contain high activity.

"Do you know where you are?" I asked her.

She sat up on her gurney and looked around the dull white room. She looked at her clothing and slowly kicked her legs. She watched the long hospital gown dangle around her legs. Her gown was white with blue trim.

She looked at the one-way mirror and then to the machine on the table against the back wall. Then she looked to Tressa and one of my scientists standing in the corner of the room.

"I need you to say something," I said as she continued to look around the room.

She looked at me. "No. I don't know where I am. I don't know who you are or why I was chosen or what I was chosen for and what this freakin mark on my arm is! I want answers, om rau!"

I only let her see a bit of surprise. But on the inside, I wanted to flip the table. "om rau?" I repeated after her. I turned to the scientist standing behind me with the notepad. He wrote down what I said. He spoke every language in the world, but he had to keep transferring words to make sense of it.

"Romanian for 'evil man', sir." He said. "Her intelligence is above average."

I turned back to the girl. "You're very smart, aren't you? Well, you are in a very special place," I explained. "A place where history starts with you."

She rolled her eyes. "Really? You're gonna start with *that* crap. I want straight answers. Not riddles."

"You want answers? Well, you got it. This is a place where I am going to put you into another test tube and-"

"Another?" She interrupted.

"Can I finish?!" I raised my voice. "You were born in a test tube which makes your DNA and every little piece of you easy to manipulate. Especially your new blood type and special brain cells."

Her eyes grew wider after every word I said.

"My old name doesn't matter in this place. We can restart here. I am President. You were chosen because you are very special. Just like the other three after you and young Tressa here."

Tressa didn't even flinch at this new piece of information. She threw away her old life. This new one shouldn't surprise her.

"That mark on your arm..." I said. I let her try and guess.

She looked down at her left forearm and spoke with a dead voice, "... Is my new life," she finished.

"How old are you?" I asked her after a long silence. "17."

I turned to face the mirror. The two guards on the other side leaned towards the microphone ready to respond.

"Take her to her chamber," I said and left to my office. "Yes, Sir." Echoed the room.

The guards came in and grabbed her by the arms and dragged her to her chamber. They walked to the threshold and let go of her.

She stepped in and looked around. In the middle of the room was a tube with a rounded glass door. Behind it and against the back wall was a wall-to-wall computer. The left side of the room had a window with metal horizontal shades and so did the right side.

She turned around and Joan, the clothes maker, stepped in and handed her another hospital gown and then Joan left. The guards closed the door and stood off to the sides and faced the hallway.

She changed into a newer hospital gown and did everything she could to do to avoid going into the tube. She looked around and learned that the tube will be her new life. Where she talked to us. Where she slept. Where she would be experimented on.

She paced in front of the computer and wondered what it did. She realized she didn't want to know and started to swing her arms again.

Faster and faster she swung her arms. She did one final swing to the computer and...nothing. No disk, no explosion, and no joy from the destruction of her captures' equipment.

She walked away from the computer and the tube and sat against the left side of the room. "The rest of my days are going to be so much fun." She said sarcastically to herself.

She put her knees to her chest and rested her arms on them. She took one final look around and scratched at the corner of the room with one finger. There were aluminum corners in the room for more support to the building.

"Aluminum? Malleable but never broken. I think I'll be Aluminum now." She crossed her arms again and laid her head on her arms and fell asleep.

CHAPTER 3

# TRESSA

Even though President let me wander around and told me to trust him, I could tell that he didn't completely trust me. He let me go wherever I wanted as long as it was in the building and out of his office. He wanted me to always use the eyes of some kind of animal, so I could see but it always took too much concentration, made my nose bleed, and wasn't as fun as blindly memorizing the maze layout of the building.

Whenever I passed by President's office, he glared at me and called someone else. He was telling someone about my condition and why I was doing. He was always on the phone. It was a strange phone too. I couldn't remember where I saw it before, but it was a silver tube with a button at the top. He pressed the button and out of the side was a hologram that was about 4 inches long. He turned it and dialed away.

But he was right to not trust me.

When I got my shapeshifting ability and developed the sight ability I looked into the future as I was going to throw away all of my past life.

There was no way to avert what was coming so I made a file that looked exactly like the digital incinerator, shape it like a bowl and then put it inside of the incinerator to catch the data before it burned. I learned the truth about what they were doing. I was a pawn. And so were all of the others.

I've been trying to warn the new girl about what I saw. President is going to use her for something and I think she should be ready for it. I can never manage to get close enough to her. MANDS-A2. I think her name was Aluminum.

I walked down the hallway that leads to five rooms with only two of them being marked. I finally used eyes of a wolf to guide me through the halls. Once again Gardo stood in my way.

He stood at the end of the hall in all of his heavy armor except for his helmet. His head was square, and his black hair was spikey and hung just above his eyebrows. He was a big guy with broad shoulders and a barrel chest.

"Going somewhere?" He said with his deep voice.

I slowly leaned forward and whispered in his ear. "If you don't let me pass, you will be visited by a wolf while you sleep."

Gardo laughed, and his deep voice echoed down the hallway. "You don't have enough control for that."

I thought about it for a while. I remembered looking through his file. He was afraid of spiders. His initiation into MANDS was simply crushing a camel spider in his hand. He crushed it, but he never truly got over his fear.

I raised an eyebrow and my glowing, yellow, irises flashed. "I have enough control for a spider."

Gardo's face was pure terror. He didn't even think about how much control I need in order to actually do that. I managed to scare a wall of muscle. He flew to one side of the hall and let me pass.

I turned around a corner and saw Aluminum's chamber. I also saw guards on both sides of her door.

I leaned back around the corner and against the wall. My mind swirled with all of what they could be doing with her. I closed my eyes and took a deep breath.

I swung around the corner and bumped into President and fell to the blinding linoleum floor. "Ah. Just the one I was looking for." He said with a smile as he held his hand out to help me up.

I kept my eyes closed. I knew it was President by the way his glasses hit the top of my head. By the way my nose hit his silk tie and I smelled the aroma of ink and that strange lemony smell of paper. I knew it was him when I slid and bounced off of his padded suit and hit his steel toe dress shoes.

Each and every physical characteristic that I couldn't see only made me angrier. I could feel the anger of the terrifying creatures I could become in my head. It was getting hard to control. It was like an instinct that told me that he was going to hurt me unless I did something. A painfully brutal version of fight-or-flight.

I tried to choose the most calming one. I was helped up and I slowly opened my eyes.

"Are those squirrel?" President asked and then scoffed. "You're thinking too small, Tressa. Come on. Think bigger."

My heart was racing. I didn't want it to be a squirrel but if it was the only thing keeping me from, once again, wanting to rip out his throat, it had to do. It made me angry that every time I ran into him, he demanded me to use my ability.

I stared at President. I could feel my heart going a thousand miles an hour. I twitched a little and looked behind me. A few guards were staring at me and laughed as I twitched. I twitched back to President.

He put away his excitement. "Very well. To harness your ability better, we put together a classroom environment. Your lessons start..."

I looked behind me. The guards were gone. I looked forward. The old-git disappeared. "Now!"

It echoed down the empty hallway and all of the sudden the walls started the close in.

I saw Aluminum's chamber door and I ran for it. A blast door dropped, and the ceiling began to fall. I thought as fast as I could.

I thought about a cheetah. I took a look around as I ran from the chamber. Everything was getting too small too fast.

I turned to a mouse and was able to scurry ahead of the blast doors.

The closing walls directed me to a room. I threw myself inside and felt my human lungs come back as I turned back into myself.

I gasped for air.

"That was pretty good." A calm voice said.

I captured the rest of my breath and studied the man sitting behind a desk. He had short, spiked blonde hair and tried his best to give the teacher impression. He even had the sleeves of his white dress shirt rolled up, but he hid his left arm more than his right. That either meant that he was left-handed, and his sleeve fell when he wrote or that he was hiding something.

I still had my mouse eyes and with those, he looked like a giant despite the fact that he was about my height.

I turned my eyes back to the standard gray ones I was given and looked at his eyes. They had a sort of gold in them. It happened to my eyes when I was first changed. The more I thought about it, the clearer everything became.

I somehow managed to slowly imitate his eyes.

"And that was even better," He said with a smile. It was strange how calm and smooth his voice was. Smooth yet unnerving. He walked around his desk and examined me.

"Where is she?" I asked.

"The other girl? She's not ready yet. She is only in her first phase. She will join us when she phases up," He said.

He leaned on his desk and introduced himself. He put out his left hand for me to shake. So, he *was* left-handed. "I'm-"

"One of us." I gasped. On his left forearm was: H. It was made exactly the same way my mark was. A needle went under my skin and burned while a needle on top of my skin tattooed.

All of the sudden I was filled with excitement and couldn't help but bombard him with questions.

"What's your ability? How old are you? You couldn't have been here long." I kept pacing quickly around the classroom. My excitement was confusing my own mind and I started mixing mutations. "How long have you been here for? Can you fly? Can you die? That's ridiculous. Of course, you can."

My eyes changed colors. One brown, the other green. One black, one purple. One cat, one lizard. One snake, one squirrel. In my excitement, I didn't pay attention to how everything was changing.

My own physical characteristics were changing. My hair was shortening like a rodent's and my hands looked like an ape.

"Tressa-" He tried to calm me down.

"I saw someone with super strength in a vision. Was that you?" "Tressa. Calm-" he said again.

"No that couldn't have been you. Do you have telekinesis? But he had *black* hair. Can you manipulate your cells and DNA like I can?"

"Tressa!"

Everything went dark. I opened my eyes and saw everything as I usually do, various shades of darkness. I tried to pick eyes of anything that could help me see. I couldn't think clearly.

"He's wrong," I heard a smooth voice say. "And he's worse for forcing you to use the ability you just got. You're thinking too big, Tressa. Don't think big. Think small. Narrow your mind. Concentrate on one thing at a time."

I closed my eyes and when I opened them, my teacher looked like a giant once again. He helped me up and handed me a strange bottle with a glowing clear liquid in it. Like it was made of liquid diamonds.

"Take this. It's a serum that will help with your mutation. It slows them down a bit so they're easier for your mind to grasp. Courtesy of Jason." He walked back to his desk and leaned against it again. "This is why we are training. President finally let me see what you are capable of. But, while I get to see you, your lessons will consist of just visits for now. And doing some work for me."

"Visits?" I squeaked like a mouse as I leaned against the lonesome desk in the classroom with a yellow strip of paint across the top.

"Visits to Aluminum. This place isn't as shiny as it looks. There's some dirt on the walls and I would like my students to know what not to touch."

"But won't you get in trouble? President. He could kill you." I said.

For the first time in a long time, I cared about someone. I didn't know who this person was or why I instinctively felt like I had to protect him, and he would do the same for me.

He walked forward and rolled his sleeves up as far as possible. I could see needle wounds that healed as welts.

"I am going to tell you something that you, being as intelligent as you are, would only guess at. Something that you must not tell the others until the time is perfect. I want you to leave the others hints though."

He pulled out a dark orb with a shadowy liquid swimming around in it. I could tell he wasn't supposed to have it by the way he kept looking at the door behind me.

"Jason and I have worked on this with...a third party. We are a part of something much bigger than either of us. We are MANDS..." He said as he held out his marked forearm.

I showed my forearm. "And MANDS is us," I said.

"Take this to your room and look into it when you are supposed to be asleep. There are some things in here that MANDS is hiding along with some precautions I need you to take."

"What do you need me to do?" I asked. Why the hell was I so forward with him? I barely got a name and I was already willing to do whatever he asked me to.

"I need you to watch over the other girl and make sure she is safe until she gets to me. Watch President's every move as well." "You know I'm blind, right?"

"Act like you are President's most willing servant." "Servant?"

"Tressa, I need you to do this. It is very important. Can you do that?"

I took the orb and leaned forward and let gravity catch me. Before I hit the floor, I was a cat. And I was heading straight for my room with the orb. President's office was my next stop.

CHAPTER 4

# ALUMINUM

I've been here for quite a while now and no one has come in. I keep getting the feeling that I'm being watched but I am convinced that it is just the camera in the corner of the room.

I started sleeping in the tube and found it rather comfortable. I forget I'm standing up and just sleep.

I'm actually starting not to trust the tube. I sleep in it and wake up feeling strange. I don't eat for days after one night of sleeping in the tube. It's like everything that makes me human just disappears.

I keep telling myself I will go back to sleeping on the floor, but something tells me otherwise. Something under my skin.

A guard in grey and white armor came into my chamber and motioned for the tube. I didn't listen. I looked at the door and saw three scientists behind the guard waiting for me to go back to the tube. They cowered behind him.

I stood up and stepped inside and the guard locked the glass door. The door's outline vanished and became the rest of the tube. I started to panic but told myself nothing would happen. I was wrong. The tube extended towards the ceiling and the scientists got to work on the computers against the back wall.

A thick bluish fog filled the tube and I couldn't see what they were doing. I was running out of air. I put my hands against the tube and started pounding and screaming.

"Let me out! Hey! Let me out of here! Please!" I screamed.

The female scientist turned around and I saw worry in her eyes. I recognized her as the one who gave me the other hospital gown. Another scientist nudged her, and she turned back to the computer. I slid down the tube and tried to find air at the bottom.

It was like the fog was coming from everywhere. They talked amongst themselves as I suffocated.

"Vanish." One said. Buttons were mashed. "What if she's found?"

"Shield."

More buttons.

"What if one of them tries to kill them?" "Doesn't matter." Buttons were mashed.

"What did you just do? Jason! Did you just do what I think you did?" "All I did was make her-"

They were gone. The fog was sucked away through vents on the floor and ceiling of the tube. Then the door to the tube became visible and opened automatically.

I stood up and got out of the tube and went directly to the giant computer to see what they were doing. The screens were blank, and it looked like they were all turned off.

I looked around and saw that they left a mirror. Must have been broken or something. I couldn't see myself. I realized what they did and dropped the mirror. The mirror exploded into multiple shards when it hit the ground. I backed away; scared of myself. I looked at my hands.

*What hands?*

I picked up a shard of the mirror. The shard fell through my hand. I went to pick it up, but it exploded like a force had come from my hand and exploded it from the inside.

*What did they do?*

I tried to gather some kind of logical explanations or excuse, but nothing worked. Nothing fit.

I ran to the door but hit everything on the way there like it was invisible too. I stopped at the door. I looked down.

I could see myself again. I went back to where I had slept when I first got to my room. The corner of the room. I forgot everything and sat down.

The door opened again, and a guard came in and motioned for me to follow him.

I followed him to President's office. The guard shoved me further into the office with President and closed the door.

There were a few moments of silence between President and me. Then he spoke. "Fascinating isn't it? What some money and geniuses can do. I've done a bit tampering with your genes and DNA and-"

"I hate you."

"Oh, I know." He said. A black cat with blonde slits of fur vertically over its eyes jumped onto his desk and glared at me. Its yellow eyes stared at my every move. "What was the name you chose? *Aluminum* was it?" He said as he stroked the cat.

"How did you know that?" I asked. I forgot he had a camera in my room.

"I am the President. I know every little thing that goes on in my White House."

"I hate you," I said again. The cat still stared at me. "Is that Tressa?" I said as I pointed to the cat.

The cat hissed at me and I could have sworn that she smiled. It was really creepy to see an animal smile.

The cat jumped off the desk and turned back into Tressa. "I thought I'd try it out. I still like the wolf though. Hairballs aren't exactly my thing."

"Whatever," I replied. Tressa stood behind me. More silence.

"Can you control it yet?" Tressa asked with a snooty tone. "I can. It's quite simple if you think about it hard enough." President leaned forward excitedly for my response.

"Control what?" I asked suspiciously. Evidently, it wasn't the answer they were looking for. "Take her back to her chamber and message Jason. Tell him he's needed in the second room at his scientist station."

"Jason? He-" I started.

The door shot open and the guard nodded and took me back to my chamber. Tressa followed us and walked passed me to her chamber as I was being put into mine.

I walked inside, and my tube was gone. In its place was a metal table.

I wouldn't have been panicking if there weren't leather restraints and a creepy headrest.

They laid me down and strapped me in. They put IVs in my arms and pulled out a scalpel. A female scientist walked over by my head and nodded to another. Her face mask and gloves were blinding white under the bright lights.

I could hear some of them making notes.

"I want you all to notice how blue her veins are. Both ways." One said.

"Her restraints are invisible, but the chain gives evidence that they are still there." Said another pointing at the chains with his pen.

I closed my eyes and when I opened them, they were gone. I was really getting sick of them just vanishing.

I wiggled around and went straight through the leather restraints. When I turned around though, they were broken.

I walked to the door that was left open and looked around. I looked down a catwalk instead of a hallway. I didn't trust what could be below, so I ran across.

Halfway across the catwalk I fell through and landed in the middle of a forest. I was outside. I was free. I didn't know how but I was free. I ran for what looked like a blue tower with a blue A2 on it. On my way, I became trapped in a force field. I figured it must have been my own doing, so I sat crisscrossed and closed my eyes and tried to focus. The force field became a full sphere half full of dirt. It began to sink into the ground.

I sunk slowly and as soon as it broke bedrock, the field broke and I was free-falling. I landed in the middle of the woods even further from the blue tower.

"Well, I guess this still counts as being free," I said confidently to myself. I walked only a few steps when I heard twigs breaking and creatures growling. I froze. All around me, predators of the woods stepped out of the shadows. A wolf stepped in front of them all and spoke.

"Is something wrong, Aly? Did you think we couldn't see you?" The wolf turned into Tressa.

"I'm Aluminum," I said as I spun around and watched the others as they all turned into Tressas. "Is that what you think." They all said in sync.

They all snapped their fingers and guards with real guns instead of dart guns stepped to each of their lefts. The guards waved two fingers in a circle in the air and scientists with scalpels stepped from the right side of each Tressa.

The main Tressa stepped in front of me, held up her hand, and snapped her fingers.

Guns fired, and scientists ran at me. My eyes shot open. A doctor was taking off her bloody gloves and stepping away from my head. "All done." She said smiling as she took off her face mask. She threw her gloves to the other doctor next to the incinerating trash can and he threw away the gloves.

"What was her score?" Said a scientist by the computers.

"41. Guards killed her. She was smart enough to find her way away from MANDS, but she couldn't stay close to the tower." Said the nearest doctor to me.

Then it hit me. A rush of information swirling around my brain. I didn't want them to know that I knew. So, I spoke to myself:

*This is all connected. Their army, doctors, scientists. They are all the same people. Some clones, some blood. The army is going to be the same people until the test is complete. The test with the five kids and the clone. Once that is done then we will replace the army and then replace the world's armies and split the world up into districts and keep the entire planet on lock-down until they find another planet or even Galaxy that they can travel to and make their own little fun zone!*

After all of that, I couldn't stop myself. "WOAH!" I said.

Jason came up to me. "I bet." He leaned closer to my ear and after slightly removing his mouth-cover he whispered, "I bet you just figured out what President is doing. You can thank Tressa and Harry later. My part was your enhanced intelligence."

He leaned away and smiled at his female co-worker, the doctor, who was wondering what he just told me. He had his mouth-cover on, but it was easy to tell he was smiling by the wrinkles next to his eyes.

"Just calming her down." He said and smiled. She turned back around. He leaned back down to my ear again. "The name's Jason." He whispered.

He looked down at me and got rid of his smile. He looked back up at the other two scientists, put his mouth-cover back on and said,

"Hey, umm can you two clean her up? She's got class tomorrow. I've got to go talk to President."

"You got it, Jason." One replied.

The other nodded and put me to sleep. I made sure it was actually a dream and not another hallucination or test before letting the darkness of my dream fall over me.

That was another effect of the tube. No dreams.

# CHAPTER 5

# TRESSA

I was meditating. Ignoring every little piece of the real world. Listening to the trickling water from my fountains. Watching the flickering candles through my blind eyes.

*What did President do to that girl? Why did he need her so badly? Why* **her** *next. There was another girl. And I thought there were two boys.*

Then I remembered the mental test he did on her. He was getting in her head and I could feel it. I could see it. I could see her dead if I didn't do anything about it. At least I think it's her. I needed to talk to President.

I went to turn into a small insect but thoughts of President sucking lives away filled my mind and I was a mosquito.

Before I made it to the vent in the ceiling the door opened, and a guard came in.

"Tressa you have been summoned." He looked right at the little spec in the room. Finally. An informed guard. President was getting real guards that prepared themselves for the unknown.

I turned back to myself and walked past the guard and down the hallway maze. I had been in MANDS long enough to know which hallway to take. I found the office and waited for the guard to open the door for me before I stepped in.

Before stepping into the office, I took off my shoes. One less piece of clothing to tear through if I needed to transform. I stepped in and took a seat. I planted my feet flat on the ground.

"So, do you know where the next girl is?" He asked. "Really? Another girl? Why in that order?" I complained.

"It's a long story and the answer is hidden in the company." He waved his hand around as he tried to circle back to the subject. "Do you know where she is or not?"

I rolled my eyes. "Of course, I know where she is. I know where she will be two days from now which is dead. So, we need a plan *now*."

President reached into his desk and pulled out a glowing red orb. He threw it and it opened into a 3D map of our location. "Where?" He asked.

I stood up and walked to where the holographic map was. I put my hand on it and pushed away. Across forests. Across lakes and rivers. Across the lonely city. I put my fingers together and then threw them apart. I zoomed in. Then again and again. I dragged carefully this time.

"This one has already been experimented on. There is one other that targeted her and he still has her. She's here."

I zoomed in one more time, so it was just one building. A building with JI above the door of a skyscraper.

President put his face in his hands. And looked up again dragging his baggy eyes. "Jonothan Industries." He stood up and walked to it and crouched down to the map's height. "Our plan." He said. "Today we write down every variable in obtaining the girl. Tomorrow we tie up some loose ends and the next day we take what is mine."

"Yours?" I said confused.

"Yes, Tressa. *Mine*." He assured me. "You have helped me capture one girl and showed me to the most difficult one. The boys will be easy. We already located them. But given that you and Harry are doing your own things, I'd say you've lost your place. Do you want the truth? When you reach your full potential, which will be *very* soon, I am going to clone you, and have you executed. It's dangerous when you start questioning too much, Tressa."

I shook my head and set my mind to the new target. He's the one who allowed me to question. Why would he cast someone aside so easily?

I thought Jonothan was his best friend. Or his partner at least. Why would he kill him? Why was Jonothan going to kill the girl?

All of the sudden I felt heavy footsteps, and something being banged against the floor heading towards us. Like someone was struggling. Like someone was being dragged. The door burst open and two guards motioned like they threw something into the office. I felt something hit the ground. The guards left and slammed the office door behind them.

"About time." He said to a spot on the ground. Aluminum appeared and struggled to regain her breathe. "We have a bit of a plan. It requires a talent that you have recently come into possession with."

"I won't do it. I know what you're doing, and I won't be a part of it. I won't play your game anymore!" She yelled. President walked to Aluminum who was on her hands and knees and crouched down.

"What are you talking about? You think this is a game? This is a reality, Aly." He stood up and walked to his desk and sat down. "You will have the entire day in the training room to learn to use your power when desired. To your full extent. Do so or go without rations."

The guard walked back in and next to President and whispered.

"Oh. Well. Do so or we triple your ability sessions. You know, those surgeries and those moments where you can't breathe. *Those*. Oh! And those tests. Your score was not very impressive anyway."

Aluminum stood up. "Fine. I'll play a part in your little *reality*." She walked out of the room and found her way to the training room. But I heard a whoosh sound like she was invisible again and guards screaming and running. I turned to President.

"She won't help you."

"Doesn't matter. She won't know how long she's been in there. More of a chance of passing the test. You need to learn a little more as well. Other DNA will be put into your blood."

"Like what," I said very curiously.

"Other people. Old creatures. Creatures that aren't even supposed to exist." He smiled

"So, to training it is then?" "Go." He waved me away.

<T1 A2 S3 K4 S5>

Training wasn't hard. All I really had to do was think. I was able to turn half of my body into a horse. I became a centaur and a bow and arrow were provided. I thought I would use that to capture the new girl, but I really had to think about Jonothan. Was he a bad guy? I never met him, so I prepared myself for the worst.

The next day President and I drove to Jonothan Industries and went to Jonothan's office. It wasn't the tower that was on the other side of the mountain. It was a bigger tower on the opposite side of the city. President was so angry and looked like he had been betrayed so bad that he nearly broke the door off its hinges when he kicked it open.

"Give us the girl, Jonothan." President said angrily.

"Sir?" I said; trying to figure out what he was doing. We were supposed to get the girl tomorrow.

He turned around and whispered. "We try to get the girl now. If he refuses, then we will get her from the rubble tomorrow. He turned back around for an answer.

Jonothan stood up and pulled a tablet from his desk.

I studied everything I could from Jonothan as he stood in front of me. He looked almost exactly like President. I looked at President. President had graying hair throughout his jet-black hair and bags under his eyes while Jonothan had all black hair and a soft face. President was developing wrinkles too. Jonothan looked like President's little brother but with so many identical features like height, eye color, nose shape, jaw and mouth, they were undeniably twins. And President was going to kill him.

"You can take them both," Jonothan said as he slid the tablet across his desk.

President picked up the tablet. "Why did you take *two* pictures. Wait. Did you say both?" President looked up from the tablet.

"Yes, you idiot. We gave her a power, but it was getting out of control. So, we split her into two and now they each have full of what we gave them and send things to each other. Thoughts. Emotions. Abilities. They killed the other specimens that we had and took their abilities. One is deadly enough. Take them both."

President looked back at the tablet with live footage of the girl and her clone. "Did you mark her...them?"

"No. They wouldn't let me get close enough." He went to the cupboard and pulled down an old bottle of whiskey. The bottle was so old that the glass was yellowing, and the label had peeled off long ago. "You should see the ones who *did* manage to get close enough. Their funerals are next week." He poured the whiskey into a glass of ice and drank the entire thing. He filled it up again and slid it to President.

President stared at the red release button on the tablet. He looked at me. "You see the future. Do we make it back?"

I looked at the worry in his eyes. I could see he wanted to change his mind if they were too dangerous. "No," I said. Without them, I would still be useful and hopefully, he wouldn't kill me.

"She's lying," Jonothan said calmly.

President shot me a distrusting look and pressed the digital release button. The two girls walked out of separate spheres. "We have a special van for you, Charles." Said Jonothan. "The good clone gets to sit up front."

President took the cup of whiskey and drained it. He slammed it on the table, cracked his neck twice and we headed for the gray van with JI on the side.

"Drive safe, brother," Jonothan called from his office. "And best of luck." So, they were brothers.

We got in the van and locked down the evil one. It wasn't hard finding out which one was evil. We just watched as she tried to take a knife with her on the way out of the building. That and the black demonic eyes.

The good one chose to sit with her twin. They talked but not out loud. In their minds. It looked kind of funny; the way they gestured around. I just wish I knew what they were talking about. Or arguing about.

I was getting curious and I tapped the one I knew to be good on the shoulder. "How old are you?"

"16." She said.

I was seeing a pattern with President's kidnappings, but it was making less and less sense. Two 17-year-olds and two 16-year-olds. If my theory is correct, he will capture two 15-year-olds and they would be the two boys.

# CHAPTER 6

# PRESIDENT

I hadn't seen Tressa for several days. She was no longer at the top anymore, so I figured she was with the clones and possibly trying to explain things to them. But it was no use. The clones looked after themselves. It seemed like only one of them understood English, anyways.

I hoped she was with the good clone, but I had been wrong before. It would have been better if she was with both of them and gaining their trust. I could let her back at my side if she gained trust, and therefore control, of the clones.

I left my office and went to check in the third room. The one marked: MANDS-S3.

On my way, I went to the training room where I left aluminum. I peeked my head in. "Hello? Looks like you've mastered it."

I couldn't find her. Then something ran passed me and pushed me into a wall. She was breathing heavy and I could see distortion in the air as she ran.

"Guards!" I called. They caught her and put her back in her chamber. We put her tube back in after her surgery. We locked her in the tube as punishment.

I went to the third room where the clones were living. Their room was the biggest. We were thinking about if it was more dangerous to keep them together. I thought that together they would balance each other out and control each other. It didn't matter. We still needed to find out what Jonothan gave them and how it made them so dangerous.

I went into the room and saw Tressa teaching the clones fighting methods. Tressa was a lion and the clones were working together to try to beat the lion. But Tressa had been training for a much longer time and she could turn into so much more. She felt too small against the clones, so she turned into a gorilla. The impressive thing was the extra arms.

Before they went onto round two I pulled Tressa out. She turned back into a human and went back into her chamber. I motioned for the clones to follow me and they willingly did so. I brought them into the infirmary with the branding machine and marked: MANDS-S3 on their left forearms.

As they were getting their marks, the guards went into their room and put metal tables in the middle of their room. They were released from the infirmary and they walked back into their room which was now divided into two rooms. I figured that until we figure out what they can do, they stay on separate sides of the room.

We strapped them to the tables and put IVs into their arms. I had to leave and get some paperwork that Jonothan dropped off.

On my way back there was an alarm that meant someone had broken out of their chamber. I hoped it wasn't the clones. I ran to where the alarm blared the loudest and found guards holding down a pocket of air. They pulled out a needle and plunged it into the lower air beneath one of their knees.

Aluminum gave a breath she was holding and became visible. Her hands were being held behind her back and one of the guards had their knee between her shoulder blades. She looked up at me and her eyes slowly rolled into her head as her eyelids fluttered. She was unconscious. The guards picked her up by her arms and brought her back to her chamber.

When I came back to the third room, the scientists were outside of a locked door. Guards stood on both sides with their guns drawn and never took their eyes off the door.

I opened the door and walked into a scene I found rather interesting.

Both clones were sitting up on their tables. One absorbed the metal from the IVs and the other absorbed the leather from the straps. The tables were missing straps and the IV tubes had no needles. They were sitting on the tables and looking at their hands.

Not to mention, they also pushed their tables closer together. When I left, they were on opposite sides of the room.

They saw skin but felt much more under their skin. I walked up to them.

"You two have been here long enough and we made your marks identical. I think it is time you give yourselves names for your new lives. What are you calling yourselves?"

One put her hair up in a ponytail and said, "I will be Scarlet."

I chuckled a little. "Like the witch?" They both looked at me with confusion. I forgot they had their minds wiped so they had no idea what I was talking about. The 50-year gap didn't help.

The one now called, Scarlet, threw a hand out and leather shot out of her hand and wrapped around a guard's neck. She held onto the part that was still in her hand and she yanked it towards her.

The guard launched forward. His head angled towards the ground and, when it hit the ground, his neck snapped. He collapsed and lay motionless in front of the table. If that was the good one, I didn't want to know what the evil one was capable of.

Scarlet played around with her power a bit while her clone thought. Scarlet threw her hand to her clone and everyone thought this could be a there-can-only-be-one moment. But the other one caught the other end of the leather and absorbed it.

Then she dropped it and messed her hair up a little and spoke, "I am a part of her. I will be Scar." She let the IVs slide through her fingernails to look like claws.

She looked at the second guard by the door and flicked a finger. An IV went straight into his helmet. She flicked again. Then again and again. The guard died with needles in his helmet and neck.

I ignored the fact that I had just lost two men.

"That makes everything so much easier. Scar, your room is over there." I motioned to the divider sliding into place. When the divider was in place, a steel door swung open.

They both ignored me. They flicked IV needles back and forth.

Scar eventually walked over to her room. The inside was completely empty. It would stay empty until we find a chamber that they can't absorb. We emptied out the room we were all in to match Scar's.

In a few days, Jason would return with the next specimen; a young boy. We knew that both boys had already been experimented on and we knew that they wouldn't go without a fight.

# CHAPTER 7

# SCARLET

Scar keeps telling me things. Through telepathy that is. She figures out various ways to break out of her chambers and then gives me step by step instructions to do exactly as she did.

But she keeps getting caught too. Every time she gets caught, they change the layout of both of our chambers and keep a close eye on me. She's trying to corrupt me.

Jonothan told me that if she succeeds in corrupting me, then no one will be able to stop us. I know that I was created to keep Scar under control. If I'm evil, then we are even more powerful. Jonothan once told me that I am good, and Scar is evil so that we can become one and become neutral. If I'm evil, we will be the same and everyone knows: opposites attract. So, everyone in this place is trying to keep me pure. Especially President. But he's just as corrupting.

When Scar was created, Jonothan tried to lessen her abilities but only succeeded in giving the original amount to Scar and myself. If we are merged it could either kill us immediately or cause us to go insanely rouge...and then probably kill us. Jonothan's scientists and guards told us stories to try and scare us. Scar showed *them*.

President has it wrong. It's not just the ability to absorb. We adapt to survive. The other day when I absorbed the leather, I didn't trust President coming closer to me and I wanted armor. Scar chose a more offensive tactic but requested some armor from me.

Tressa's freedom has been taken away. Or at least that's what they tell me. They say that all specimens are on lockdown for a while. I don't know why.

## <T1 A2 S3 K4 S5>

President came into my room without any guards and approached the bulletproof glass box that I had recently been imprisoned in.

"You and Scar will be training with everyone after we get the new one. Tell Scar." Said President's muffled voice.

I let Scar into my mind, so she could listen through my ears. She did more than listen. I could feel her presence in my head become stronger and stronger. It felt like being crammed into a box and then falling through the bottom while Scar sits where I sat in the box. Scar decided to use my body as her own and spoke for me. I unwillingly stood up and stepped closer to the side of the glass box.

"Why don't *you* tell her?" An evil smile went across my face.

President smiled back. He's caught onto Scar's tricks. "Oh good. You're here, Scar. Training is tomorrow." And he walked out.

I could see what Scar was doing on the other side of the wall through my mind. She walked up to the divider and put her hand on the concrete to absorb it. Scar walked over to the metal door and, with concrete fists, punched down the metal door.

"Still in your glass box?" She said surprised as she walked over the fallen door. She shook out her hand and pieces of concrete fell from her hand. On her way to the box, she knelt down and touched the cold metal floor. She continued walking to me and punched the box. The glass box shattered, and thick glass shards surrounded me in a square shape. The alarm sounded.

"Looks like you tried. You do know that scratching the bottom of the box won't get you out, right?"

I put on a sarcastic look, "Yeah, because that's totally what I was doing. I was just bored."

Scar shook the metal out of her hand and crouched down to see what I had scratched into the concrete floor.

"These are names. Who is Fabian?" "Don't know. Heard it in a dream."

Suddenly a guard kicked the door open and shot a tranquilizer at Scar. The dart went into Scar's leg and she fell to her knees. She looked at the guard who shot her and got right back up. She was angrier this time. She limped toward the guard.

I could tell he had been given specific instruction to shoot only once. He pulled a small cylinder off of his belt and threw it out to the side. It extended a couple of feet and started to buzz with electricity. Then, a younger guard came in whimpering and emptied his tranquilizer magazine on Scar.

"This is for my brother!" The young guard cried as he continued to pull the trigger on his empty gun.

Scar fell to her hands and knees. She tried to stand up, but she fell forward and stopped moving.

"You idiot!" The older guard said as he ran up to Scar's unconscious body. "President said only one dart! She could die! Or worse, lose her power."

The skinny little guard dropped his gun, "Is she alright?" He walked forward. He got closer and when he saw me, I saw a look to kill on his face. His tears were gone. "Is *she* dangerous too?" He pointed at me.

I sighed and hopped off of my bed and let the IV needles protrude from my fingertips. To try and save herself, Scar transferred the tranquilizing drug to me. The drugs stopped her from giving it all and, within seconds, we both were unconscious.

I woke up strapped to a table next to Scar. We were in our same room, but they took out all of the broken glass. They left the door open.

I lifted my head up and dropped it back. The table rolled backward toward the open door. I couldn't see outside of the door yet, so I did it again. Still nothing. I did it until I get to the door.

When I was beyond the threshold of the door, I looked and saw Jason (who I recognized from JI) leading some guards down the hallway. Each of them holding empty magazines in their hands.

Behind them, I could see two more guards holding a little boy by his arms and dragging him down the hallway. Another guard that was walking behind them noticed me and pushed me back in my room and locked the door.

Before the door closed I heard one of the guards say something about super strength and healing. I actually put them together rather fast and came to the conclusion that they were going to be giving the boy super strength and regeneration.

I didn't know what to think or when those doctors/scientists would be back. I felt pity for the kid who looked no older than 12.

Tomorrow we train. Probably with the kid. For now, we rest.

CHAPTER 8

# PRESIDENT

I've put together a council. A group of people to help me think things through and make sure it all works out. People to assist me in looking at every variable from every angle possible.

The council has 12 people plus me. I make 13. It's split into two groups. The most successful group is the one that I put Jason in. He's proved himself rather well since I let him back in. He might just make it back up to where he was. Especially since he caught the next specimen. That little boy is tough.

We were losing trust in Tressa. She spent too much time with the clones and it was possible that she was telling them everything she learned since she joined us. I saw two options: Brainwash her or clone her and start over with her clone.

As for the boy. I assigned him the ability of super strength and regeneration. His regeneration would be slight. We want him hard to kill, not impossible. His interrogation would have to come first so we could see how much of his past he would remember. His age makes it harder for him to accept all of what we give him. At the age of 12 he will block certain things and accept others. That's the experiment.

He will be marked: MANDS-K4 when he wakes up in a few hours and be put immediately into training. The training will be set to each of their powers.

The training is not just going to be fun and games. It will be brutal. It will be torturous. It will help us find their breaking point and fix it, so it can never be found again.

<T1 A2 S3 K4 S5>

We interrogated the boy and gave him his rest. He didn't tell us anything we needed to know so we took it. He had his chance to sleep and he didn't take it so we took that from him too.

Then it was time for his mark and training session. We gave him the mark: MANDS-K4 in the infirmary and sent him straight to his training room with some new clothing. As he left the room I pressed the holographic "release" button on my tablet and opened all of the doors. I stood in the hallway and watched their marches to training.

Each specimen was provided a hoodie in their color, white tennis shoes, blue jean, and a white silk t-shirt.

Tressa walked out of her room with her head down. She stopped outside of her door, zipped up her yellow hoodie, and looked up at me. Her weak eyes burned through me. She looked as if she knew what was in store. Maybe she did. She continued walking and passed Aluminum's room.

Aluminum was nowhere to be seen. Tressa knew what she was doing and her sad, pale ocean blue eyes, turned to fire. She roared and scared Aluminum. Aluminum lost her breathe and was visible again in a blue zip-up hoodie. They continued the walk to their training rooms. Tressa saw no point in trying to hide from this.

The clones walked out of their room through the same door. Scar wore a black hoodie that she didn't bother to zip up and Scarlet wore a red zip-up hoodie. I noticed Scar was trying to leave with a scalpel again. She looked up and our eyes met. She looked around and saw that I wasn't the only one who saw the scalpel. The guards at both ends of the hall pointed their weapons. She backed into the threshold of the door. I gave a signal and the guards put down their guns. I figured she may need the scalpel. She followed behind Scarlet to their training room.

At the end of the hall, outside of the door to the training rooms, the boy stood in an orange pullover hoodie. He watched the four girls walk towards him and into the main room to the training rooms. When all four of the girls had gone inside, he looked at me. His face fell like he was trying to piece something together and he went inside. He hadn't said a word since we found him. It was fine. He was bottling up his words and emotions. The training would make him explode.

Each specimen walked into their training rooms from the main room. In each room was a one-way mirror so we could see their progress. The rooms were all white and empty. Inside the walls, floors and ceilings were mechanics designed to change and give the strongest illusion the world has never seen and give a realistic effect of each training program and challenge.

First was Tressa. She walked in and stood in the middle of the room in her yellow hoodie, blue jeans and white tennis shoes and waited for her test. Since Tressa strategically chose what to turn into based on the environment and the enemy, we designed her test with the four elements in each corner.

Even though the room was a perfect square, the illusion of the test was expansion. In each element, stood an elemental guard. She had to choose wisely because a Phoenix would kill the Groot that stood rooted at the edge of the forest element but the Hippocamp that circled around in the water element may have her beat. None of the things were real.

The creatures and objects generated in the rooms are able to cause damage but once the creature or object got to a certain point that counted as a victory towards the creature or object, it would vanish. The creatures and objects were in the specimen's heads and special technology created by Jonothan Industries (JI) helped us see them. The room was empty to the naked eye. Once we press a certain button on the console, the window we look through, digitally shows us what the specimen is up against.

Tressa stood in the middle of the room and kept staring at the mirror. She widened her stance and put her hands behind her back. She was waiting. She was preparing herself.

Tressa stared at the one-way mirror almost as if it was a window. Her eyes flashed to the gray ones we gave her. She looked to the wall left of the mirror. The wall was pushed down by a raging ocean. She looked to the right where a volcano had pushed through the bottom of the room.

She turned around so her back was to us. To her left was a forest. To her right was more forest but the wind blew violently and lifted the ceiling off of the room.

She put her arms to her sides and prepared herself for whatever came at her first.

First was the oread from the forests. The oread was a guardian that looked human except for her dark green skin and wood splinters growing out of her head like hair. She walked out and pulled her bowstring back to her cheek. Her outfit held close to her body and was made almost entirely of bark, vines, and moss.

The winds blew, and her hair trembled in the wind. Tressa turned to the wind part of the room and noted as she turned:

"Forest guardian."

The winds picked up, but nothing swooped down so Tressa ignored it for the time being. Tressa looked at the water and saw a Hippocamp jump out of the water. It looked like a regular majestic creature but when it jumped it caught Tressa's gaze and didn't let her out of its sight. It jumped out of the water and landed on what was left of the silvery linoleum floor. When it did, it showed its fanged teeth of pearl. Though it was in an attack position and was more than capable of killing, it was hard to not think of it as majestic and beautiful. It kept its tail in the water. Its body was pure white with a few blue scales that could make anyone over-look it's horse hooves and whale-like tail.

"Water guardian," Tressa noted.

Tressa broke her gaze and looked to the part of the forest that was on fire and mostly in ashes below the volcano. There were giant cracks forming in the ground. A burned dog jumped out of one of the cracks and landed in an attack position. It burned and the flaming cracks in its skin let lava glow from inside of the beast. It growled and molten lava dripped from its obsidian fangs.

"Great," Tressa said. "Hellhound. Fire Guardian"

Tressa was ready to go for the hellhound first when but then the winds picked up again. She turned to the open part of the room and a giant blue dragon dropped straight down in front of her. Tressa turned to where she last saw the one-way mirror.

"A dragon!?" She yelled. "Are you serious?"

I smiled at her frustration and confusion. It was difficult to make a feathered dragon. It was hard to make a dragon at all. I assumed that it was anyway. Harry, Jason and my brother designed it.

The dragon roared and as it did, the feathers on its head danced from the vibration of the roar. Then the dragon took to the sky and flew so high Tressa lost it.

Tressa quickly turned into a Phoenix and headed straight for the oread. She burnt the oread just by flying in circles around her. The oread loosed as many arrows as possible. She kept putting more and more arrows into her bow and the tips glowed green as they flew past Tressa. Tressa fought and let her fire burn. Her feathers were more of a yellow than they were a red. She watched the oread lose her breath and start to burn alive.

She was almost through with her when the Hippocamp came after her. It bounced into the air and slapped her with its whale-like tail and put out her fire. She fell to the ground and changed back to a human in her soaked yellow hoodie.

She faced the Hippocamp and turned to a fish and dove into its waters. The hippocamp slid into the water and tried to eat her and she turned to a shark and turned to face the Hippocamp. The water splashed and rolled. When the water had calmed it turned red with the victory over the Hippocamp. Chunks of the creature floated on the surface.

Before Tressa could find time to rest, the dragon flew down and snatched her from the water. She turned back to a human to get her normal lungs back. The dragon dropped her and she lost her re-found breath.

The dragon landed and slowly walked forward. It got to her face and opened its mouth. Saliva on the side to watch. Tressa tried to lift herself up and saw exactly what she expected. The hellhound.

Though its size was nothing compared to the dragon, it was 100 times more dangerous. It stepped forward and pulled its paw back to claw out Tressa's throat.

Tressa closed her eyes and after a while of nothing happening she opened them to see the hellhound putting its obsidian claws down and backing away to lay down by the dragon. The dragon yawned and pulled in the air which made the hellhound's ember body burn hotter.

Tressa stood up to see what was going on. She slowly spun around. The oread was a pile of burning ember and the Hippocamp was shiny chunks floating in the water.

Then all of the sudden the sun appeared in the sky and an orb descended from it. The orb turned into an elf. Her dress was bright and made of materials that could have come from the gods themselves. Her arms were long and made of light as bright as the sun. They touched the ground and she swung her arms slightly. Then, as we didn't plan, she spoke. It was a strange language, but she translated it after every sentence.

"I am Ljósálfr." She said.

The sun was partially eclipsed by the moon and cast a shadow on half of the room. When the eclipse passed, a shadow hung around. It all of the sudden stood up and looked like the silhouette of a human.

"What's going on?" I said to the people on the computer next to me.

They quickly went all over the computer. They mashed every button on the console. "Not sure, Sir. We didn't put any of this stuff in." Said one of them. The other leaned back; completely shocked. He gave up on the console and watched through the one-way mirror. "It's taken over." He said "level two. Jason's doing."

A little puppy walked out of nowhere and stayed in between the elf and the shadow and Tressa.

I put my arm out and pointed to the puppy. "What the hell is *this?*"

The dog yawned and in the back of its throat was a blue light. The dog closed its mouth and looked around at the curious faces. He then opened his mouth and chomped down. The blue light shot horizontally around the room and everyone started to float off of the ground except for the dog.

Surprisingly, even stuff on *our* side of the mirror started to float.

The elven girl said something to the puppy and it chomped down again. A blue light shot out of the pup's mouth, vertically this time, and everyone slammed on the ground. Tressa hit the ground and the air escaped her lungs. The puppy barked and wagged its tail with joy.

The dragon helped the hellhound back to the ground, chunks of the Hippocamp were now outside of the water, ashes of the Oread were all over the room, the sun-elf floated safely back to the ground and the shadow never left the ground. Tressa was sprawled out on the ground and once again trying to regain her lost breath.

"Shut it down!" I screamed.

"We're trying, sir." Said one of the computer people.

Then all of the sudden a little lemur with big sad eyes crawled out of the shadows nearest the volcano.

The test was playing its own game and getting too dangerous. Jason and maybe Jonothan created a level that wasn't letting us stop it. "Kill it!" I yelled and pounded on the table.

"Us?" Said the two computer people. "*Somebody* kill it!" I said.

"What's this?" Tressa asked the elven girl.

"This is the beast." She answered after she spoke in her elven language.

The lemur stretched, and its arms started to grow. They grew to triple its size. Its legs expanded, and its entire body grew to muscle and pure power. Its friendly eyes were glowing red and that innocent look was no longer there.

I quickly went to the other side of the room and slammed my hand onto the power off button. The room went dark and all that was left was a particle of light. It was the elf. The particle expanded back into the elf form and glided over to Tressa.

"This isn't real." Said the elf. "They want you to believe it is. Use your true instincts and remember that. Find us, Tressa. Soon."

Her beam arms turned to hands. Just by looking at them, I could feel how soft they were.

She shrunk down one of her light beams to form an arm with a hand. "Not here," she touched Tressa's forehead with one finger. "But here." She put her hand to Tressa's heart and faded away.

The test was designed to hurt and wound but never kill. In her punishment, we clouded her into. She fell to her hands and knees and tried to block it out. The sound was so bad and so unbearable that she passed out and we stopped the sound.

"Return her to her room," I said to the research board I gathered. "She needs another dose. I want her able to be those other four...*things*. Bring the others to their rooms too. If *she* can't handle it, and she's been here the longest with no limitations, then everyone else is screwed. Put them all back in the hospital gowns as well."

All would be trained tomorrow. I looked through the windows as each specimen was given the news.

Each one gave their own sigh of relief before they were tased unconscious. All but the boy showed any emotion towards ending the test early. I could still see the anger and hatred in his eyes. He was young and being taught to hate. Something that, so far, was sticking.

"The boy," I said to myself. "We will train him when we get the other.

They can use their hate and skill on each other." I walked back to my office and called Jonothan to update him.

"Tressa is too weak to help us find the other boy. Any ideas?"

"Uh," Jonothan started. "You have the clone girls. Why would you use Tressa? Anyways we uh...saw him."

"What!" I yelled. "Do you have him?" "We *had* him."

"What do you mean *had?*"

"We had him in the car and he pulled on the steering wheel and crashed the car to escape. We chased after him but he lifted up the car and trapped us under it."

I was in shock. This may be the hardest one to catch. I thought for a while which seemed long enough for Jonothan to ask if I was still on the line.

"Where did you last see him?" I asked.

This time Jonothan went silent for a while. He wasn't thinking. He was stalling. "Well?" I said impatiently.

He replied quickly and with a huge sigh. He didn't want to say it, but he did. "Around...MANDS."

I hung up and walked fast down the halls. I walked through the halls and yelled as I walked. This wouldn't change the training schedule.

"I want guards pulling security! No one rests until the boy is found!"

All the guards stood around waiting for something. I was getting even more impatient and was already angry.

"Did I stutter? Find that damned boy!"

<T1 A2 S3 K4 S5>

It had been 2 weeks and we were still looking for the boy. He was actually seen inside of MANDS once. He was trying to open the door to Tressa's cell when we saw him. Then he took off running and waving his arms and wrecking the halls behind him. We haven't seen him since. He did manage to take some stuff too. We just needed to find out what his ability was. Then we could capture him.

Tressa passed her test. She was to face all 8 elementals (earth, air, water, fire, light, shadow, gravity, and beast). She killed them all by changing single parts of her body and becoming one giant beast. She had traits from every enemy in that training room. Her instincts were getting stronger.

Aluminum barely passed her test. She was supposed to fight simulation guards through a pretty thick fog. She had to judge where they could be based on the small changes in the fog. She also had to attack the simulation guards with nothing but discs. She had to make the discs completely invisible and leave no trace as they cut through the fog. As they hid, so did she and she won.

Scar and Scarlet trained together. They fought one giant creature that Jason and Jonothan created. A hydra. Scar and Scarlet were allowed to take the test together because 1) this creature cannot be killed by one person unless you're Percy Jackson and 2) Scar and Scarlet are mentally linked. It is because of this link that they successfully defeated the hydra.

The last test was MANDS-K4. He refused to tell us his new name. He hasn't spoken at all. His test was to break down as many walls as possible to stay away from the fire behind him. It was fine if he fell in the fire. He would heal but the fire would still hurt.

The floor moved towards the incinerator and walls would burst through the ground. In order to not get burned he had to break down the walls and run as fast as possible.

When he broke a certain number of walls the floor would slow down and allow him to jump to the stable ground to rest. By the end of his test, he was so tired that he didn't have the energy to be angry. He walked a few steps out of his training room and passed out. The test was passed.

The next day we decided to let them all meet each other in the room we made to be their but we came to the conclusion to empty the room. The last thing we needed was them throwing tables at us. Tressa and Scarlet (and technically Scar) were talking about their tests.

Aluminum and Scar and the boy were in a little triangle and playing with their powers. Scar threw a knife and it stuck in the middle of the triangle. Aluminum turned it invisible with the wave of her hand and the kid found it and smashed his hand down. The knife went five feet underground.

"Mine was pretty successful," said Tressa. "I had to choose dragon a few times, but it helped a lot."

"I wish *we* could have been a dragon. Scar and I had to face a stupid hydra. Can you imagine a dragon vs. dragon battle? Does a hydra count as a dragon?" Scarlet said still shaking out concrete from under her skin.

"How did you do it?" Tressa asked.

"Attacked all of the heads to distract them. Scar jumped on their backs with her sharpened metal arm and cut out their heart. Or hearts. I'm not really sure. I was too busy trying to not get eaten."

Tressa was surprised at this. Then some other topic came to mind. "Have you heard about the boy? The one they can't catch."

Scarlet shook her head. "I heard he tried to break some people out."

"That was me." Tressa thought a little bit. "He knows something that we don't. What if he knows how to escape?"

"He doesn't have to. He was never captured. And besides, I think *I* know how to escape a car." Scarlet said confidently.

Tressa leaned closer to limit who could hear them. "But can you escape MANDS?" Scarlet sat quietly. The guard came into the room.

"You have been summoned, Tressa," he said in his deep voice.

Tressa went to my office and sat quietly in the comfortable leather chair in front of my desk. "Let's get straight to the point. We've spent all this time looking for the boy and now-"

"He's found *you*," Tressa interrupted.

I nodded. "We need to know his next move. He can't be *that* unpredictable."

Tressa stood up and went behind my desk. She went through my cabinets and pulled out a box. She carried it around to the other side. She pulled out a blue orb containing locations. She threw it and it opened into a green holographic globe.

From a distance, she opened her hand and the globe zoomed into a building marked: MANDS Incorporated which was now neighbored by Jonothan Industries.

"He's been here and here" Tressa pointed to where Jonothan tried to capture him and MANDS. "His next move will be here." She pointed to an abandoned warehouse on the edge of the city closest to the mountain.

"A warehouse?" I said confused. "What's the point of a warehouse?"

Tressa turned around to face me. "He's proved his point. He's taken his turn and moved to form a triangle with a predictable third point. Now it's your turn. This spot means something to the both of you."

"Then there is only one way to do this."

Tressa nodded. "I will tell the others the plan."

I stopped her just before she left the room. "That's not the only thing you told them." Tressa quickly snapped her head so one eye was on me. She slowly faced forward. She continued to walk to the others.

I pulled out another orb. I first retrieved the orb to my hand and put it back in the box. I opened the other. It was the surveillance I closed before Tressa came in.

It was a recording of Tressa and Scar during the first month that Scarlet and Scar were captured. She's telling Scar about a plan to escape.

"But not all of us make it out," Tressa added.

"But which of us don't make it?" An actual look of worry took over Scar's face.

"I couldn't see very well but that part doesn't matter. How do you think we make it? I can't see far enough."

"Well, I know exactly how I'm getting out of here, "Scar said. "Once those idiots get all of us, I'm killing President. I will wait until he's alone. Or when he comes to check on Scarlet and me."

I closed the orb and put it away. Nearly forgot about the plan to kill me. Tressa had been looking into the future and telling the other specimens. I figured that the plan to clone the specimens would have to start before the mountain test. I would have to capture the last boy, train them a bit, clone them, kill the originals to erase rebellion, and then put the new specimens straight on the mountain for the final test.

Tomorrow, instead of the physical tests, I will have Harry teach them again. A portion of the mental test. And I *will* find that boy. Even if I have to find him myself. Without Jason. Definitely without Tressa.

If this boy is as dangerous as everyone is making it seem, I may need something equally as dangerous. I have two.

# CHAPTER 9

# SCARLET

"Good morning, lab rat" Scar said as she casually walked through the door in the divider. I was surprised. She actually used the door properly this time.

"How did you get out?" I asked. I put my hands up to the bullet-proof glass wall that was three inches thick. Every corner and every edge of the box had strips of metal from top to bottom with bolts two inches thick and made of titanium.

Scar looked down to avoid eye contact and then looked back up. "They *let* me out." They didn't trust her. It made no sense to let her out.

"Who?" I asked.

"I don't really know who. He said his name was Harry or something. Then he left. I was debating on whether or not I should kill him on his way out, but something told me not to. Something stopped me. I couldn't."

"How did he get in? Your room is only accessible by mine. I would have seen him."

Scar looked towards the only door in the room. "See that door? See that piece of metal the exact same size? That piece slides over and it trades which side is accessible."

"And?"

Scar reached into her pocket and pulled out a fist. "And he gave me a key." She opened her hand and a very technical looking key was in her hand. A special key that was impossible to copy. A cubical key with thousands of little grooves in it.

Scar opened the door to the box I was in and we left. Something wasn't right though. The walls. They were different. They weren't where they were when we got here. They were set up differently. They looked like they were set up to lead us somewhere. I followed the walls and Scar followed closely behind me.

I could feel her fear. It was something that made me want to fight. I wasn't afraid though. It could have been because I felt like she was playing me. If she managed to trigger fear in me, I could easily be the evil one.

Then a huge tumbler sound froze us just a few feet from our room. We turned around and the wall opened. It was Tressa. Her door opened, and she walked passed the room marked: MANDS-A2 to catch up to us.

"Not helping?" Scar asked her.

Tressa took a few steps forward and a wall blocked it, so she couldn't go back to her room. She faced us again and kept walking. "Guess not."

I didn't know what they were talking about, so I ignored them and continued walking. We took a few more steps and a door in between the first and third room (Tressa and mine) opened.

Aluminum walked out. "What happened to the walls? I thought we were free to roam." "I don't know. The walls are leading us somewhere," I told her.

She joined us and the four of us kept walking. Then a wall blocked her from going back to her room. Then my room. We kept going and then another door opened. We paused and waited for the next addition on the strange journey.

It was the boy. He looked around and joined us without a word. We kept walking and he stopped. He turned around and a wall covered his room. He punched it and tried to go back. Nothing.

We walked and eventually came to a room. We cautiously walked in. The walls were all white and in the middle of the room were five desks with different colored strips on them plus a bigger silver desk against the wall on the left. Behind the desk was a huge board.

The silver desk had a bunch of different colored orbs in trays that matched the colors. All different colors. Yellow, blue, red, black, orange and green.

The desks were marked with the last parts of our marks. Tressa sat at T1, Aluminum at A2, Scar and I had a joined desk marked S3, and the kid sat at K4. There was an empty desk in the back corner marked S5.

After we took our seats a man came in. He had messy light brown hair that was almost blonde and funny-looking glasses that looked like he didn't even really need them. He wore a white lab coat like the doctors and the scientists. His voice was smooth and almost unsettling.

"Good afternoon class. My name is Xavier." He walked to the board and wrote his name on the board. Tressa crossed her arms and leaned back in her seat.

Aluminum decided to speak first. "Is that your first name or your last name?"

He turned around. "That doesn't matter here. What does matter is that here whatever you choose as your name, will be your name." He pushed his left sleeve down to make sure it was down.

"Your name is Harry." Scar said.

"How did you know that?" He said confused.

She stood up at our shared desk. "On our way in I saw a nameplate that said 'Harry' on it. You said your name was Xavier but you're the only one in here and you look like you've got the whole independent procedure of teaching down. I assumed it was someone else's but you assured me just now that your real name is Harry."

He waved his hand and the letters on the board behind him broke apart and rebuilt themselves to spell out 'Harry'.

"Very good, Scar. You are very good with attention. Which just so happens to be one of the two categories I am supposed to be teaching you today. Attention and memory." He threw the black orb to Scar and it hit her desk and bounced up a few inches and opened. "It's extended for speaking out of turn."

He threw the rest of the orbs to their respective colored desks. My test was attention. I looked behind me and saw that the boy had a similar test. We all had attention.

"Anyone care for some tea?" Harry asked. Aluminum raised her hand; doubtful that she would actually get tea. Harry walked over to her. "Unsure? Or are you just wondering?" He put the tea on her desk. "Go ahead. Assure yourself."

Aluminum picked up the tea and put the small teacup to her lips. She lifted the cup and drank. She put in back on the desk and passed out. Her head hit the desk.

Tressa sighed. I looked over to her and she adjusted her crossed her arms. "Was that Aluminum?" "Unfortunately," I said.

Tressa put her crossed arms on her desk and rested her head on her arms.

"She's done well to question herself," Harry said. "Doubt is a strange thing. It could save your life or end it and while Aluminum is not dead, she could be. She could have also prevented it."

The boy leaned back and spoke under his breathe. "I think he's put something in his own tea." We both tried to hide our laughter.

"Looks like *some* of us want to go on to day 2 of the test." He reached into the glowing trays and threw out the different colored orbs. They all opened.

Aluminum picked her head off of her desk and rubbed away a headache. She looked at the holographic test in front of her and scoffed as the questions changed from 20 questions to 30 questions.

"Memory!" He bellowed. "Some things are easy to forget. Remembering is the hard part. Can anyone give me an example?"

The boy leaned back and mumbled to himself, "Who we were."

"Yes!" Harry said. "As I said, it doesn't matter who we were. You could be anyone."

He walked to the front of his desk. "History is the most important part. Those who forget history are doomed to repeat it. We have forgotten who we were, and we are in danger of returning to the mindless, destructive, beings we once were. War has been raged and innocent people have suffered the same fate as the guilty. The world is dying at an alarming rate. Class, they want me to lie to you. They want me to tell you that Earth is in a certain state that doesn't exist and only you can change the world. I will not do that." He reached into the trays and threw out more orbs. "I want you to learn."

By the end of the day, my head felt like it was being split apart and information was being crammed inside. The memory and attention tests were combined with the history and altogether made absolutely no sense.

I saw a fox run through a winter wonderland and a blue tree chasing

George Washington with a yellow ax and I think Benjamin Franklin was there somewhere. Three tests at once. And the worst part, we had to test like this until the other boy was found. Then we would move to physical and mental tests.

"Great," I said under my breath. "Captured and given supernatural abilities and I *still* have to go to school."

# CHAPTER 10

# ALUMINUM

"There is nothing special about you or your friends. Especially you." President said. "You were simply another name of a test tube baby that was in a hat. If there *is* anything special about you, it is because I made it so. Anything special about you came out of a bottle. It came from Tressa. Actually, you aren't anything like Tressa. She had a real position. Scar and Scarlet are the next best thing. You all passed your final tests. I don't need any of you. You, Aluminum...you're just a spare."

His voice was as dark as the shadow cast across his face. I couldn't see his smile in his dark office, but I could feel it.

I looked up. Sadness and fury began to grow in my eyes. "Then why am I still here? You clearly don't need me anymore. I helped you get what you wanted and now you have it."

President bent down and grabbed something from under his desk. He kept it out of view as he walked to the front side of his desk. "You're right. I *don't* need you anymore. We've got the boys. You did first. Goodbye, Aluminum."

He pulled out a machete and held it to my neck. He pulled it back and held it over his head and swung.

At the very moment the machete came in contact with my neck, my eyes shot open and my hands went to the sides of the tube where I slept, and I tried to push the sides out. It was just a dream. I thought I couldn't dream anymore.

I calmed down and moved my hands down to the small glass door and stepped out.

Just as I closed the door behind me, President came in. "I need to know *now*. What is your answer?"

I turned around and faced the chamber tube. "I still don't understand why you won't have Tressa do it."

President rolled his eyes. He's told me the same thing three times now, "because I don't trust Tressa anymore. And the easiest way to find someone who doesn't want to be found is with someone who can't be found. Along with someone who equals them. And two of those people assure victory."

"You mean capture," I corrected

I stared at him as he stood just past the threshold of my door. I said nothing. Only stared. "You will not be harmed." He promised

I rolled my eyes in response. "Fine. Just give me a minute...and better clothes" I said as I pulled the hospital gown away from my body by the blue trim around my neck.

President snapped his fingers and Joan, the clothes-maker, dropped off a blue jumpsuit that fits perfectly to the body. She pointed at what it was made of. It had a rubbery feel to it. The entire thing was light blue with dark blue around the neck, wrists, waist, and ankles. It wasn't much of an upgrade from the gown, but it was a start. Then she left. President turned around to leave but paused.

"You have five minutes." He turned back around and headed to his car.

I quickly got dressed. I didn't know if there were any other cameras but, I knew that they had them somewhere. I hid behind my tube, so the camera couldn't see me and I changed.

I walked out of my room and two guards met me outside of my room. They escorted me to the garage. They actually got lost on the way. One of them had to pull up a map on his armor's GPS located on his forearm.

When we got to the garage President was pacing around a silver Prius with a cigarette and he was talking to himself. The guards waited until he was done.

"....and if she helps me, I could promote her. No. That would be too complicated. But she doesn't have her old life anymore. What about

Tressa? Doesn't matter. What about the next one? No. That will come soon enough. As for the boy...."

President looked up and his face turned slightly red with embarrassment. He threw down what was left of his cigarette and got in his car without a word; stepping on his cigarette as he got in.

I walked to the passenger's side of the car and stepped in. We didn't leave until the two guards got into the back seats.

As soon as we left the garage to who-knows-where I turned around to inspect the guards. I started with personality. I made mental notes.

*The guards were obviously new and excited to actually get out of the lab and go on an outside mission.*

As for their appearance.

*They respected their orders and rules of not taking off their white helmets covering their entire heads. They are covered in white and grey armor that looked almost plastic and shaped specifically to their bodies. The thicker parts being around the neck, chest, stomach, and thighs. Certain aspects of the armor actually gave the possibility of them being women.*

Before I could finish my observation, the braver guard saw me and pointed thier gun at me. The more curious guard leaned forward to look out the front window at the dark and abandoned warehouse being lit up by the blinding LED headlights.

I pulled down the sleeves of my suit and made sure my mark was covered. It didn't matter that anyone could see it. I just hated it. "So, are you sure this will work?" I asked, staring out of the windshield.

President looked at me. "The suit or the plan?" And he stepped out of the car. The two guards followed him towards the warehouse.

I stepped out and turned invisible before I started toward the warehouse. I stayed close behind to listen to President's little speech.

We all walked in. The boy dropped down from a beam and landed in front of President. Dust shot up from the ground as he landed perfectly. Then he slowly straightened up. The guards lifted their guns. President waved his hand and they lowered their guns.

The boy was wearing black combat boots, torn jeans, a torn once white t-shirt and a black sleeveless hoodie that probably zipped up years ago.

"Listen," President said. "We mean you no harm."

The boy moved his front foot to a strange stance. "Unless I don't cooperate, right?" He was getting ready to run.

President continued. "Well, yes. Just come with us and you won't get hurt. It's as simple as that."

The boy brought his feet back together. "And if I refuse you will hurt me and force me to go anyways. Like you did to *them*."

President brought a hand to his forehead and wiped away invisible sweat. That was my cue and the sign of his frustration. I walked to a doorway that was the boy's closest exit and laid on my back taking up the way out. I was still invisible. The suit was too.

President kept talking. "Yes. There is *that*. Haven't you always wondered why you feel so shaky? Or why things fall slower around you? Or even why your thoughts seem so much louder than normal?"

The boy backed away slowly, confused at how he knew all of this. "What game are you trying to play, old man? You already-"

"There are others like you. One was blind and now she can see through the eyes of any creature she wants to become. One enjoyed the feel of every little material and she became two and they can absorb those materials. They now use those materials however they want to."

President took slow steps forward and put out a hand. Trying to show the boy that he didn't have to run. Or that he shouldn't run.

"One, very young, was able to lift incredibly heavy objects and now he could lift this whole warehouse. He could lift my company building if he wanted to." President chuckled but ended the laugh too quick for anyone to feel comfortable.

President put his head down and allowed the evil in his eyes to show as he slowly lifted his head.

"One, who had a talent for staying hidden, can now hide whenever she wants. And she isn't going to let you leave."

I didn't think President would give me away. President had caught the boy's attention. The boy stopped backing up.

"You see, at MANDS, we simply take people like *you*, with incredible talent, and make them better. And *you*...could be great."

The boy imitated President's chuckle and stopped as quickly as President did. "They all would have been great if you hadn't murdered them." The boy ducked in case someone shot at him and so he could run faster. He tripped over me as he ran through the doorway and his momentum sent him flying face-first into President's car. He stood up and held his head.

I jumped up now with a bruised rib and I, by instinct, started swinging my arms. I had never felt power like that before. I became visible and blue bolts of some kind of new found energy traveled from my brain and through my veins to my arms and grew larger. I finally jumped into the air and spun for more of a charge. I landed and flung my arms forward. Two large blue discs, slightly distorted, shot towards the boy and barely hit him.

He threw his arms forward and the discs slowed and stopped in place. The boy fell to one knee and I could see the strain on his face. His arms fell, and the discs continued their speed and course. The discs cut his left leg and his right shoulder. He fell to the ground but quickly recovered. The discs put huge gashes in his leg and shoulder. He pushed himself up and was exhausted. He looked up at me and I saw shock and terror in his eyes. He hopped on one leg.

President nodded to me and then looked to the guards and waved his hand in a circular motion and said,

"Wrap it up."

The guards tore off the thick and heavy armor and threw it to the ground. It was Scar and Scarlet.

Scar wore an all-black suit like mine but with red around the neck, wrists, and waist. Scarlet wore red with black around her neck, wrists, and waist.

The boy crouched down and used his power to pick up President's car and he threw it at Scar and Scarlet.

Scar and Scarlet put their arms out and caught the car. The car froze. They looked at each other; shocked. They had no idea they could do that.

The boy got angry and waved his arms in an upward motion. The ground under Scar and Scarlet's feet began to rise. A chunk of solid dirt began floating 150 feet in the air. The car was thrown through the air and landed on its wheels behind the boy. I looked at President. He cringed as it fell through the air. The car landed on its wheels and President let out a breath of relief.

The boy then threw his arms to the ground and the chunk of dirt fell to the ground. Scar and Scarlet somehow grew wings and glided safely to the ground next to the missing chunk of dirt. Their wings shrunk into their backs and out of sight.

They were next to their guns, so they went to grab them. The boy pulled the machine guns towards him and caught them. As soon as he caught them he started shooting at Scar and Scarlet with a machine gun in each hand.

I thought that Scar and Scarlet would be dead for sure with blood flowing out of hundreds of bullet holes. I was wrong. I originally thought that their power was just absorbing things. But their power seemed to be the ability to adapt to survive. Most likely what President or Jonothan had intended.

When I looked at Scar and Scarlet they were covering their heads and had their faces away from the gunfire. They were completely covered in whatever tough material the armor was made out of.

The boy ran out of ammo and watched as the girls examined their skin changing back to normal. They looked at each other and gathered his power from the air. They mirrored each other and kept circling from in front of them to their hearts. When It built up enough they threw their arms forward and the boy flew backward into President's car; folding the car almost completely in half.

President didn't want that to happen, especially to his new car. He walked over to the clones and put a shock sticker thing on their necks and it zapped them unconscious. "You idiots! He could forget! Get him in the van, Aluminum."

I walked over to President. I held my side where the boy's boot made contact and tried to find my lost breath. Whatever I did to make those discs took a lot out of me. "I would have preferred the ability to hide pain instead of myself."

"Help put the boy in the van or I'll hide you in the rubble of that warehouse." President snarled.

I wanted to punch him just for telling me what to do. I held back because I was curious. That and the pain. He then had all of the pieces to his wicked game. I needed to know was his next move was.

<T1 A2 S3 K4 S5>

As we were driving back to MANDS in Gardo's van the boy woke up. His eyes shot open and his first instinct was to kick President in the head and crash the car. President slammed on the brakes, turned around and knocked him out again. He faced the wheel again and kept driving.

When we got back, President paced while we got the boy out of the van and went to the interrogation room. Then he stopped us.

"I don't want to see if he's lying. I want him to know what we are doing." President looked at our faces to see if we got the idea. "We are going to throw him straight into training. We don't have a moment to waste."

First, we went to the interrogation room. President walked into the nearly empty room and sat down with the boy.

"Do you know why you are here?" President asked.

"So, I can get a better chance at killing you?" The boy said groggily but with a smile and dried blood on his upper lip. His hands were chained to the table with a weird type of handcuff. The cuffs kept his hands apart and did not bend or allow him to use his ability. There were also more of those stickers, but they were on the boy's temples. Most likely blocking the energy flow or making it harder to focus enough to move things. The boy looked around the room. "Have I been in here before? This room looks oddly familiar."

"What were you doing in a warehouse next to a junkyard?" President titled his head.

The smile vanished from the boy's face and he leaned forward and spoke through gritted teeth. "I was burying *them*." Blood had stained his teeth and turned them yellow. "You killed *them*. They were like me! They were my friends! My family! I taught them the power! They were like *me!* I had an entire race!"

"*You're* the one who taught them and gathered them there. *You* killed them. They did put up a good fight though. But they weren't like you. They didn't reach what level you have reached now." President stood up and excitedly walked around the lonely table in the claustrophobic room. "On a scale from 1-10, how lucid are your dreams?" He asked calmly.

The boy looked confused. "What are you going on about, old man?"
"How old are you?"

"I'm 18. What does that have to do with-"

"Can you fly yet?" President kept going around the table. "Can I wha-" the boy was interrupted.

"Can you throw fire?" President yelled with excitement. He started pulling a shocking sticker off of its adhesive.

"Are you drunk?" The boy questioned.

"Can you use the elements? Can you stop time?" "Stop." The boy said groggily while shaking his head.

"Can you teleport?" President said as he hovered the sticker above the boy's neck.

"If I could, I wouldn't be here." The boy said slowly making eye contact. President put the sticker on the boys' neck and it zapped him unconscious.

President stared at the unconscious body. "No." He said. "You wouldn't." He looked up to the one-way mirror.

"Take him to the training facility now," President yelled to the one-way mirror. "Set it to his second training level. Prep it for Friday. We train *now*. He's a basic level 5."

<T1 A2 S3 K4 S5>

We went to the boy's training room and President let me watch along with Scar and Scarlet. Not the kid though. He had been in lockdown for days. Through the one-way mirror, I could see the boy wake up and jump to his feet. He still wore the torn clothing he wore when we captured him.

President walked into the observation room just as the boy woke up and a group of researchers followed him in.

"Take notes," President told them. "Start with how what he immediately does and how fast he performs it."

The boy looked around at the strange white room. He turned around and a hole in the wall opened.

President reached for the microphone and spoke to him, "This is your test. To show us what you can do, all you have to do it stop the bullet."

The boy didn't look away from the hole. "And not let it hit me in the face?" There was no answer. The boy stared and waited. "Oh, this should be fun." He said under his breath.

Then a bullet shot out of the hole and froze just before it made contact with the boy's face. It dropped to the ground and the boy fell to his hands and knees.

"That was a real bullet!" The boy said through ragged breaths. "I could have died!"

"Now for round two. You might want to get back up," President said into the microphone. He turned to the control person. "Three sides. Stand him up."

The ground shocked the boy and he jumped to his feet. He was still faced away from us. A hole opened on each side of him now. He braced himself. He stopped the one to his left. He turned his head to his right, raised his hand and caught the one to his right. He faced forward and prepared for the last one. It shot out quickly but slowed. It still kept its spin, but he held it with his mind.

The boy started shaking. He dropped his arms to his sides and the bullets to his left and right fell to the ground and bounced with a metallic clink. The bullet slowly sped up. It was a foot away from his face. Blood dripped from his nose. He lost it. The bullet caught its full speed and flew passed the boy's head. It ricocheted from wall to wall and finally hit him in his exposed shoulder. The bullet hit something important and the boy passed out from blood loss.

"To his chamber." Said President. "Three doses and *strap, him, down.* He is on full lock-down. We will train him with the kid."

He turned to me. "Sorry Aluminum." He injected something into my neck. I passed out. When I woke up I couldn't remember what happened the past three days.

I was wearing my boring hospital gown and a bruise was attacking my ribs.

All I could remember was something horrible and a terrible dream. A dream that was all too real.

*What have I done?*

# CHAPTER 11

# TRESSA

I slept in longer than I used to. I woke up and did my daily meditations in the triangle of mats. Since Present didn't trust me enough to let me roam around, meditations were all I had.

Today we were allowed to actually eat together. We were on lock-down until the boy was found.

I folded up my mats, blew out the candles and left for the lunch hall. I traced my finger down the hall and felt for sudden changes and corners. I blindly found my way to the lunch hall. I changed my eyes to my standard gray ones and studied the lunch hall. The lunch hall was a room that was completely empty and gave no evidence that we were supposed to actually eat there. It didn't have any tables or even one of those ugly lunch ladies. They changed it.

I didn't mind sitting on the floor. I was already pretty used to it. The kid felt more comfortable knowing he wouldn't break a seat or a table.

I arrived and Scarlet jogged to catch up. We were both in our hospital gowns. Scarlet's had red trim.

"You beat me." She said with a smile.

"I slept in," I told her. I sat down, and she quickly sat next to me and waited for the others. While we were waiting she leaned closer to me.

"Did it work?" She whispered. "Yes and no."

She shook her head in confusion.

"I sent the message in the form of dreams after President gave her the offer. She completely ignored the message and accepted the offer."

"You said that Aluminum was the one who doesn't make it out." Scarlet put her hands to her face. "Your visions suck." She groaned and fell back, letting the groan echo through the empty room. Her clone came in and joined us.

"Don't be a baby, Scarlet. We still have...how much longer?" Scar asked me. Her white hospital gown had black trim.

"Don't know. All I know is that we can't let Aluminum be alone with President. He will kill her for sure if we aren't there."

The kid strutted through the cafeteria doors of the room in his orange trim hospital gown. "But he will also grow suspicious if we follow her. You should really talk quieter. I could hear you from down the hall."

We let the kid in on our plan in order to keep everyone alive. We all arrived here alive. We plan on leaving alive. We need all the help and muscle we can get.

"The kid is right. We need to help. In secret." Scar said.

Aluminum entered the room. We hoped she didn't hear what we were saying about her and acted like we weren't talking at all.

"Do we have to wait for the other one?" She said as she took a spot next to me. "The other boy?" Scarlet asked. "What do you think?"

We waited and waited then the doors finally flew open and the boy was thrown into the room in a white hospital gown with green trim. He had strange cuffs on his wrists. The same ones he was interrogated with, but they weren't connected. He turned onto his back and lifted himself up on his elbows. He raised one hand like he was trying to open the door without touching it.

A guard outside of the door groaned and a gun fell to the ground. I could hear the guard groaning as he was being pushed into the walls. I could feel him hitting the walls and the floor and then the ceiling. The boy put his hand down and waited. Apparently, the ability restricting cuffs did nothing.

He had a smirk on his face while the bloodied guard followed by six others marched into the room. They pulled small white cylinders off of their belts. We thought they were gas canisters so we all backed away and got behind Aluminum who was ready to make a shield around us if she had to.

They pressed buttons on the cylinders and they snapped open into batons. They hit him with all they had. Then they put him on his stomach and got on top of him. A guard got on each side of him and put a type of sticker on each of his temples. The boy shook violently and passed out. Then they let him go and left the room.

The doors closed behind the guards and the boy rolled over. The boy quickly got up, still smiling, and pulled the stickers off.

"Is that all you got?" He called after them. Blood stained his teeth.

I heard a guard yell angrily and try turning back for round 2 but the other guards stopped him. The boy looked at the cuffs. A green light turned green and his arms twitched. They had blocked his telekinesis. The boy got to his feet and walked around this new room. It was his first time being in here.

"Why is it so empty?" He finally asked walking to us. "Trust," I told him.

"I suspect a lack of it." He said. I nodded.

He and Scar joined our circle and we waited for the food. A slot in the door opened and six trays slid through. Of course, the trays were colored too.

I grabbed yellow, Aluminum grabbed blue, Scar grabbed black, Scarlet got red and the kid grabbed orange. Leaving the new boy with green.

We sat back in the circle and ate. The boy didn't really touch his food. He just stared at it. When he finally looked up he asked, "how come I can't remember my name?"

Aluminum told him. "None of us can. That's why we came up with new names. See this last letter on my mark?" She showed her mark: MANDS-A2. "I chose my name based off of that. We all did. Except him." She pointed to the youngest of us. "He hasn't really chosen one yet."

The boy looked at his mark: MANDS-S5. "Do they know the names you've chosen?"

The kid answered the question. "All except for me and I plan on keeping it that way. They have my past. My new name is a new life. I control this one."

The boy put his arm down and finally ate. "We have class next." He said as he pushed the oranges off of his plate and the purple lettuce out of his salad.

"How do you know?" I asked him.

He stuffed his mouth with the partially green salad and cardboard-like steak and pushed the tray to the middle of the circle. Under his steak was a torn piece of paper. On the paper it said:

*You have class next*

*-H*

I stressfully ran a hand through my hair and ate. I needed my strength. If any answers were wrong in the new test we had to take, we would get electrocuted from the floor and more lab-work. If we tried simply lifting our feet up, the current would always find us.

"Not looking forward to this." I said to the group.

"No one is." Said Aluminum. "I think President is trying to kill us." She said jokingly with a smile.

My eyes widened, and I looked to Scarlet. We put our widened eyes down and finished our food.

The boy chuckled and watched us gag as we ate the terrible food. He was the reason the food was as terrible as it was. Until he could behave, President would punish all of us. He didn't believe in individual punishment.

<T1 A2 S3 K4 S5>

"Welcome back, class. Today you will not have lab-work." Harry told us. We all cheered and everyone gave high fives. The older boy sat confused.

"No. Instead of work in here," he grew an evil smile. "You will work in your training rooms. So everyone pack up your stuff and head down to your training room."

"What stuff?" The kid asked.

Harry was packing up one orb for each of us into a grey sack with a faint glowing hexagonal pattern and the mark 'J. I' on it. He turned around and said, "Your brains and muscles." He paused and smiled. "You're gonna need them."

We all groaned and slammed our heads down. Even the other boy. He was put into the test without getting his dose. As he groaned his tray fell over and hit Harry in the shin. Harry cried out and jumped on one foot. The boy, still with his head down, laughed.

Harry put the pain off. "Before we go, there are two things you must do: one physical task and one mental task."

He grabbed a random yellow orb (one he didn't pack up) and turned to me. "Here is your question." He threw it and it bounced off the top of my desk and opened. It was multiple choice. A-E.

I cheated by trying to look into the future at which answers would zap me. I found the one and put my finger to it. It said CORRECT in big yellow letters and did another question. There was only supposed to be one question.

"What the heck?!" I yelled. I looked down and saw a surge of electricity swimming around my desk. I looked back at the question. *What does MANDS stand for?* I had no idea. That one wasn't multiple choice.

I told Harry I didn't know. Instead of giving me the answer he watched the surge reach my feet and me jump out of my chair. He laughed and gave me my physical test.

"Please give the sound of a lion as a squirrel." He said. I did so, and he grabbed a blue orb and walked over to Aluminum. Those involved in Aluminum's protected all tensed.

She got her question right and CORRECT was in big blue letters. She got the same second question as I did and was electrocuted shortly after admitting she didn't know. She then moved to the physical test. "Alright, Aluminum. Move across the room and take that pencil," he pointed to a pencil in his desk, "without any of us seeing you. She turned invisible and four seconds later she was visible in her chair with the pencil and a paper that she found in Harry's desk.

"Let's see here." Aluminum said as she unfolded the paper. "MANDS stands for-"

Harry snatched the paper and brought it back to his desk. Aluminum was electrocuted but not as bad as me. Harry grabbed a red orb with black snakes swimming inside and walked over to Scar and Scarlet. "You two do this together. He threw the test and they were completely lost.

"How are we supposed to know what the Scar Origins are and when it started?" Scar protested. Harry didn't acknowledge that they said anything.

He just waiting for them to put in an answer. They plugged in a random answer and got the question wrong. Surges swam across the floor and zapped them both.

"Now your physical portion. Absorb something. Both of you." Harry said. They pressed the same answer that they got wrong and knelt down to collect the surge of electricity before it could harm them. They stood straight up with the surges or electricity flying around their arms and walked over to Harry. They slowly reached out to Harry and, ever so lightly, tapped his chest.

He went flying across the room and through his desk.

Then all of the sudden he stood up and was perfectly fine. He pulled down his sleeve but before he did I saw the H that was marked on his forearm. I looked around to see who else saw it. The older boy looked like he saw it but couldn't make sense of it.

Harry walked to the orange tray and pulled out an orb. He threw it to the kid. He got it wrong but on purpose. The surge went through him and only made his arm twitch. Harry nodded and gave him his physical portion.

"Break that wall," He said, pointing to the 10-foot thick wall of concrete. "with one punch." He finished holding up one finger.

The kid walked over to the wall and punched it. Harry put a ruler in the hole that the kid had just made. "8 feet." He said and went to his desk for the final tray.

He pulled it out and an evil smile spread across his face. He threw the green orb to the older boy. It opened, and the boy just stared at it. "Is there a problem?" Asked Harry in one of those partially sarcastic ways. "Oh. Your test seems to be blank. What's your answer?" He smiled and stepped back as the electric surge found the boy's feet. The surge went through the boy and he tried his best not to show his pain. It didn't work very well.

"Man." Said Harry. "First we can't get you to shut up and now we can't get you to talk. Come on. Say *some*thing." Harry gave the boy his test as he leaned on his desk. "Lift...me."

The boy looked up with surprise on his face. From the surge and the test. Harry started walking back to what was left of his desk.

"The purpose of this company is to take what *we* give you and turn it into instinct. This is the less painful way to do that. So, do what you're told. Even if you don't want to and even if you are incapable of doing so. There's no point in not-"

The boy lifted his hand and Harry started to levitate. Then all of the sudden, the boy looked really angry. Not like how the kid looked but like an agony type of anger.

He threw his hand on the concrete wall that was the kid's test and Harry followed.

The wall broke all the way through and fell. The boy took his green orb out of the 'J.I' bag and walked to the door. "The kid passed." He said and walked out. He then turned around and crouched over Harry's body. "*Something.*"

We all grabbed our assigned orbs from the bag they were packed in and left. I turned around before I left the room to see Harry's broken body but, never saw a broken body. I saw a man who was back at his broken desk in his swivel chair and typing in our results to another orb. I left and went to the training room.

We went down the hallway and stopped at our doors. We all went in at the same time. I went in mine and didn't expect what I saw.

Guards, control operators, battle categories, 5 serums (probably all the same), personal bodyguards, combat researchers, 2 giant control panels and President.

"Time to show what you're made of," President said with a smile. He pushed me through the door into my training room and all I saw when I looked back was myself. The intercom came one. "This test has a physical part and a mental part. Solve the problems while fighting an equal opponent: yourself."

# CHAPTER 12

# PRESIDENT

I kneeled down next to their mangled bodies. My suit jacket was long gone, my white dress shirt was no longer white, my tie sat loosely around my neck, and I was covered in blood. Wether it was mine or where it was actually coming from was a mystery to me.

*How could I have let this happen?*

"Charles?" Came a gargled voice. I looked around to find who the voice belonged to. I turned over body after body.

Gardo. Joan. Jason. Harry. Even Jonothan. All dead. I turned over another body. The kid. I stared at his lifeless body. His orange sweatshirt was peppered with bullet holes and stained with blood. Then suddenly he coughed, and his eyes opened. He raised his head towards me.

"You! Did. This..." Blood slowly spilled out of his mouth. His head fell. He was dead as fast as he had woken.

"Charles." I heard again from the same gargled voice. I turned around. Tressa was looking in my direction. Half of her body was buried in the dirt. I crawled over to her. She wore a bloodied yellow suit and her hair was covered in mud and slightly scorched.

"Is that you?" She asked. Her eyes were the same pale blue they were when we found her. "Yeah. It's me. You're going to be okay."

"I tried to warn you," She whispered. "All would die."

She was fading. She turned her head towards the black cloud infested sky. Fires all around us lit up her face.

"Your intention was to save the world." She said. "You can't even save yourself. You're going to die, Charles." She turned her head back to me. "YOU'RE GOING TO DIE!" She screamed, and I heard it echo in my ears.

I launched myself out of my bed. As soon as I regained control over my breathing I walked into my bathroom and turned on the hot water and watched the stopper slowly drown in steaming water. I dunked my head in and pushed my short, yet stubborn, greying hair back. I looked up at the fogged mirror and wiped away the fog. The bags under my eyes returned for another day.

*Who is this man who ruins lives? The children's lives. My own life.*

I splashed away the monster in the mirror and got dressed in my regular grey suit and black tie. I prepared myself to go back to MANDS and check on the daily progress.

I decided it wasn't a good idea to sleep at MANDS anymore, so I gave Harry my room and had a house built on the hillside. I took some of the gas that I once used to erase the children's memories. But it wasn't enough for me.

Sometimes I just wanted to forget but it all came back to me. I wanted to forget when I found out every little thing Tressa told Scar or that Aluminum was protected and planned to use her power to kill me. I wanted to forget how the clones were using their surroundings as an advantage or how the kid killed over 40 guards in the past week.

The other boy wasn't speaking. Every time we came close to getting him to talk, he impaled people with different objects. Even in empty rooms.

I got in my new car, Maybach Icarus 2067 XIV, and drove to MANDS, still wiping the crust out of my eyes.

"Sir, you have a visitor", Jason warned at the front doors.

"Send him on his way", I told him. Jason grabbed my shoulder and turned me around. "It's your brother."

My eyes widened, and I went immediately to my office. I threw the doors open and he was in my chair. I slowly walked into a surprise visit and sat in the guest chair.

Jonothan rose out of my chair and went over to my liquor cabinet.

"Remember when we were kids?" Jonothan started; pouring himself a drink. "Remember when we would have the others sleep over and we would plan for our future? Or when we got older and planned on building a house together and rule the world?" He laughed and took a drink and shivered as the whiskey coolly burned its way down his throat like lava and pooled into his stomach.

"Of course, I remember. It wasn't that long ago that we were kids."

"It was too long ago. But that's not why I'm here." He drained another glass. "And why *are* you here?" I said slowly growing impatient with my brother.

"Charles, I thought we could do this together. We completely combine MANDS and Jonothan Industries. I move here, and we work together. Maybe attach the towers. We will make yours taller, so the heights match and we could both have top floors."

I glared at him. It was like he was trying to steal my ideas. "You do realize that *that* was my original idea, right?"

"Well, of course, brother." He said pouring me a glass. I grabbed the glass as he slid it across my desk. As I caught it, some of the alcohol spilled out onto my white desk.

He kept talking. "There are some things we need to talk about first."

I put the glass of sweet poison down just before it touched my lips. "What kind of things?" "Well for starters, Scar and Scarlet."

"What about them?" I asked, pushing the glass of alcohol aside.

"I split Scar thinking that it would split the power. It was Jason's idea. She was too dangerous with that amount of power. But It didn't work. All it did was make a copy of her and take away a sliver of the ability from Scarlet. I did it one more time with Scarlet to see if I make one more that would either balance the two out or come out as human. The other never got the power but she was just as strong and just as telepathic to the others." He avoided eye contact with me.

"And?" I urged him to continue with this new information.

"I had to kill her. I suggest you do the same with Scar and Scarlet." He avoided eye contact again.

I took a drink of my alcohol and waved him to continue.

"As for the rest of them. I had them all before you did." Jonothan said as he finally met my eyes.

I forced the burning liquid down my throat. "What! How? When?" I said breathing hard. I demanded all answers at that very moment.

"I'm getting to that part. I wanted to show you that I can do this stuff myself. So I captured them and put slight abilities in them. I realized that even a little bit of power with this sort would be dangerous. So, I had Jason make-"

"How long have you and Jason worked together? I just got him." I interrupted. Jonothan threw his hands at his sides, tilted his head and glared at me. "Can I finish?" I nodded.

"I had Jason make a serum to take their powers away, but he didn't give them the right amount of dosage. I brainwashed them of those few short weeks and dropped them off back at their homes. Not all of them went home. A couple could feel the power in their blood and searched for a new place to live. A way to live. Then you found Tressa; the last one I dropped off. I thought I could do something with Scar and Scarlet, so I kept them. I was wrong."

"Damn. Anything else?" I said.

"Yeah. When you picked up Tressa...did she have any bruises?" Jonothan asked slowly stepping around the desk for a clear answer.

Tressa *did* have bruises. And they quickly faded into nothing. "That was you? Why?" Jonothan continued, "It was all a part of the breaking point of their training. She had broken ribs too."

"Broken ribs? I never noticed any br-" I was cut off at Jonathan's enthusiasm.

"Exactly!" He smiled. "They heal. I mean, the 12-year-old heals the best but, they all heal, Charles."

I thought about it. "All of them?" I took another drink.

"Every last one of them. Faster than any human. But not extremely rapid. Aluminum! Tressa bit her in her wolf form, did she not?" He asked pacing around excited.

"She did," I answered while trying to keep track of Jonathan's quick movements through my office.

"Scar and Scarlet. They heal each other. Right after an injury, they help each other. One cannot live without the other. They cannot die if the other is living. If they are merged, then they will immediately die if they are close enough to death. They are dependent upon each other."

I followed him and as I was going to comment I was cut off yet again by Jonathan's excitement. It felt good to see my brother acting the way we did when we were kids. The only difference was our appearances. I looked much older than him, but it was still us.

"The little boy. What is his name?" He calmed.

I thought before I answered. "He never said. I assume the others call him *something* but in the lunch hall they get in such a tight circle that the cameras can't pick up much of what they say."

Jonothan threw his hand. "Anyways. Did he not have scratches when you got him?"

"He did but they were from Tressa." I thought a little more and let the memory resurface. "...and they quickly-"

"They quickly healed, didn't they?" Jonothan got excited again. "And the oldest-I doubt you got anything out of him-he had major gashes from when Aluminum threw those discs, right?" He held out his hand for a response.

He was exciting me. I smiled. "True. The discs did a lot of damage and he quickly recovered. This is incredible!" I tried to get serious. "And he healed too. I get it." I looked at the orb that Jason and Jonothan had constructed for me. "So, what do we do?" I asked.

Jonothan calmed himself. He put the alcohol glass back in the cabinet and sat back down in my chair. "First, we join. I'll move my closest tower even closer. The next move is up to you."

"I say we brainwash them just one more time." "No," Jonothan said firmly.

"You *just* said that *I* get to make the next move."

"Every time you brainwash them, you have to give them another dosage, so they won't forget their abilities."

"So?" I asked shrugging my shoulders. "We have plenty left."

"So, every time you give them a dose, they become more and more of what we don't want them to become."

There was a moment of silence before I broke it. "They will be the ones that secure the future of mankind. They will take us to a new planet and help the humans. They will be heroes."

"They will be mindless *freaks*!" Jonothan snapped. "They are our future!" I snapped back.

"Don't you care what happens to them?"

"Why does it matter what happens to them? Jon, I'm thinking about the future. I'm thinking about *us*!"

"You're thinking about yourself, Charles! You always have. Stop thinking for one minute and look at the current situation. Look at their eyes. Have you not seen their eyes, Charles?!"

"I *have* seen their eyes. Yellow, blue, black, red, orange, green. I've seen it all!"

"It is almost complete. Tressa's irises are solid yellow. Aluminum's eyes have dark blue flakes in her eyes. Her eyes are already blue so that's not a very good marker. Let the oldest boy be your marker. His left eye is still brown, but it has green flakes in it. By the time both eyes are green, it will be too late."

"Listen. I know Aluminum can't take anymore brainwashing and I know how close it's getting to that start over mark. I brainwashed her after I went to get the older one and every time she made a plan to kill me but, they are strong, Jonathan. You said so yourself."

"I said they can heal. I never said how strong they are," Jonothan said monotonously. "They're stronger than you give them credit for." I pleaded. Jonathan sighed.

"What are we going to do with her?" Jonothan asked, playing with the short hairs that made up his beard.

"Well she constantly seeks freedom." I watched as Jonathan leaned forward and slowly understood where I was getting. "I say we set her free... from this world. Rumor has it that she wants my life."

Jonathan's eyebrows rose. "She wants to kill you?"

I continued. "Using the power that *I* gave her." I sighed.

"And how did you find this rumor?" Jonothan asked. I pulled out an orb that had the security on it and played back one of the previous meetings that Aluminum took charge of in the lunch hall.

Aluminum told of how they have to get away and how she would gladly take the life from the man who took hers.

She said revolution when Jonothan closed the orb by putting his hand straight down onto it. "I get it." Jonothan said. He brought a hand to his temple and rubbed away yet another headache that was being caused by me.

"Very well. We will brainwash them now. We will kill her soon. But not before we clone her and start again with her. Despite the success of the Scar Origins" He looked up from the closed orb. "the others will most likely know of this very moment and seek to protect her."

"You can use my own private project to kill Scar and Scarlet. Action starts now. Welcome to MANDS, baby brother." I said as I offered my hand to Jonathan.

"You're older than me by 14 minutes. Don't let that go to your head. Welcome to Jonothan Industries." He said as he shook back. Then he left. I sat back in my chair. I couldn't help but wonder if I was doing it all right and if it would work.

*Am I doing the right thing? I saw the enthusiasm in his eyes and the same worry I have now. But is it all the right thing to do? Of course, it is. The world is mine. The world is ours.*

I looked up and saw Jonothan with a smile on his face. He stood in the doorway and shook his head and said, "You have got to stop doing that." He turned to leave. "Stop doubting yourself. You're supposed to have faith when no one else does. Only then will this project work."

As he walked down the hall he glanced at the oldest boy's room. He stood there for a while and when a scientist came up to him he told him something.

The scientist nodded, and the rooms filled with fog. It was done. The final test would soon be activated.

# CHAPTER 13

# SCARLET

I didn't know what happened. I was in my chamber and then it flooded with fog and I must have passed out before I made it very far from the dome-like prison. The fog, or whatever it was, was still in my lungs. I couldn't remember how I was there or for how long. All I knew was that I had to get out. Me *and* my twin. I had almost forgotten about her.

I felt the link to my twin and could tell that she remembered just as much as I did. So basically nothing. I laid on the ground and I thought about my twin. I was told that we were twins, but we were too similar to be twins. We were more of clones than twins. And if we're clones, how many others are there?

The metal door in the concrete wall opened and my clone stumbled out holding her head. Every door in the room was open after the fog cleared.

"You alright?" She walked over to my body on the floor.

"I think so," I said. "Where are we?" I got to my feet. Just as I got to feet I felt light-headed. I felt a rush going through my entire body and going straight to my head. I heard a whisper in my ear and it echoed around in my head.

*Scarlet? This will only take a moment. Don't forget why we are here.*

I tried to stay on my feet, but it was all too much, and I stumbled. The room spun as pictures of faces went through my mind. I fell to the ground and screwed my eyes shut hoping it would all stop.

I opened my eyes and looked over at the clone and she was doing the same thing. She fell to the ground at the same time I did, and it was like looking into a mirror. We rolled onto our backs as pictures flashed on the ceiling.

The pictures stopped, and, at that moment, I felt nothing.

I stared at the blinding white ceiling. I looked at my clone. She looked dead. Or traumatized at least. I tried to get to her to see if she was okay. I kicked myself over to her while I was still on my back. And then it all came back. The pain. And that pain brought back memories of pain and even more memories. Who I am, who the clone is, where I am, who runs this place. I turned over onto my stomach.

I tried to lift myself up, but my arms shot out from under me. Weak and drained, I turned my head with the little strength I had left. I saw my clone. She was staring at me. I thought she was dead. Then she opened her mouth and yelled as the pain came back to the both of us,

"Scarlet!"

I rolled over on my back again and let the pain in. I stared at the ceiling and saw more images flashing faster and faster. Memories. There was another. A girl with strange pale blue eyes surrounded by golden flakes and she had blonde hair. Tressa. Tressa was somehow making us see the images. We saw images of people and a memory swam around them that was their power.

I saw myself. But it wasn't me. The hair and clothes were different. It was Scar.

Scar must have seen the same things I did because when we saw Tressa she yelled, "Traitor!" Scar knew something I didn't, and it was restored. They had a deal and based on our lack of memory it seemed like Tressa broke it.

When it was all over for sure, we struggled to get to our feet. Scar stumbled, and I caught her. I looked at her closer. Her eyes were pitch black. Not just the irises. It was her entire eye. Almost as if they were black holes. She gasped; looking into mine.

"What's wrong?" I asked. She put her hands on my cheeks and shifted my head around at weird angles still looking into my eyes.

"Your eyes are red." She said breathlessly still moving my head around. "Well we haven't been sleeping much and I got the fog stuff in my eyes." "No." She said. "Not the white parts. But the irises."

"Must have been the fog. Come on. Let's go check on the others." Scar nodded, and we left the room through the thick metal door to the hallway.

We walked into the chow hall and Scar saw Tressa.

She ran at her and jumped on her, placing her hands at her throat. Tressa tried to pry Scar's hands from her throat. It was no use, so Tressa started to shapeshift. We could see the form of a bear slowly take place, but Scar was cutting off too much air.

Then Scar was tackled by the little kid into the concrete wall. The wall crumbled on top of them. The kid stood up and looked at me. His eyes were glowing orange.

He was pulled from the debris by an invisible force. The older one held Scar in the air with his power and then dropped her but caught her just before she hit the ground. I looked at his eyes. Only his left eye was glowing, and it was green. He dropped Scar and she landed back in the pile of debris.

Tressa tried to explain what happened.

"Jonathan is with President now more than ever." She said with a heavy sigh of frustration. "They are working side by side and their first action was to brainwash us. I was able to save a few of everyone's memories but not all of them. And it didn't work so well for everyone." Tressa looked at Scar who was brushing herself off. Tressa got to her feet and walked over to Scar. "I'm still going with the plan."

When it turned out that the deal wasn't broken, Scar calmed down.

The girl who could turn invisible came in and sat down next to me. Not even questioning what happened to the room.

We couldn't remember her name. Only that we had to keep her safe. Though the plan and what she was being protected from was lost for me, I was relieved to know she was okay.

We sat in a circle in the middle of the room like we'd always done. Tressa spoke first. "They tried to take away our memories." She looked around the group.

The girl who could turn invisible spoke, "I've still got most of mine."

Tressa stood up. "Well, Aluminum, with my Found Power to see into the future I can also look into the past. Your Found Power is super intelligence, so you should be able to look back too. That allowed me to look into your head pretty easily. *He* was the easiest." She pointed to the older boy.

Scar stood up. Anger was growing in her eyes black voids. Tressa was about to speak but Scar interrupted. "You told, didn't you? Why else would they have tried to take away our memories? So, we would forget it all!"

"Scar, you have most of it back. I am following with the-"

Scar was still standing, and she tried her best not to kill her then and there. "Shut up! You're not one of us! You're one of them! You just want to have your old position back, so you told President what we were trying to do!"

Tressa shot back, "Just when I thought you couldn't get any dumber! I mean honestly, Scar! Do you hear what you're saying? I bet that if you didn't have any of your memories you would be smarter than you are now."

They both met in the middle of the circle. There was tension growing between them. The tension felt normal, but the strange part was the fact that we could see it.

Black particles emitted from Scar's chest and met in the middle with the bright yellow particles from Tressa. The two clouds collided and swam around the two; forming a column of rotating black and yellow particles.

The older boy stood up. I couldn't remember his name either or if he even chose one. He walked away from the group. He stopped about five feet away. He turned around and raised both arms out to opposite sides.

Tressa shot to one side of the room and Scar to the other. The two-colored particles followed the ones they had emitted from and returned. "Why don't we all have seat." He pushed his arms down and Scar and Tressa face-planted into the ground. He let them go and sat back in the circle.

Scar stood up and brushed herself off once again, but something wasn't right with Tressa. She just laid there. Her eyes were glowing bright yellow. After a few minutes, she sat herself up and joined the circle. She didn't talk for the rest of dinner.

"We need a name," the kid said after too much silence. "Like what?" Aluminum asked.

"Well, they're trying to get us to use our power as instincts, right?"
"Yeah?" I responded.

"Let's do something with that." Kid said. "Instincts?" The older boy asked.

"Yeah but with a twist."

"It needs to sound like there's more than one of us." The older boy said. "More than five or six of us. An army of us." Aluminum added.

"Like The Instinctsion." The kid said cheerfully as he uncovered an invisible title above the group. "And any super who stays alive by using their instincts, is a part of The Instinctsion."

The boy shrugged. "I like it. Why not? Long Live The Instinctsion."

Scar eventually got up and stomped to our chamber. Something wasn't right. She was purposely blocking our link, so I couldn't see what she was doing from the mess hall.

As we left Tressa stopped me in the hall and pushed me against the wall and waited for everyone else to continue walking out of sight.

"I know you have a link with Scar. Am I wrong?"

I looked into her still glowing eyes. "Yeah," I said trying to look away.

"The link was rebuilding itself and already restoring memories. I had to stop a few. Is it possible for you to block certain parts?"

I managed to look away from her eyes, but my eyes fell on the redness on her neck. "Yes." I choked out as her forearm began to crush my windpipe.

"Block the link and buy me some time. Let Scar think what she wants."

"You want her to continue thinking that you are betraying us?" I said, looking back into her eyes. The glowing was going away, and they were returning to their normal pale blue.

"She has to. She is no longer apart of the plan of escape." Tressa looked away from me. "She never was. I think that she is the one who doesn't leave here so from now on, her only purpose is to keep you alive. Okay?"

"You do realize that she will kill you the first chance she gets, right?"

"I was wrong about the vision. Aluminum isn't the one who won't make it out of here." She brought her eyes back up, "Trust the boy. Tell Aluminum too." She removed her arm and walked back into her room. The wall moved to block her way back.

"Which boy?" I said, knowing that she couldn't hear me.

I went to my room and Scar was looking around my room. She had managed to put a hole in a wall big enough for her to squeeze through and was now digging around in a scientists' desk. She was throwing things around the room.

"What the hell are you doing?" I yelled while dodging scalpels and stethoscopes.

She didn't answer. She pulled out a fillet knife and paused. She turned it and watched the steel flicker. Then she threw that too and gave up. She went into her own room which was just as messy as mine.

She began to panic herself. She was curling up into a ball and held her hands over the back of her head. Her fingers were buried in her dark blonde hair. She sounded like she was crying.

Then small damaged wings shot from her back. Bones broke and then healed. They curved, and she had legs similar to that of a werewolf. I felt everything, but the physical changes only happened to her.

She crouched and jumped up into the vent and began to crawl to Tressa's room.

"No," I said. "It's too soon." By Instinct, I grabbed scalpels and did as best as I could to delay her. I threw them through the vent, so she would have to stop. She stopped crawling. All of the sudden a scalpel was pulled through the vent to Scar's side. She pulled three and then kept crawling. Blood dripped through the vent as Scar crawled further over the scalpels she didn't want.

"Sorry, Tressa." I went to my chamber door and waited. I heard guards and scientists. The plan was being activated. That day, we escape.

# CHAPTER 14

# KID

I woke up face-down on the white linoleum floor of the room that was my chamber. They never gave me a bed to sleep on and I was not going to sleep on the table, so the floor was my best friend when It came to sleep. I heard someone crawling through the vents.

*Must be that clone.* I thought to myself

I hadn't heard much from the other boy, but I was sure he was planning the same thing that we all were; escape.

I thought I had gotten all of the schedules figured out. It was all mental times though because the clocks didn't work. I guessed the clocks were just supposed to add a *home* feeling.

I pushed myself up off of the ground and looked around my chamber. The only thing in my chamber was a horizontal table. Everything was in order. Then I remembered.

"Tressa," I said as I pushed myself up onto my feet. I stumbled to the door and tried to make my way to Tressa's room. The wall was in the way. Again.

I followed the way that the walls were set up. They led to my training room. I looked around. There was no one there. No guards. No people on the control panels. No boss. No one.

I walked into the middle of my training room. I looked around and saw that the power was turned off. The room actually seemed peaceful for once. I remembered that the floor moves so I quickly stood against the wall. It was a force of habit. Almost instinct.

I looked up from the floor and to the mirror. I had gotten so used to people on the other side of the glass. No one was on the other side of the glass nor was there a glass at all.

I walked across the floor and looked through the empty frame. I saw a blur go by the door. "Aluminum," I said under my breath. I jumped through the frame and ran through the door. I looked left and saw nothing.

I looked right and saw a circle of guards in the hallway. Nothing was in the middle of the circle. But that's only how it looked. One guard threw a smoke bomb and then I saw what they did. They made Aluminum partially visible.

With Aluminum visible enough, the guards took aim and shot little darts into her and she fell flat to the ground. Surges of electricity journeyed through her body and she shook from the power.

"You have *got* to stop escaping," said one guard while grabbing her by the blue trimmed collar of her hospital gown and dragging her back to her room. "How do you escape a locked door without opening it? Are you the one who can phase? That would explain it."

As the guards dragged Aluminum back to her room, one guard decided to hang back a little. He slowly turned around and saw me.

"Well, well, well. Who let you out, little guy?" He said. He slowly walked toward me. I didn't know what to know to do. There could have been others around the corner and I didn't want him to call the others back.

He brought himself to my height. New guy obviously. He clearly didn't know which powers I had, and he wasn't being cautious. I tilted my head and allowed a smirk.

The guard's expression changed. "What are *you* smirkin' at?" He started to back up.

I walked closer. I punched him, and he went through the wall that he backed into. Before I ran I looked at the damage I did to him. His skull had become concave and I could see his brain. Or what was left.

"Cool!" I said. I looked down the hallway that I was going to go. Guards were running my way.

"The beacon in his nervous system stopped working over here!" The leader said. "Not cool!" I said as I ran the other way. I had no choice but to follow the walls.

I thought I remembered Aluminum and the others plan to escape. Yeah. I was the wall-breaker and Aluminum would keep us all invisible and protected. But with walls that just won't break, the plan was pretty useless. Now that I think about it, it might have actually been another dream.

I followed the walls and they led to my room. I turned around to run the other way, but guards blocked my way back. I looked behind them and saw a stretcher with a body on it. I looked behind that stretcher and saw another stretcher.

The guard I 'accidentally' killed, and Aluminum lay on two separate stretchers. I put my hands up and put a smile on. Two guards cautiously stepped forward with weird cuffs.

The cuffs were controlled with a trigger at the end of an eight-foot pole. A trigger on the side of the pole controlled the electricity in the cuffs.

"Sorry, kid. Can't take any chances." A guard said. He pulled back his gun and was going to knock me out with the butt of his gun. I ducked and pushed it so it hit the other guard.

I grabbed that guards foot and swung him around and launched him at the group of guards. I broke the cuffs apart. I jumped over them all and ran. I ran and then stopped. Not by choice of course.

A new device. One I hadn't seen before.

"Oh, you like this little gadget? Got this from the boss's brother. Jonothan." The cocky guard kept his thumb on the button controlling the energy force and used his other hand to push a button on the neck of his suit that folded his helmet away into the collar of his armor.

With my strength, I was able to move but it was in super slow motion. I tried turning around to grab the controller from him, but he was moving too much.

"I think it's a little much but with people like you, it's just my style." His smile disappeared, and he pushed the button forward. The energy force quickly pushed me to the ground and then I couldn't move at all. It was crushing me.

The smile returned to his face as he walked up to my body. He pulled out a lightning sticker and put it on my neck. I was zapped unconscious.

I woke up but everything was blurry. I noticed I was vertical, but it wasn't my legs that were keeping me up. I turned my head a little and saw a table. The same metal table in my room that had kept me up in the surgeries was doing its job once again.

I looked down. Not to my feet but to my hands. They were in small box-like machines with no covers. I could see my palms. The machines had two little mechanical arms for each of my hands. One of the arms had a scalpel and the other had a needle.

The mechanical arm with the scalpel cut open my palm. Blood squirted from my hand and pooled up in my palms. It flooded my palm and dribbled onto the floor.

The other arm with the needle injected the needle into the cut. A timer started at the bottom of the box. 77 seconds and my palm had completely healed.

The timer reset, and the needle refilled itself. Then the scalpel cut again. 76 seconds.

My arms were at 90-degree angles for the machines. My entire upper body was covered in needles. Giving me more muscle power. This much could kill anyone though. But at that point, didn't think they cared anymore. I was fading. My head fell, and my vision blurred.

At least I went out with a little fight. And so, did everyone else... hopefully.

Tressa was probably going to die from Scar who didn't believe that Tressa was still on our side. Scar was in the vent above Aluminum's chamber. I can hear her absorbing different things. She was so angry that she kept switching between the metal of the vent and the strange thick,

plastic of super screws.

Aluminum was thrown back into her chamber. Probably locked up or just unconscious and the guards were given the task of finding out how she kept getting out.

Scarlet was probably just sitting in her chamber letting it all happen; waiting for when everyone meets their end.

As for the other boy. He is probably breaking more stuff. Again. And killing guards from inside his chamber. Again.

And then there's me. The one who is probably going to die first. But

I went with a fight. I actually didn't mean to hurt anyone. It felt natural. It was like instinct.

"Long live The Instinctsion." I whispered to myself as the floor blurred to darkness.

# CHAPTER 15

# STEFANO

I was laying on the horizontal table in the middle of my chamber. I woke up from the same dream I had been having for days. Tressa explained that it was a message from her and what it meant. In the dream, I get struck by lightning and go to a floating city for help. Angels descend from the city and help me. Tressa told me that the dream was something I had to make a reality.

I've been tased enough to say that I don't look forward to being struck by lightning.

I lifted myself up and put my face in my hands. I pull my head up and dragged my cheeks with my hands. I looked at my left forearm. There was a faint scar in my forearm that told me that I was injected with something. Perhaps, I was given something to make my telekinesis weaker. Maybe it was something to make it stronger.

MANDS-S5. Since day 1 of being locked up, I didn't choose a name. I thought on it for a little while.

"How about...Stefano?" I said to myself. For some reason, the name sounded closer to home than any other. I looked around. That day was the day I would leave.

I inspected my chamber door. It was still locked. As if I expected anything different.

I raised my hand a little and played with my telekinesis just a little more as I thought of a plan for escape. I levitated the tray on the back counter.

I watched my veins glow bright green and create a trail from my fingers, around my arm, over my chest, up my neck, and making my eye glow. But only my left eye.

As I did that, a thought popped into my head. I turned to the only window in my chamber and threw the tray at it. The window was on the thick metal door. A small target but it looked thin enough.

I threw the tray, but it didn't even scratch the glass.

I heard a sound come from the door. I shook my arms and my head and got the glow to go back to the normal slight pink glow under my skin.

I lay back down and pretended to still be asleep. I listened as they worked. "Hey, Bill."

"Hey, Lance."

"What happened to the tray?" Bill asked.

"I don't know. I just got here." Lance Replied.

"Isn't this the kid who almost killed everyone on his way here?"

"Yup. Crazy bastard tried to flip the car while he was still in it. Anyways, guess what." "What?"

"Caught that inviso-girl again," Bill said as he puffed his chest.

"They let *you* on guard duty?" Lance said surprised.

"Of course. Every great scientist is an even greater guard." Bill bragged.

"Is that why that kid beat *you* with *Rick*?" Lance tilted his head and waited for Bill's excuse. "You heard about that?" Bill said; trying to act like he was actually working on something.

"I work with you. Of course."

"I do too. Sadly." Said Harry as he walked in. "Shut up, Harry!" Lance and Bill said in sync.

"Did you two see the plans for President's new project? The memory force field thing? I think he's already set it up." Harry asked.

"Nah. Too busy. Fill us in."

While the idiots were talking about something I probably should have listened to, I thought of a plan. I couldn't think straight for some reason.

*They got Aluminum and the clones were most likely locked back up in something far worse than before. Our only two hopes of escape; behind locked doors.*

A determination was filling my body. I was rapidly turning it into adrenaline. I improvised the rest of what little plan I had.

I jumped up onto the table and slammed who I could have guessed to be Lance and Bill together. I got to a position to crush the last guy's heart.

It was Harry. I wanted to kill him but at the same time, I wanted him to run away. He smiled and slowly started to walk toward the table I stood on. I slammed my foot on the table hoping he would at least flinch, but he kept walking. He placed a folder on the table.

"Jason helped out a bit too." He said

He put his hands up in surrender and started to back out of the room; still with a smile on his face. He leaned forward and whispered to me,

"Perhaps we will see each other again." He winked and started to walk away. His sleeve fell as he put his hands up. Before he turned around I saw his mark: H. He was one of us. "Long live The Instinctsion." He left the room and left the thick door wide open.

I jumped off of the table, grabbed the folder, and walked out. I walked into the hallway and checked for guards. Harry was gone. The coast was clear. I hurried out of the room with my hospital gown waving behind me.

As I headed towards the hallway I believed to be the way out, I heard a voice. A feminine voice that made me feel like I should have recognized it.

*Don't forget the boy.*

I didn't think twice before I turned around to the door where I believed the kid lived. I lifted my arms and threw them to the left. The door followed and crashed to the ground. I walked over the door and saw the kid. Apparently, I could only use my ability on the outside of the door.

His body was covered in thousands of needles and his hands were in small machines that cut his hand open and injected him with something that made him heal almost immediately. Blood was pooled on the once spotless linoleum floor beneath his hands.

I put one hand up. The bed laid out flat and levitated out of the room. The needles slid out of his skin effortlessly and fell to the ground. The small machines tried to hold onto his hands but eventually joined the needles on the floor.

I looked through the folder with my other hand. There was also a key card.

*You can't do it alone.*

I pulled out the key card and used it on the pad next to Scarlet's door and the pad next to Aluminum's door. When I got to Tressa's door, the door was already open ajar. My hand reached for the handle but froze when I glanced down. Seeping beneath the heavy door was a pool of bright red blood. I was forcing myself to come up with excuses so that the truth would hurt less. I heard a crash and looked down the hallway. Guards were coming. I backed away from the door and continued to run with the table floating after me. Kid was unconscious but groaned in pain.

I used the key card on every door I came to. I heard guards running down the hallway and coming straight for me and the kid. The doors were taking too long to unlock and then open, so I threw down the key card. I stood next to the kid and waited for that voice to help me out. Nothing. I looked at my glowing green veins and then to the kid.

"Sorry, kid," I said. I ducked and threw the table over my head with both of my arms. The table went straight through the wall. I ran to the table to see if the kid was okay. If he wasn't unconscious when I threw the table, he definitely was then.

I looked behind us at what remained of the wall. It worked pretty well so I picked the table up and used as much telekinetic energy as I could to throw the table through the next few walls.

After five walls I could no longer pick up the table and the kid slid off on the last throw. I looked down at the kid and wiped the blood off my upper lip; a result of what President called a *Telekinetic Overload*.

I looked around to see if the others had followed. I must have gone in a partial circle because through a window I could see all five specimen doors. I never took a turn, but the hallway must have turned without on the left side of where the kid's table was had a small sign on it. The sign said: Private Project. Plan B. Below it was an F.

I cautiously walked inside. On the left side of the room was a single tube chamber. Thin tubing fanned out of the top and connected to the ceiling. Connecting with the floor and the ceiling.

The wall to the right of the tube, opposite the entrance, had five more tubes. Each one with a different color square above it. The first was yellow. Second, blue. Third, black bordered with red. Fourth, orange. And fifth, green.

I walked up to the empty tubes. They were empty but some kind of thick liquid dripped from the ceiling of the tubes and oozed down the sides. They had been used. I looked to my right.

Attached to the wall was a glass case that took up the entire right wall. It had holes in it every couple of feet. Inside the case was a baby crib.

I opened the case and peered inside the crib. There was a baby in it. The baby had gray eyes and dilated pupils even though the room had plenty of light. Inside his pupils were small specs of white. The baby boy looked at me. He didn't cry.

He looked over to the table in the middle of the room. Somehow, I missed it. I closed the case and walked over to the table. On the table were five strange looking bottles. T1 was labeled on the first bottle. Each bottle had a golden cap and they had all been slightly used.

A slow creaking sound echoed through the hall. I looked back to the baby in the crib. He smiled at me. But not the smile one would normally expect from a baby. A more sinister smile.

I walked back out into the hallway and closed the door.

Aluminum slowly opened her door and looked around to see if there were any guards nearby. She stepped out and took a deep breath and vanished. Her hospital gown flourished and then disappeared too. The only door between us opened. Dust from what was left of the walls behind us rose and fell. Aluminum was heading in our direction.

I looked through the dust that slowly fell back down to the ground and saw Scar edge Scarlet out of the room. They saw me and ran towards me. I was a little confused at the moment. Scar saw me and got really angry. Probably because we beat them out. Or that they actually needed us to escape.

I looked around for guards and a few walls back I saw another door. I ran for it and hoped there was something useful inside.

I stepped inside. It was a storage room. The gray room was empty except for a silver button in the middle of the room.

I walked up to the button and stopped. It could have been a trap. I studied the room carefully but quickly. With no threat present or possible, I pressed the button. The button sunk into the floor and a wall opened up in front of me. A faint green light came on and illuminated weapons, clothes, backpacks, and dog-tags. Weapons on top, hoodies on the left, jeans in the middle, shoes under the hoodies, dog-tags next to the jeans and backpacks in the lower right.

I admired the bow and the staff. I reached for the bow and examined it. It was a strong compound bow with a gray rubber grip. I held up the bow to get a feel for it and saw the gray grip turn green. I dropped the bow in surprise and watched the grip flash back to gray.

I slowly pulled the staff down from the rack and touched the grip. It turned green. Then a small button slowly appeared on the side in the top part of the grip. I pressed it and it snapped open into a better version of the bow I had before. I flung the bow forward in my hand and it collapsed back into a staff.

I then grabbed one of the gray hoodies made of a strange silky fabric with a glowing hexagonal pattern on it. I put on the hoodie and it turned green and the material of the hoodie turned to cotton that hugged my body. I grabbed a backpack and threw it onto my shoulders. It turned mostly black but the gray pattern on it turned green. I put the folder Harry gave me into the backpack. There was already stuff in it but there was no time to examine the contents. I found my dog-tag, put it on, grabbed jeans and the only kind of shoes they had. I stepped back, and the wall began to close and the button began to rise.

On my way out of the room and back to the kid I saw him standing in the doorway of the room. He weakly leaned on the frame. The table was just outside of the room. Almost like he dragged it there but there were no drag marks.

He watched the green light go away and the button rise out of the floor again. He looked up to me. "Can you help me get my stuff?" He asked.

I helped him up and walked him over to the button. He slammed his hand down on the button and the wall opened again. The items were illuminated by a faint orange light this time.

"What's your name again?" The kid asked me.

"It's Stefano. Is it cool if I just keep calling you Kid?"

He shrugged his shoulders but in an accepting kind of way.

He pointed out items and I grabbed them off of the wall. His weapon of choice was the giant war hammer. They never turned green for some reason.

When we were done I sat Kid back on his table. I looked at the wall of items. The wall restocked itself and closed. The silver button that the kid pressed rose from the ground. We left the room and left our hospital gowns on the floor.

I looked down the trail of broken walls to check for the girls. Tressa must have either been way ahead of us or looking for Harry.

After a few quick breaths, I helped Kid back onto his feet and we moved on to what should have been the exit. The only problem was that it had five extremely complicated and high-tech locks on it. They looked like puzzle locks. The kid stood on his own and examined the door with me. Breaking the lock systems would most likely lock the door more or drop a blast door.

I turned around and saw Aluminum walk out of the room we were in and zip up her blue hoodie. She looked up at me, gripped her machete and vanished. Still no sign of the other two.

I waited awhile and saw Scar and Scarlet walking out of the room. Scar had a black zip-up hoodie and her hair was thrown over her right shoulder. Scarlet followed her and wore a red hoodie and had her hair in a French braid. They both had throwing knives.

I turned back to Kid. He was still standing in front of the door. Eventually, he just decided that punching the door would be more efficient than trying to solve the puzzles. He merely dented the door. He punched again. Then again and again. I gathered as much energy as I could and threw my arms forward at the same time Kid punched. The thick door fell, and Kid grabbed his stuff and we ran.

We broke through the exit door and ran towards the mountain.

"Come on, Kid!" I yelled. Being the youngest of us, the name sounded right.

We ran to the base of the mountain and I looked behind me to see if everyone made it. Guards poured out of the door.

Scar and Scarlet came from a nearby hallway and ran in front of them. The guards that were already in front of them stopped and turned around.

"Fire! Fire! Fire!" One guard yelled.

They shot, and everyone emptied their magazines. The gunfire only stopped when they pulled new magazines from their belts and snapped them in their guns.

All of the sudden a huge blast louder than a sonic boom sounded.

Bullets went in every direction. Kid and I hit the ground and covered our heads. We looked up and saw Scar and Scarlet walk out of the circle of bodies.

They looked at each other in surprise and then continued to run. More guards came out of the building. Scar and Scarlet put only a small dent in the number of guards that MANDS had.

Scar turned around as she ran and threw knives at the guards. When she only had about five knives left, she kept running.

Then a trail of the guards fell over and a few were bleeding. Aluminum became visible and stopped and stared at her bloodied machete. She shook her head and continued to run.

I didn't see Harry or Tressa. I hoped they made it out before us. I was so distracted with Harry and Tressa that I didn't notice that Scar disappeared. I assumed she went back to look for the others.

Aluminum caught up with Scarlet and they were only about fifty feet behind the kid and myself.

One guard ran in front of the rest and held his arms out. "Stop!" He called. Whether it was to the guards or to us, everyone stopped. Another lifted his gun and pointed it at us. He pulled the trigger and a burst of pops whistled out of his gun. They whistled through the air and three of them sliced through my left shoulder. I put my hand to my shoulder.

"Run!" Everyone yelled. I looked up and saw the guards advancing. I turned around and followed Kid.

We ran through what looked like a force field.

Everyone stopped running. I couldn't remember anything except what I knew to be instinct. My ability. My telekinesis.

I turned to Kid who had the same look on his face as I did.

He pulled his war hammer from the side of his bag and swung it at me. I angled my staff, so his hammer handle slid to the ground and got stuck because of how far into the ground it went. I used my left hand to push him back with as much power as I could. He fell onto his back but quickly got up.

He pulled his arm back to punch me in the face. I dropped my staff and backpack as fast as I could and wrapped his arm in an energy shield. It only slowed his punch. We both strained. I could feel blood running out of my nose as I tried to push his arm away. Then I heard a voice again.

*Your fight is with them. Not against them.*

My shield broke and he punched me. I was on my stomach. He was walking towards me with anger in his eyes. He picked up his hammer and continued in my direction.

I knew he was going to try to kill me with the hammer, so I tried to time it perfectly. I lay on the ground and pretended to be unconscious. He swung the hammer over his head. He turned his hammer so the part with the giant spike was facing me and he brought it down. I moved just in time, but the spike still hit my left leg. At the same time, I grabbed my staff and tripped him. He face-planted into the ground. He slowly lifted his head and looked around. Blood was collected in one of his eyebrows.

"What was that?!" He said; panicked.

"I have a hunch," I said as I got to my feet. "I just hope I'm wrong. Now's not the time. Right now, we need to stop *them.*" I pointed to Scarlet and Aluminum.

Aluminum was disappearing from one spot and reappearing in another so fast it was like she was teleporting. Scarlet was moving just as fast. Every time Aluminum threw a punch, whether she was visible or not, Scarlet countered it.

Kid and I ran back down the small hill to try and break up the fight. I was limping at first but as I kept running, the limping went away. I healed.

Guards were flooding out of the building. A sea of gray and white armor with black guns were rushing towards us.

Eventually Aluminum landed a punch. Scarlet tried to capture all of the punch's force and use it for herself but only succeeded in knocking them both down. At that point, they decided to use their weapons.

Scarlet threw almost all of her knives. Aluminum put her machete up and deflected every knife. She held it over her head and prepared to swing down, Scarlet caught her arm and grabbed her by the neck. She bent Aluminum's hand and Aluminum dropped the machete.

I could suddenly hear what was going through Scarlet's mind. I could hear her thoughts. I could read minds. I got closer to them both and tried to get into their minds. I figured that if I could read minds, I could write them too.

"Get out of my head," Scarlet said; still staring at Aluminum who was slowly losing breath. She raised Aluminum off of the ground.

Blue veins began to crawl over Scarlet's hand. They stretched over her hand and crawled on their way to her eyes.

I kept trying.

*Scarlet, this is Stefano. Put her down, Scarlet. She is not the enemy.*

Scarlet dropped Aluminum but then turned to me. The blue veins faded before they got to her eyes.

"I said to get out of my head!" She said as she grabbed me by the neck. She raised me off of the ground.

Now green veins crawled over her hand. They kept crawling and when they got to her eyes, the veins turned red and headed back to me. They touched my skin and I could feel them.

I looked at Scarlet's eyes. They were burning red. She dropped me, and the veins felt like a thousand bugs that were on fire were crawling into my ears and nose and mouth. It was like I ate a pepper and the only way to make it stop was to dunk my head in lava.

Then I could only see what Scarlet was trying to do. I saw an electric red hand dragging itself over my brain. It was surrounded by darkness. It pulled back and then attacked my brain.

I rolled around at the splitting headache. The hand then simply plucked away a green orb. The hand and orb vanished from my view and I could see everything again. The pain had stopped.

"What did you do?" I said.

"I told you to stay out of my head." She replied.

I couldn't look into her mind anymore. As a matter of fact, I couldn't look into anyone's mind anymore. I looked around. Aluminum stood there staring at me. I took her place. Her gratitude was hidden behind fear.

Our necks partially matched. Her neck was mostly reddened and slightly bruised while mine was mostly bruised and slightly portrayed what looked like a burn.

I looked to Kid. He was shocked at what had just happened. Scarlet took away one of my powers. He stared at Scarlet and then me. He still had a cut on his eyebrow, but it looked like it had healed since we ran to stop the girls from fighting.

I looked back to Aluminum. She wasn't snapped out of it. She backed up and began throwing her arms in circles. I got into a stance to catch whatever she threw. "Aluminum, it's me. It's Stefano. I am just now realizing that my name means nothing right now because you didn't know it in the first place, but I would ask that you not throw those again." Her eyes narrowed, and she crouched down. "Please?"

She jumped into the air and when she landed she threw her arms forward. At the same time, I heard Kid call my name. "Stefano!" He yelled.

I turned around and saw him trying his best to hold back Scarlet. I looked back to Aluminum and saw two discs flying my way. They looked like distortions in the air but when you could see them, they looked almost blue.

I tried to stop them with my telekinesis but once again they only slowed. I could feel the field breaking. If I didn't do something, this was going to be my end. I let my field break. The discs flew at me. One hit my left arm and the other hit my left leg. I fell to my knees.

"GAAAAAAAAAH!" I yelled. "Same *damn* leg!" I groaned.

Kid tripped Scarlet and as he waited for her to get up, he pointed at MANDS. Everyone, even Scarlet followed his gaze.

I looked towards the guards pouring out of the building. They were heading up the hill after us. Most looked exhausted just from the slight incline of the hill. But they had numbers. Guards continued to flood from the building. Everyone watched in awe. Even Aluminum. Scarlet calmed down.

"I thought it was just a giant square." Kid said breathlessly. "It must be like an underground tower or something."

*Run you, idiots!*

She spoke to me again. This time louder. I looked to everyone who was still staring towards MANDS. Scarlet and Aluminum still didn't have very much of their memories. I held out my hand and my staff flew into my hand. I swept it and tripped Aluminum from behind and then swung it at Scarlet's head. Aluminum fell backward and hit her head but quickly pushed herself up onto her elbows.

"What was that for?" She asked while rubbing the back of her head.

Scarlet was on her knees and had her chest to her legs. She wrapped her arms around the back of her head where I hit her. She winced for a while and slowly got to her feet.

"Did you have to hit me so hard?" She asked as she helped Aluminum up with one hand and kept the other on the back of her head.

I looked towards the guards. They gathered on the other side of the force field. Waiting for it to be turned off.

"We have to go," I said. I ran in the direction of the massive mountain and everyone followed. Everyone but Scar and Tressa. Not even Harry.

We ran as fast and hard as we had ever run before. Away from MANDS. And hopefully towards home.

# CHAPTER 16

# ALUMINUM

I stayed behind Scarlet as we went up the mountain, but Scar was nowhere to be seen. I figured she must have gone back to find Tressa and Harry, so I shook the thought from my head.

The boys were ahead of us and went a different way. We ran further up the mountain to catch up to them. We jumped over logs and giant rocks. We came to a fallen tree that made the shape of an 'A' and we stopped for a while.

We were about to keep going when the boys emerged from the woods.

"Where have you been?" Stefano asked angrily as he pulled twigs and pine-needles from his hair.

"We were right behind you," I said.

Kid looked a little confused and angry. He pointed at Scarlet. "Where's the other?"

"Don't know. We lost her just before we went through the force field. She must have gone back." Scarlet answered. Stefano groaned.

We were all standing in a small circle when we heard a branch break behind us. "Their coming," Stefano said worriedly.

We all snapped our heads from the noise to the 'A' tree. We dove under the leaning tree and kept running. Then Kid stopped.

"What are you doing? We have to keep moving." Stefano tried to tell him.

Kid faced the trail of trampled grass that we made. It was easy to follow. And the five guards proved that. No, ten guards. Fifteen. Twenty. Their numbers increased as they came around the corner.

Kid finally moved. He swung his heavy war hammer straight through one tree on one side of our path and punched a tree on the other side. And he kept punching and knocking down trees until they blocked off the way we came from. It didn't cover enough so he went to the other side and punched another one down. And another and another.

He turned to Scarlet. "I can slow them down and buy you some time! Cover your tracks! If I haven't caught up by dawn, assume I'm dead and keep moving!" "But, Kid-" Stefano and Scarlet started.

"GO!" Kid yelled as he punched a tree. The tree fell between us and Kid and blocked the way back. He then jumped into the air and punched the ground when he came down. Dirt shot up from the ground and roots lost their hold. The trees fell around him and formed a wall of fallen trees. Kid was hidden in a silo of trees.

We did exactly as he said. We ran and covered our tracks. Stefano stayed behind us and ran backward. He used his power to push the trampled grass upright.

The narrow, hard to see, path that weaved between trees, became harder and harder to see. We began to move slower and hoped for a place we could stop. Stefano kept urging us to keep moving. Every time we stopped he would back into us and yell "keep moving!"

Finally, we came to a perfect place to stay for the night and we were losing light fast. The guards behind us went quiet when we left Kid. We came to a bunch of spruce trees that had naturally fallen into a wide crevasse to make a perfect shelter. But not enough for three or four. Or even six if Harry and Tressa were found.

Despite Scar's temper, she was nice to have around and had great ideas. I hoped she was still alive and still behind us. The guards. They could of either gone through Kid, who would not go down without a fight or go around him and try to cut through the trees. Either way, there's no trail for them to follow.

As for Harry and Tressa, they could be dead.

"Alright," Stefano said. "We are going to need a few things. Fire, water, and shelter." "I'll get the shelter stuff. We can use what we break off of trees for fire." I said.

"I'll get the water," Scarlet said. "Should just be down this hill a way." She pointed to the small grassy cliff.

"I guess I'll gather tree limbs and try to get a fire going," Stefano said. "Nothing too big. Just big enough for Kid and Tressa to find.

"And Scar," I added. He nodded, and everyone gathered what we needed.

I started to move my arms in small circles. The circles gradually got bigger. When I thought the discs were big enough, I jumped into the air, spun, and when I landed I threw my arms forward and cut down several trees with two slightly transparent discs.

Stefano dragged the trees over with his power to the shelter spot and then gathered twigs and branches for the fire. He leaned over and tried to catch his breath.

"Take a break," I yelled. "You're going to kill yourself before MANDS gets the chance." Stefano stood up straight and shook his head. He wiped the blood off of his upper lip and dragged the trees and branches by hand; still slightly out of breath.

"It's like a muscle," he explained. "If it's worked hard, it will start to hurt. Mostly in my head. If I expel the energy all at once, an event happens I call a Telekinetic Overload. If the muscle is stretched too far, it will snap. If that happens I will either die or lose the power completely. And with the amount of dosage I received," he paused for a while and caught a few deep breaths. "One of those is coming really soon."

Scarlet backed up the small hill. She was dragging something.

"I found a tarp." She said. "I put it in the pond down there and trapped water in it. Maybe some fish too. Stefano, I need a place to put this."

I glared at Stefano. If he continued to use his power, he would die.

He smiled and shrugged his shoulders and walked over to the shelter. He put his arms out and made a circle in the air towards the ground. Then he lifted his arms up and a chunk of dirt rose out of the ground and fell next to the hole.

Scarlet dragged the tarp to the hole and then opened it. A few Minos were swimming around in the almost clear water. A few fish, couple twigs, and some moss but I would say it was useable water.

Everyone took a knee and opened their backpacks and pulled out a few things. We all had water bottles so Stefano and I threw them to Scarlet, so she could fill them up. Stefano had a flint stick and Scarlet had a water purifier and more throwing knives. I looked around in my bag for something useful. The only thing useful at the moment was rope. I walked over to Stefano.

"When it comes to what happens after your Telekinetic Overload, let's hope it's neither of those options," I said to Stefano as I handed him the rope. We walked over to where the shelter was going to be built and started making a place to stay for the night.

By the end of the first night, we had a small fire. We dug it into the ground for more heat and less flames.

We had water. With the tarp being put in the ground, it doubled as a rain catcher.

We had shelter...kind of. We had to dig it into the ground for more room just in case the others find us. Without a place to actually go, it was the last hope we had. The frame was four trees pushed into the ground. The walls were smaller trees with branches weaved through each other. I used my machete to make notches, so it looked somewhat habitable. The trees that fell to form a shelter were laid on top, so it made a roof and made it less easy for guards to see. We just hoped the others would be able to find it.

By dawn, no one was back. Kid said that if he wasn't back by dawn, to assume that he was dead. Stefano kept pacing around in front of the shelter. He took the first-night watch but never woke us up to trade shifts. He never went to sleep.

He saw me as I crawled out of the shelter and he stopped pacing. "We need food." "I know." I said.

Scarlet stumbled out of the shelter and fell to her hands and knees.

"You alright?" I asked.

"What's wrong?" Stefano asked.

Scarlet looked up and she had glowing red irises in her eyes. "I don't know. I can't control it. It hurts!"

Stefano and I made eye contact. "Scar!" We said in unison.

When we looked back to Scarlet, she jumped into the air and turned into a giant black wolf and sped off through the woods. Stefano looked at me. Without saying a word, I knew what he was thinking. Tressa.

Scar hated Tressa. I didn't know why. All I knew was that she did. Apparently enough to take her power and kill her. Scar was obviously able to take abilities because Scarlet was able to take Stefano's. So that meant that Scar was alive. Harry was still a mystery.

We stood there for a while waiting for nothing. "I'll get some traps laid out." Stefano's said. "You're going to kill her?"

"I'm going to kill whatever walks into these traps. I don't know about you but I'm starving."

Stefano walked over to the door of the shelter and began thinning extra bits of rope and tying them together.

I looked in the direction that Scarlet ran and waited.

<T1 A2 S3 K4 S5>

The traps were set and all we had to do was wait.

Then there was breaking coming from where I was. Stefano ran out of the shelter with his staff in his hand.

He pressed a button and it sprung into a bow. An arrow quickly shot sideways from the side of the staff. He caught it and put it on the bowstring. He pulled back the arrow as far as it would go and waited for whatever was in the woods to show itself.

Scarlet walked out of the woods. She wiped blood from around her mouth and held up a rabbit. Then she threw down three guns.

"Weapons." She said as she threw down some machine guns. "And food." She held up the rabbit.

Stefano put down his bow and put the arrow back. He flung the bow forward in his hand and it collapsed back into a staff. "I'm sticking to my staff. Where did you even get all that stuff?"

"Well," she started. "I *think* it was because I was starving and part of everyone's instinct when they're hungry, is to get food. So, I did. And while I was going to eat the rabbit, I saw a group of guards and kind of went on a killing spree. I killed three or four groups of guards that were heading in our direction. Bought us a bit of time. Before and after that is a bit fuzzy."

Stefano nodded in a sort of not-bad kind of way.

I looked at Scarlet. "How many guards in each group?"

"About 32 or so. Not very many. They were fanning out and trying to find even the smallest trace of a trail."

"What about the bodies?" Stefano asked. "Well let's just say I'm not hungry anymore."

Stefano walked off into the woods to find his traps. He returned shortly after with a handful of squirrels.

"We've got enough food for everyone. I'm not eating Scarlet's catch though. She pretty much already ate it." Stefano said with a first-ever smile.

"We are going to have to eat fast," Scarlet said. "Chances are they are going to send reinforcements when they figure out they are missing about five groups."

"Wait. You said three or four." I said.

"How many reinforcements?" Stefano said over me as he leaned his staff against the shelter

"Maybe three times as many."

"Is it three groups or is it five groups?" I asked. "What does it matter? There was a lot."

"Because we can definitely stand against 96 guys. We can hold our ground for a while with 128. But we are in a bit of trouble against 160."

"All the better reason to leave." Said Stefano. "We will go that way." He pointed to a small clearing to the right of our shelter.

"Who made *you* the leader?" Scarlet said; taking a step back from him. Her reaction wasn't like her at all.

"It doesn't matter who the leader is. We just-"

"If it doesn't matter then I'm not going." Scarlet retaliated.

"We can't divide anymore, Scarlet. We have to stick together!" Scarlet slowly shook her head and started to turn around. "Where are you going?!" He yelled.

"To find Scar." She said. She walked into the woods where we came from. "Enjoy your breakfast."

Stefano and I watched Scarlet leave. There was nothing we could do. She was heading back to MANDS.

Before she left I saw something in her eyes. It was like a glitch. The red drained and the entirety of her eyes were pitch black. Then, in the blink of an eye, they were red irises again.

Stefano looked at me. "Well?" He said.

I looked at him. "Well, what?"

"Where do you stand?" He said calmly.

I looked to where Scarlet was last seen. "I want to go after her," I said. I looked back to Stefano. "but you're right. We can't divide anymore."

He was silent for a while. Then he spoke. "This isn't real. But at the same time, it's far too real." "What do you mean?" I asked.

He kneeled down and opened his backpack. He pulled out a folder and threw it to the ground at my feet.

"Harry is dead. Tressa is dead. I think we can assume Kid is dead. Scar could be dying and Scarlet is going to follow." He threw out the plan that he and Tressa wrote on the back of the broken food tray.

"What are you getting at?" I asked.

"The project that we were unwillingly put into is real. They were testing us in a simulation for the complications of the real world. We were not allowed to die in the sim. We broke out and now Tressa is dead, Harry is dead, Scar could be dying, and Scarlet is close behind her." he said as he studied the trees. "And I think certain aspects of the simulation are real too."

I stepped forward. "What do you mean?" I picked up the food tray and studied the back of it.

*President is going to kill Aluminum.*

*It would be easiest for her to escape.*

*President would think that because she can escape, she can easily get into his office and kill him. She's got the motive to do it anyways.*

*She could help us all escape. We need to keep her alive.*

*Keep her safe I will buy you some time.*

*From who? And what will you do? How will you get out?*

*Scar isn't who we think she is. I will get her away from you guys. When that happens, you have to get everyone out. I don't plan on following. Promise you won't come back for me.*

I *will find a way to save everyone. Including you. PROMISE!*

*I Promise.*

Maps were drawn all over the tray with arrows and circles and X's all over it.

"You're the one who can't be seen but apparently *you* can't see it. You know that hydra that we all had to face individually and then together in the training rooms?" He said. I looked up at him and nodded. "I saw a scale about three miles back." Stefano pointed behind us. "Everything in that building that was supposed to be computer generated or in our heads is really in this world. MANDS and JI are stronger than we thought. Not to mention all of the cameras."

"Cameras?"

Stefano looked like he was getting even angrier. He walked around to certain trees. "They are watching our every move. Camera!" He walked by the shelter. "Camera!" He stood in the middle and pointed as he spun around. "Camera! Camera! Camera! Camera! Cam-"

Something cut him off. His face turned white like he saw a ghost. He just stared at the tree. His arm still pointed towards the tree top.

Then he slowly lowered his arm but still watched the tree. He snapped out of it and went silent. He looked back to me.

"What?" I said.

"I-I think I just-just saw Tressa."

"That's impossible," I said. "Scar killed her."

Stefano turned to me and picked up his staff. "Wait a minute," He opened his staff into a bow and put an arrow in. He pulled it back and aimed it at me and said, "maybe we *can't* die."

He let the arrow loose and it came flying at me. I put out my hands and screamed, "No!" The arrow never hit me. It was lying on the ground in front of an energy shield. An energy shield that *I* made.

"Tressa must have developed another ability. An ability to help her survive easier. She could also be dead but she's also in my head. That means that they made it, so we can't kill each other but they can kill us if they want."

"What are you talking about? Scar killed Tressa!" I said; getting frustrated.

"If she killed Tressa then that means Scar was never one of us. She was always one of *them*. And we were lucky that Harry and I guess Jason weren't fully one of *them*."

"Then how did you just see her?!" I said; slightly scared.

"Maybe she is dead and slowly coming back. Maybe she's wounded, and she has astral projection."

"What's that?"

"She can move her spirit while she sleeps." "What does all of this mean?" I asked.

"Open the folder," Stefano said; pointing at the folder at my feet.

I did and there was a very detailed map in it. He held out his hand and I put the map in his hand. He gently folded it up and put it in his pocket. "We could go home."

"Or?"

"Or we can go back and get back the only family we know. We can expose MANDS for what they truly are and what they are doing and how they are doing it. We can shut them down. We can destroy them. Then, we can find a new home with them."

I thought for a bit. "On one condition," I said to Stefano. "I get to kill President." Stefano walked up to me and put his left hand out.

I grabbed his left forearm and he grabbed mine. "Do you think we will find Harry?" I asked him.

"I don't think he's really dead. He can heal himself. He took everything we threw at him. I doubt a simple bullet from one of those two maniacs will kill him."

I smiled, and we started to fortify our shelter. In order to prepare ourselves for what we were about to do, we needed to be ready and with full abilities.

"Today or tomorrow," Stefano said as he put more branches on the shelter and the fire. "MANDS falls."

We fortified the shelter, trained with our powers and stretched them to their limits and killed every guard we saw. Soon we would be ready.

# CHAPTER 17

# KID

I opened my eyes and looked around. There were bodies everywhere. The walls of fallen trees were broken and I was surrounded by wood splinters and slivers. There was a path going straight over my body. I looked at my body.

The orange hoodie that I wore was ripped and covered in dirt. There was bloodstained around multiple bullet holes. I moved the hoodie around to see if there was any other evidence that I had actually been shot. Everything had healed.

I grabbed my bloodstained hammer and my slightly torn backpack and tried to find the trail left for me.

I walked on the slight path that was left and it was easy for me to tell that Stefano had used his power to push the grass upright. I just hoped that the guards that got past me weren't able to figure that out.

I continued on the path that slowly vanished and hoped that I would find them soon.

Just as I was about to give up I found a wall of trees. But they were all standing upright and had been growing there for some time. I squeezed through and looked at a building that was the complete opposite of MANDS.

While MANDS was white and a giant flat square, this building was gray and reached for the sky. It was a skyscraper with JI above the door and at the very top.

I looked at my hammer and saw two letters flash.

*JI.*

I looked back to the skyscraper and headed for the back door.

There were no guards, so I walked right in. Everything was as clean as MANDS but had more of an eerie feeling to it. There were boxes everywhere like whoever was there either just moved in or was moving out.

"What else?" A man's voice said.

I froze and held my breath. I felt like I could still be heard so I hid by some boxes and held my hand over my mouth.

"They were running away. The kid stopped running and told them to go on." Said a familiar girl's voice.

"So, he's alone?" "Yes, sir."

"What about that insignificant clone of yours?" "She is just now waking up."

"Bring her here. I want to test how well you blocked the connection. Will she know what is going on?"

"No, sir. I blocked the connection so it's only a one-way connection."

"Good. Stay here. I need to talk to someone." He stopped and turned around. "Actually, when she gets here, change places with her. Separate yourselves from that group. We are going to make things right."

The man continued to walk out of the room with the girl and got into an elevator. As soon as the doors closed I peeked around the corner to see who he was talking to.

It was Scar. She closed her eyes and took a couple deep breaths. I quietly walked past her. I looked at the elevator the man got into. CRASH!

"Uncle?" I heard a boy's voice say.

I ran through a door with a sign of a stick figure walking up some stairs. I ran all the way to the top and hoped the man I heard earlier was there and that the boy hadn't seen me.

I slowly opened the door and looked around. The top floor of the building had the exact same layout as the only floor of MANDS. Minus the confusion and secrets.

I walked down the long hallway and heard the man's voice again. It was coming from an office. I hid in the room next to it and locked the door. I put my ear against the wall shared with the office and listened.

"Whatever it is, Uncle, I'm ready." Said the boy's voice.

"You keep trying but you're not old enough, Fabian. Not yet."

"But, Uncle Jon, surely my father told you how fast I age. I'm ready. Give me the assignment and I will train until the time comes." Said Fabian pleadingly.

Jonothan sighed heavily. "Charles did do something right with the aging process. Alright. Are you familiar with the Final Five?"

"My father told me stories. He told them with six though."

"Well, there are six if you include Scar downstairs. But it's not supposed to end that way. Not with six. But with five. That is where you come in."

"You want me to kill them? All of them?" Fabian said with a sadistic smile that could be felt from the other side of the wall.

"No," Jonothan said. "I want you to kill two."

"Which ones? Stefano and that annoying kid? Aluminum and Scarlet?"

"I want Scar and Scarlet."

"But, Uncle-"

"I need them. The girl they came from is still with them. In their conscience. Transferred through both of them. I need their bodies here in order to recapture it."

"Are you going for a dead or alive kind of thing?"

"I would expect dead. You won't be able to get them any other way."

"How much time do I have to train?"

"Ask Scar on your way out. What abilities did your father give you?"

Fabian reached into the pocket of his hoodie and pulled out a folded-up piece of paper. He slid it across the desk.

Jonothan unfolded it and read it. He took a while to get through the entire thing. "Everyone's powers. Nice. How many have you unlocked?"

"Enough."

"Alright. Go talk to Scar and then talk to your father about your training room."

I ducked behind the desk and looked out from behind it to see the boy called Fabian.

He wore a white hoodie. It was tight against his body like all of ours. His sleeves were rolled up and on his forearm was a mark like Harry's. His mark was F. It looked like the same machine made it. His hair was brown, and it kept falling into his eyes. His eyes were gray with white flakes and he walked around with a sadistic smile. He looked about my age.

I waited for the sound of the elevator doors opening and closing. As soon as they did I snuck into Jonothan's office.

Jonothan was standing in front of a giant window. His hands were folded behind his back and pressed against his grey suit.

I turned my hammer to the side with the small jagged spikes and held it above my head. I gathered as much power as I could. I was going to bash his skull in. "I wondered when I would see you again."

I froze. Jonothan turned his head slightly over his left shoulder. "What do they call you now, my friend?"

I raised the hammer higher. "I'm not your friend."

He faced the window again. "I suppose we aren't anymore, are we? But what *do* they call you?"

"My name is Kid," I answered immediately. I was the youngest and everyone called me Kid anyway.

He turned around and sat in his silver office chair. "That's nowhere near your real name. Take a seat please."

"And why would I do that?" The hammer was slightly lowered but the power behind it was still just as much.

"Tell me, 'Kid', do you want to know about our past?"

"Why would I want to know about your past?"

"Your past is buried in it." He said with an innocent smile. "Trust me."

"Why should I believe anything you say?"

"You shouldn't. But you should *at least* consider it."

I looked at my hammer. The two letters were now glowing. I looked at Jonothan. He looked exactly like President but Jonothan's hair was jet black and he didn't have bags under his eyes. He was cleanly shaven. They both had dark brown eyes.

I lowered my hammer to my side and sat in the chair. I put my right hand on the table but kept my left hand on the top of my hammer that was under the table.

"Where should I start?"

"What is all of this?" I asked calmly.

"You were originally a part of a program that you are more than familiar with." "MANDS." I filled in.

"Exactly. It all started in elementary. We were all the smartest in all of our classes. And-" "Who's *we*? "I said.

"Tressa, Aluminum, Scar, You, Stefano, me, Charles, Jason, Harry, Joan, Gardo. All of us. We decided that the world needed a little bit of order and a lot of safety after the recent wars. We saw on the news that Earth was dying so we devised a plan to leave Earth. We just needed someone or something to get us to a safer planet. So we planned to make a super army to put everything back in place and then look for another planet similar to earth to promise maximum peace. You and your friends are in a simulation designed by each of you. Or you were, anyways."

"What? We didn't make this! Why would we subject ourselves to this torture?!"

"You were all the brightest of us. You designed all of MANDS. We didn't ask questions. Jonothan Industries is just a distraction for me until the next phase is activated. But the first phase didn't work very well. You all volunteered to be subjects for the MANDS project. You were put into a sort of cryogenic chamber. The chambers let you age but not at your normal rate. Or it would seem like a normal rate for you while you were sleeping but it was extremely slow for us. The chambers were supposed to release you all at the same time so you would all be the same age, but it didn't work. Your friend, Stefano, was first. Then Tressa, then Aluminum, then Scar and then you."

"How long were we asleep?" I asked.

"Oh, geez. It must have been," he paused and thought. "50 years or so." "Why do you keep saying Scar and not Scarlet?"

"Scar is a part of a project I created called The Scar Origins. A long time ago I got bored with *just* Jonothan Industries. I went to the cryogenic chambers and took Scar. The power was perfect but Scar was too aggressive, so I created Scarlet and hoped to split Scar's abilities. The power was a perfect match and Scarlet was too soft. Now I don't think they can balance each other out in the slightest."

"I'd take it, it doesn't end there." I guessed.

I heard a little girl laughing and running around the office. But she was nowhere to be seen. "No. It doesn't. I created one more and I kept the chamber for Scar in *my* building. I quickly replicated it and put Scarlet in another one. The final one is perfect in every way. But the only way to finally activate the third is for the first two to be dead." I sighed and put my face in my hands.

"Charles has gone too far though," Jonothan said.

I quickly lifted my face from my hands. "What do you mean?"

"You were supposed to believe that you escaped on your own. And then find your way back for a big fight where the truth is revealed, and no one has to die. But Charles got anxious about your 'escape' and changed every dart shot at you to bullets. Before that, he added too much memory fog, so Tressa became convinced that everything that was happening was leading up to a massacre with no escape."

I pulled my sweater away from my body and showed off the bloodied bullet holes. "I've noticed the bullets."

"If it got to the point where your powers became too dangerous, Charles had Jason make certain serums to get rid of your power. One guard had those and actually managed to hit one of you. But he was the only one who carried the darts."

"I think Stefano may have been hit."

"I think so too. But Charles didn't stop there. Before you left, he took your blood while you were unconscious and created something he wasn't supposed to. Something that was never a part of the plan. He created-"

"Fabian." I cut him off.

"He is all of you and more. But-" "You altered the plan too."

"Yeah. I practiced the project for years. Waiting for all of you to wake up. I stored them somewhere only people like you can find. It's a super-city. But the last time I was there, they called it something I believe you and your friends call yourselves."

"Why are you telling me all of this?"

"You don't get it yet, do you? MANDS is you." "W-what?"

"*You* are MANDS."

I stood up and grabbed my hammer. I slowly paced back and forth. Then I put my hammer on the table and leaned towards Jonothan.

"Where can I find the city?"

"You have to find your friends first." "Where are *they*?"

Jonothan spun his chair towards the window. I walked towards the window. I could see the entire mountain. Every tree and every animal. I could see a black wolf with glowing red eyes speeding through the woods and heading straight for us with dead guards behind it. Their usual blinding white armor was splattered with blood.

Passed the mountain, in the foggy distance, I could see a city. It had skyscrapers as big but not bigger than Jonothan's main building. I could see houses and a fountain in the middle of it.

"It's somewhere over there," Jonothan said; pointing off to the right.

I followed his finger and saw a city that looked ancient. It made me wonder how long Jonothan had really been doing the project for. It looked more like a village. I could see five large towers. There was too much fog to see any real detail in them. The small houses were put together by the surrounding forests.

The fog shifted, and I could see that the entire city was located in the middle of a giant lake. Jonothan made a square with his fingers around one part of the mountain. "And your friends should be here." He said making the square bigger. As he did so, the window zoomed in on that part of the mountain.

I could see Stefano and Aluminum working on a well-built shelter. Then they both ran to the edge of the forest. They were swinging their arms and fighting something. There was no sound.

"Would you like audio? Maybe a better angle?"

"Yes! Yes! Do it!" I said panicking.

Jonothan waved his finger around in the air and the entire image spun and lowered so I could see the massive wave of guards that they were fighting.

"Audio!" Jonothan said. The audio immediately came on.

"Gah! Where are Kid and Scarlet when you need 'em?" Stefano said; swinging his staff and knocking guards away from the shelter.

"Duck!" Aluminum yelled.

She swung her arms and multiple discs flew from her arms and over Stefano as he bent backwards. They hit a few guards and a few trees. The trees began to fall in Aluminum's direction.

Stefano quickly rose up without his staff and caught the trees with his telekinesis and made them fall so they would fall on the guards.

The trees landed on the guards and killed most of them. Aluminum walked through the survivors and concentrated on their chests. She was putting a small force field in their chests and then expanding it.

Stefano fell to his knees. Aluminum ran over to him. "You okay?" She put a hand on his shoulder.

He wiped the blood from his upper lip and his brow. "I'm fine." He said; wiping her hand away. "Let's get back to work. We need to be stronger."

They disappeared into the shelter but before they did, they grabbed as many guns as they could along with the small white toolkits that were attached to the guards' belts. And minimal armor and first aid kits.

"Do any of them have syringes?" Aluminum asked.

Stefano checked the small first aid kits and pulled out a syringe. "Here's one." Aluminum grabbed it and they went back into the shelter.

We watched for a while before Jonothan said something.

"They are filling in the blanks in Stefano's dosages. This is just a recording. Would you like to see what is happening now?"

"Yes!" I yelled at him.

"Fast forward!" He said. "Present time!" The window sped through hours. The sun lowered, and dark clouds rolled in. A few quick flashes flashed in the distance and then it stopped on what was happening presently.

Scar was running through the woods and heading straight for the shelter. Nearly invisible I could see Fabian following closely behind. Scar didn't know he was there. I looked behind him. Heading at the same speed as Scar, but further behind, was Scarlet.

Jonothan zoomed out and the window returned to its normal image. He looked up at me. "They don't know the truth. You do. They need to know. Bring them here. If not here, then bring them to the super-city. Keep them safe while I try to control my brother. Okay?"

It was at that moment that I realized that the Scar Origins were based on President and Jonothan. One evil, one...less evil. One had the sole purpose of controlling the other.

I gripped my hammer and studied the way to Stefano and Aluminum. I turned to leave the office.

"But, Kid," Jonothan said quickly. I turned to face him.

"I need to ask you something."

"What is it?"

"No matter what happens, I would like you to be here when I release her." "Why? Why me? Why not your brother?"

"My brother is out of control. You still stand with me and are strong enough to make it back again."

"I could *actually* die this time. What will I do *then?*"

"Leave the right clues. I'm sure you'll find a way. Now. Enough talk. Go save your friends." I turned and sprinted out of the office.

"Where ya goin'?" I heard echo through the hallway. "Stop following me," I said to the building's walls.

On my way out, I could hear a little girl's laughter. She ran beside me in the walls as I quickly flew down the many levels of stairs.

"Are you ready?" The little girl asked when I stood outside next to the building. I stopped.

"Yeah," I said to my own shadow. "It's time for the Instinctsion to meet The Instinctsion."

CHAPTER 18

# SCARLET/SCAR

Scar forced me to run back to the strange building. She traded places with me and then came back to check that I was still in the building. I escaped from her trap and hid just before she came back. Then she ran.

I knew every way to escape because of her. She made the mistake of not coming up with a new way to keep me contained.

I waited until she was out of view from the building but before I could leave, someone ran after her. They then turned invisible and ran in front of me. I could see their distortion in the air. I knew it wasn't Aluminum. They were too fast to be Aluminum or anyone in the group. They were following close behind Scar.

We were heading straight for where the shelter was. The pace was beginning to pick up. I could barely see Scar, but I could see her jump into the air and turn into a massive black bear. The distorted person made themselves visible. It was a boy who was wearing a white hoodie that was tight against his body like ours.

He jumped into the air and turned into a giant white wolf with gray streaks that started at his eyes and went along his back and met at his tail.

I jumped into the air. I needed to keep up with them but quietly. I turned into a wolverine. All black with my glowing red eyes being the only other color.

The sun disappeared behind the mountain and dark clouds covered the sky. I felt a raindrop on my nose. I stopped.

Everything was quiet. I couldn't hear Scar *or* the boy. I couldn't hear any animals either. There were no trees rustling and no whispers on the wind. It was quiet.

Then there was a blinding flash followed by a crack of thunder. It began to rain.

I heard the two creatures in front of me continue running so I continued running after them. I could hear someone behind us as well. They were keeping up with our intense speed. I figured they were really strong and used to running through the woods.

Trees around us caught fire as the lightning targeted our wet fur. They fell into our path and made obstacles we had to jump over. Rivers began to flow past us down the mountain. The rivers of water soon turned to rivers of mud and stone. Then the rivers started picking up trees and sliding them down the mountain at us.

Finally, Scar broke through a wall of trees. I could see the shelter I had helped to build. Aluminum threw disks and then ran inside of the shelter. Stefano was in front of the shelter. He snapped his staff into a bow and nocked an arrow.

"Just you and me, Scar," Stefano said with his bow still pointed at the ground.

"No!" Came a growl from the woods. The wolf launched itself over the giant bear and transformed back into a boy before he landed on Stefano. "Just you and *me*." He said with an evil smirk. He looked 18.

Aluminum came out of the shelter and somehow pushed the boy off of Stefano without touching him. It appeared Stefano and Aluminum managed to transfer a bit of power to each other. Maybe even fill in the blanks in Stefano's dosages.

Scar turned back into herself and looked to the boy. "Who the hell are *you?*"

"Well, I'd say I'm your brother or cousin but I'm more of your son."

"What?" Scar said.

"And hers." He pointed to Aluminum. "Wait, what?" Aluminum asked.

"And his." He pointed to Stefano.

Stefano got to his feet and brushed himself off. "Hell no." "And hers." He pointed to the woods where I was hiding.

I leaped through the trees and when I landed, I was myself. "I wish I could say he's lying. I heard Jonothan say everything. He means to kill me and Scar." Stefano raised his bow and arrow to the boy. "Who are you?"

"The name's Fabian. But I also go by," he threw his left arm out to the side. His sleeve fell, revealing an F on his forearm, and he spun his hand around. A slightly transparent disc hovered and rotated in his hand. "The Angel of Death!"

He threw the disc at Aluminum. She quickly made a shield, but the force was too much and the ground was becoming too muddy. She fell backward as her shield broke into bits and faded as she hit her head on a muddied rock.

Fabian threw his other arm towards Stefano. Stefano flew backward and onto a higher part of the mountain. His flailing body disappeared into the dark stormy night.

"I didn't come for him." He said; turning towards Scar and I. "I came for *you*."

Scar ran over to Aluminum and, in the blink of an eye, took part of her invisibility power. She quickly turned invisible and grabbed my arm; turning me invisible too. We ran further up the mountain and away from Fabian.

<T1 A2 S3 K4 S5>

**Scar**

Jonothan said I had to kill my clone to keep everyone safe. To make up for what I had done. But because of the sudden realization that he sent someone to kill both of us hit me, I couldn't do it.

Fabian was stronger than us. Than all of us. For the first time in a long time, I was afraid.

I dragged Scarlet with me and ran up the mountain. We quickly ran out of mountain. I looked over the side of the cliff and saw massive jagged rocks. The ground and bottom of the rocks were blanketed in fog.

My foot slipped due to the rain and Scarlet and I became visible. Scarlet pulled me up. "What do we do?" She asked; panicked.

I was so overwhelmed with fear that I couldn't answer her. I wanted to but just couldn't.

I looked down the mountain and saw Fabian walk over to Aluminum. He stood in one spot as Aluminum tried to push herself away from him. Her once white tennis shoes only got so far before they were just kicking mud away. The rain had soaked all of our clothes. Aluminum's clothing was covered in mud as well as rain.

Fabian generated a machete of stone. He ran the blade's edge across the muddy ground and the stone rang as if it was metal. He held the sharp blade above his head and prepared to bring it down.

Suddenly, an arrow knocked the machete from Fabian's raised hand. Fabian frantically searched for where the arrow had come from until his eyes fell upon Stefano with a bow.

"You're lucky I missed. I was aiming for your *head*!" Stefano taunted.

Fabian looked down at Aluminum. Her breathing was heavy, and she readied herself to make a shield; knowing it would not be strong enough. Fabian walked away from Aluminum and towards us. Aluminum let her head fall back into the mud and her eyes closed.

The muddy slope had no effect on Fabian. He got to the top of the mountain with ease. "This is the end for you." He said.

Fabian used his telepathy and made himself levitate. He outstretched his arms and looked up at the raining sky. He closed his eyes and concentrated his powers. Lightning flashed behind him. The transparent discs came out of his arms and began to circle him. They were more than visible now. One was red, and one was black. The rest were silver and white.

Stones stacked themselves and, when they got to his feet, his entire body was encased in stone.

The stacked stones then began to levitate and then started to circle him as well. He looked at us and lowered his arms to his sides. Through the holes in his stone skin we could see that his eyes were glowing white in the raining darkness. More lightning flashed. His hands slowly turned into giant stone spikes. The discs bent and folded against the tips of he spikes and made them twice as dangerous. He hovered above the ground.

"You will know true power!" His voice was deeper and God-like. "*I am the future!*" He quickly flew towards Scarlet and me.

We adapt to survive. But not against death himself. Scarlet closed her eyes and turned away. It happened so fast, but it was also like it was all in slow motion.

Stefano flew in front of us. "Noooooo!" He screamed. He was prepared to die for us. He helped us get out. He wanted to help us get away. Fabian quickly adjusted the angle of the spikes, so they went for Stefano's heart.

Before the spikes could penetrate, Kid jumped in the way. At the same time, Fabian was struck by lightning. The electricity veined through the spaces in the stone and collected in the spikes. The spikes were coursing with electricity when they went through Kid's chest.

Stefano had built up a Telekinetic Overload when he jumped in the way. It was all a blinding flash.

My ears were ringing, and my vision was blurred. Scarlet and I were blown back. I was on the edge of the cliff while Scarlet was in front of me. We unknowingly covered ourselves in stone before the blast. It fell off of us as we sat ourselves up. We looked around the crater that had been violently formed.

Fabian was back down by the shelter. The only stones left on him was on his left leg. Aluminum instinctively made a shield to protect herself from most of the blast.

Stefano was lying against a standing tree. One of its broken limbs had gone straight through his right shoulder. Blood was dripping off the end of his nose and was slowly spilling out of his mouth. His eyes shot open. His green eye had collected with blood. He looked around and then spotted Kid's body.

"No." He said weakly. "No!" He tried to scream. He shook his head and tried to stand up but as he moved, the limb was forced down and made the hole in his shoulder worse. "Gah!" He tried to break the limb. A tear rolled down his cheek. "Kid!" His voice broke. He managed to break the limb and pull it from his shoulder. He stood up and started limping. He fell in the thick mud. "NO!" He finally managed to yell. He dragged himself through the mud and over to Kid's body. He sat down to the left of Kid. He pulled his knees to his chest and laid his arms across the tops of his knees. He didn't look at Kid's body. He looked at Fabian.

Stefano put a bloodied hand over Kid's body. He didn't touch him but flinched at the sizzling warmth of the body and put his hand back onto his knee.

I could see tears rolling down his face. He was crying but at the same time, he was angry. Fabian sat up. Stefano held his hand out to his left side. His staff flew to his open hand. He propped himself up on his staff and watched Fabian get back up.

Fabian looked up at the top of the mountain. He pointed at Stefano. "You stay out of this!" His voice was back to the normal 'you-will-pay-for-this' sounding voice. His white, skin-tight, hoodie was no longer white. It was covered in mud and had rips in it. It was even scorched in a few places.

Stefano leaned on his right leg (because the other had a piece of burning wood in it) and snapped open his bow. He loosed an arrow that barely missed Fabian's head.

Fabian put his left hand to his right cheek and then brought it out in front of him. There was blood on his fingers. "So be it." He grumbled. He held his hand parallel to the ground and a staff made of stone materialized itself in his hand.

They flew at each other and fought in the air more than fifty feet above us. I didn't know Stefano could fly.

It was an air battle. Nearly every time their staffs connected, or they punched each other, lightning flashed and crashed around the newborn crater.

Rain fell around them, and blood rained below them. Fabian had super strength. Every time Fabian swung his staff and made contact with Stefano's, Stefano's staff was pushed to one side.

Scarlet and I got to our feet. I looked to Scarlet. Rain drenched our hair and made us looks actually identical. Except for our eyes of course.

"We are doing this together." She said; still staring at the gruesome air show. She had blood collected around her red irises and small tears of blood coming from her ears.

"That's how we started. That's how we finish." I said.

She ran at me and we flew off of the cliff. We fell so fast that the rain seemed to stop falling. Once again, everything moved in slow motion. Our bodies panicked and tensed but our minds were calm. We could feel adaptations trying to save us.

I could feel wings trying to sprout from my back, but I resisted the urge. I could feel the arms of the wings moving around in my back waiting to spring out and stop my fall, but I fought it.

As long as Scarlet and I are alive, Fabian will continue hunting the Instinctsion until he kills Scarlet and I. I can't live with that.

We looked at the rising ground. Lightning flashed, and a bolt touched down below us. For a split second, I could have sworn that in the light I saw Tressa. I looked at Scarlet.

I *know. I saw it too.* She said in our minds.

We closed our eyes and welcomed the jagged boulders.

# CHAPTER 19

# STEFANO

Fabian and I were flying around in the sky. Every swing he did with his staff, pushed me back. He was far stronger than I was. Eventually, I got a good swing in and timed it with a telekinetic push. He flew into the ground. I had finally brought the fight to the ground. I looked around. Kid was in a crater. His orange hoodie was scorched away from his skin and he lay motionless. As soon as I landed, I pulled the piece of burning woods from my leg. I hoped it would heal fast.

Scar and Scarlet were nowhere to be seen. Aluminum got to her feet.

"Enough!" Fabian yelled as he got back to his feet. "I could end you. The ones I came for are now dead. There shall be no more bloodshed! You have special blood, Stefano! Stop fighting and we could-"

I snapped open my bow and nocked an arrow. I loosed it and it went through Fabian's left shoulder a couple of inches from his heart. Enough people had died. No one else had to die. Fabian fell to the ground. "Ow." He mumbled.

I limped over to him. My injured left leg was by Fabian's feet while I put my right leg over Fabian's left shoulder. I stared into Fabian's gray eyes. Every now and then there would be a small flash and his eyes changed to one of our colors and then back.

I looked at the arrow in his left shoulder and clicked my staff open into a bow. An arrow shot out and I caught it and immediately nocked it.

I held up my bow and loosed the arrow into Fabian's right shoulder. Only the feathers of the arrow were sticking out of his shoulder. He was pinned to the muddy ground.

I walked over to Aluminum and helped her to her feet. We headed for Kid's body.

"You won't get out of here! I know where you're going, Stefano! I'll tell everyone! You'll have an army at your back!" Fabian yelled.

I quickly stomped over to Fabian and closed my bow back into a staff.

"You will fear me! I am death, Stefano. I am *your* death. I was designed to be such. I am stronger than you, Stefano! Than *all* of y-"

I swung the staff as hard as I could and knocked Fabian unconscious. A horrible cracking sound was forced from his body.

Aluminum and I trudged up the hill to Kid's body. I knelt down beside him. Kid had his hammer but never used it. Aluminum picked up the extremely heavy hammer. Two letters kept flashing.

"What are these?" Aluminum asked me.

"What the heck?" I said. I turned my staff over and saw the same two letters. "Where is your machete?"

She pulled out her machete and looked at the part of it where the blade came out of the handle. The same two letters flashed.

JI was flashing on all of our weapons.

"What about Scar and Scarlet's weapons?" I asked.

Aluminum walked over to where she had last seen them. A single knife was laying in the mud. She picked it up and froze. She dropped the knife.

I ran over to her and looked down the cliff. I could see Scar and Scarlet lying among the jagged rocks. There was a huge indent in the ground where they were. It had slightly filled with water. The small creek poured down the cliff and pooled into the depression they had created.

The rain, however, was letting up. The clouds were drifting away, and the sun was returning to its place in the sky.

I picked up the broken knife from the mud and turned it over. I could see flashing from under the mud. I wiped away the mud and the letters became clear.

I put the knife down and walked back over to Kid's body. I handed my staff and Kid's hammer to Aluminum. I bent down and picked up Kid. His head fell against my chest and his arms and legs dangled lifelessly.

"Do you think Jonothan can save him?" Aluminum asked. She put the hammer and staff under her arm and gripped her machete.

"If not Jonothan, then hopefully Harry can." I adjusted my hold on Kid. "Do you think Jonothan will tell us where to find him?"

I started walking in the direction Scar, Scarlet and Fabian came from. They left a very defined trail. "Jonothan should be more lenient than President. If he doesn't tell us, I'll make him tell us."

<T1 A2 S3 K4 S5>

We walked for what seemed like miles. Kid was getting heavier with every step. The sun was coming up, but the temperature was going down. Kid's lips were turning purple with lack of oxygen.

Finally, we came to the end of the thick forest. There was a skyscraper with JI above the door and the very top reached for the sky.

"How could we have missed this?" Aluminum asked. I turned to Aluminum. "Check the weapons."

She went through all of the weapons and turned them all over. The two letters were glowing on every weapon.

"This is it." She said looking up at the tower.

We continued to the tower. I kicked open the back door; worried there would be guards at the front.

The bottom level was dark and had boxes in two corners of the room. I walked into the next room. The room had a silver chair with restraints laying on its side across the room. Muddy footprints showed that it was originally in the middle of the room. The hole in the wall above the chair gave evidence that the chair was thrown.

It *was Scar.*

The voice was back after so long.

*Find Jonothan. Bring him back.*

I looked up towards the ceiling and yelled at the top of my lungs and then some.

"JONOTHAN!"

It echoed throughout the entire building. When it died down, everything was quiet. Then came a little girl's voice.

"He's upstairs." She said from all around us. "Top floor."

Aluminum shrugged and walked into the only elevator on the bottom floor. I followed her inside. "Going up." She said as she pressed the button at the very top of all of the rest. The one marked: JI.

We slowly made it to the very top of the building. We could see Jonothan's office. It had a steel door with no handle. I guessed it was motion activated. Next to the door was a silver plaque that said:

*Jonathan Jacobs, President of Jonathan Industries.*

Next to the office was a room with an open door. I carried Kid to the room and laid him down on the rough carpeted floor.

"Stay here with him." I whispered to Aluminum. "Don't come out until I say." "But what if-"

"Don't come out!" I whisper yelled to Aluminum. "We have no idea what he's like. I'm just *hoping* he's lenient."

She nodded and handed me my staff.

I left the room and stood in front of the heavy steel door. I took a step towards it and it opened.

"Oh. Stefano. I wondered when you would show up. Where is Kid? Did he lead you here or just point you in the right direction before he headed to th-"

"He's dead." I interrupted. It hurt to state the truth I had been denying but I stayed as stone-faced as possible.

"Pity." Said Jonothan. "I liked that kid. He was a good kid."

"Can you bring him back?" Aluminum said from behind me. She sounded like she was on the verge of tears.

I sighed heavily and let my head fall in frustration and defeat.

"I did expect two of the group to come back. I just thought it would be Stefano and Kid."

I rolled my eyes. Partially just trying to stop the tears that formed every time his name was mentioned. "Just tell us how we can bring him back."

"How much did he tell you when he got to you guys." Jonothan asked.
"I...he...he saved me. Me *and* the clones."

"The clones are alive?" Jonothan asked out of confusion.

"They're dead too." Aluminum answered. "You sent someone to kill them, but he ended up killing Kid."

I took a deep breath in through my nose. It was getting harder and harder to hold back. I walked to the doorway and stood there with my back to Aluminum and Jonothan. Aluminum continued to talk.

"They felt guilty that Fabian was going through our group to get to them and didn't want to give Fabian a chance to kill them. So, while Stefano was fighting him, they jumped off the edge of the mountain."

I turned around after feeling that I had gotten full control over my emotions again. "It was only a distraction. He was too strong."

"Where is he now?" Jonothan asked.

"Probably heading back here with one arm." I said; satisfied with my answer. "Why would he come *here*? He's not mine. He's-"

"I don't care who he belongs to! He killed Kid! Tell us how to bring Kid back!"

"Alright, alright! Calm down. I can't bring him back. But someone in the super-city can." "Where is it!" Aluminum asked. She wiped away tears that had quietly dripped down her cheeks. She had her machete in her other hand.

Jonothan spun his giant silver chair towards the window behind him. He made a square with his fingers and then pulled it apart. The window zoomed in over a lake. Fog was drifted away from it.

"It should be in the middle of this lake." Jonothan said.

"What do you mean 'it should be'? It's right *there*." Aluminum pointed to the middle of the lake. "Five towers, a bunch of well-built houses, a wall around the entire thing. It's a city."

"I can't see it." "Why?" I asked.

"A long time ago I gave orders to the temporary leaders, the *watchers* I called them. I told them to hide the city from people like Charles in order to keep it safe. And given that Charles and I are twins, I can't see it. I told them not to trust even me. For as long as I am human withno extraordinary abilities or enhancements, I can't see it. Only *your* eyes can. Go there and save your friend."

I rotated my staff and went to the next room to get Kid.

"Who is the little girl in the walls?" Said Aluminum's muffled voice. She was whispering. "In the walls? Scar and Scarlet are dead, right?"

Aluminum gritted her teeth. "Yes, Jonothan. They're dead."

"She should be her chamber room. And getting ready for release. She is the final phase of the Scar Origins. Should you choose to listen, Kid will explain it to you." I could hear Jonothan lean closer and whisper as low as possible.

"She is the last hope for Scar and Scarlet. Two in one. *The final phase.* Can I trust you with some information about her? I need someone to watch her. To teach her right from wrong."

"I guess so."

I could hear Aluminum lean closer and Jonothan began whispering something to her. "Who are we even looking for in the super-city?" Aluminum finally said.

"You'll know when you find them."

Aluminum came to the room that I was in. I silently handed her my staff and swept Kid into my arms. We got into the elevator and Aluminum pressed the bottom button with the tip of her machete.

"Did he say anything that could help us?"

"Not really." She said; staring at the elevator doors.

We exited the elevator and then the building. We set off for the city and hoped we could bring Kid back soon. Or I did anyways. I sensed secrets.

# CHAPTER 20

# ALUMINUM

We journeyed through yet another forest in hopes of finding the city. Five towers were visible the entire way.

I walked behind Stefano and carried the weapons. The heavy hammer, the staff that pushed me backwards every time it got lodged between two trees, and my machete. I didn't mind my own weapon. I even picked up the broken throwing knife that the clones had left behind.

Stefano kept building up his telekinesis and trying to levitate Kid to make the trip easier. When he had enough, he tried to levitate the weapons too. But that didn't happen very often. I thought he was dropping them on purpose.

When we were in the shelter, we built a small machine that would fill in the blanks in Stefano's dosages. He needed more because he was the newest and only received one dose of whatever gave us our abilities.

We made it to the lake with the super-city in the middle of it. The city seemed to float above it. There were no bridges and no way to get up to the city. We walked further into the shield that hid the city from normal eyes. The entire city was inside of a wall that was a part of a second defense.

Stefano gently put Kid on the ground. I gave Stefano his staff and laid the hammer next to Kid. "Hello?" Stefano yelled.

A man that looked like Jason walked across the top of the wall. "State your name, ability and reason you wish to enter the city!" He said almost as if he'd had to say it every day.

Stefano walked forward. "My name is Stefano! I have telekinesis and my friend here was killed by someone known as Fabian! Jonothan told us you could-"

"Jonothan? You know Jonothan?" The man turned around and spoke to someone on the lower levels.

He faced us again. "Stay where you are. We are coming to get you." He looked at the sky and three figures with wings flew from behind him. They slowed above him and stretched out their massive red, blonde, and black wings. They froze for a moment and were silhouetted against the sun.

Two continued to circle above us while one of them swooped down and landed in front of us. "You must be Stefano." Said the winged person. He shook Stefano's hand. He turned to me.

"And Aluminum I believe." He shook my hand. Then he knelt down. "And this is Kid." He moved Kid's head to the other side with the back of his hand. Stefano twitched like he was gonna blast the winged person away. He made a circle in the air and one of the other winged people swooped down and picked up Kid and flew into the city. It was a girl with black wings.

"Who are you?" I asked.

"Oh." He laughed. "How rude of me. I'm Falcon. That," he pointed to the circling person. "Is Phoenix and the one who just flew away with Kid is Raven. We're known as The Valkyries." He shook Stefano's hand again.

"Phoenix! Get down here!" He said.

Phoenix violently landed. Dirt flew up from the ground and blades of grass spun back to the ground. His knee bent to where it nearly touched the ground. His hand touched the ground and stopped his knees from hitting the ground on impact. He landed like Stefano did when I first found him. He slowly straightened up and showed off his massive red wings that matched his red hair.

"You must be Stefano." More handshaking. We got the same introduction we had gotten from Falcon.

"I just explained all of that," Falcon said.

"Oh. You did. I *have* to say though. I am a huge fan. I heard your stories over a thousand times. Aluminum, I have studied for years to get a glimpse of understanding about your power. It's fascinating. I wish I could make invisible disks like you can."

"Um, thanks?" I said.

Phoenix put his hands together and put them to his mouth. "I do have to ask though." He turned to Stefano and tilted his hands towards Stefano. "Can you fly?"

We were growing impatient and getting more and more curious about what was inside the city. Luckily, Falcon saw this and spoke up.

"Stop talking so much. Grab Aluminum and let's get back into the city before someone sees us."

Phoenix grabbed me and flapped his giant red wings that matched his hair. We went straight up and over the city wall. He only flapped his wings one more time to slow us down before we hit the ground.

We landed in the very middle of the city and were met by a man that looked a lot like Jason. "We have waited a *very* long time for you."

"Where's Kid?" Stefano demanded impatiently.

The man stepped aside and allowed another to meet us. He had a grey cloak on and a hood that fell over his eyes. He pushed the hood back.

"Harry?!" Stefano and I said in sync.

Harry laughed. "President watched the security footage and saw me helping you, Stefano. He was going to kill me. Jonothan called me over to his office and showed me this city. Told me to run. So here I am."

"Where's Kid?" He asked a bit calmer but with just as much impatience.

"I healed him. His heart is going again, scorches are gone, and blood is where it should be. Whatever impaled him, missed his heart. He is still just as lucky to be alive. He is resting now."

Stefano let out a sigh of relief and looked around.

"I am gonna have to ask for you to not die." Harry said. "I know it's a pretty unfair request, but I can't bring back the dead again. But Stefano, I need to talk to you about something sometime."

I looked around. "What exactly is this place?" I asked. The man that looked like Jason stepped forward again.

"Stefano. Aluminum. Welcome...to The Instinctsion."

<T1 A2 S3 K4 S5>

We were amazed at the new place. A place where we didn't have to run or hide anymore. "Before we go any further," Stefano started. "can we get your name."

"My name is Jackson. I was the first one here."

"Nice." We said in unison. "Why does it sound so normal?" I asked.

"Because I'm almost normal. I have the ability to sense where others like us are. Other supers. It only really works if they are within the city. Not really useful here."

"Oh," I said looking away from him. "Where shall we start."

Stefano looked around at parts of the city and tried to find a subject.

"How about those five towers," I suggested.

"We heard stories of five heroes that would join and lead us to full freedom. And hopefully, make it so we wouldn't have to hide anymore. We've waited more than fifty years. New-comers join every few months. Recently, we've received more and more."

Jackson walked to the tower with a green S5 on it. As we did, Stefano winced and grabbed his left forearm. He lifted his arm and we all saw that MANDS had vanished from his arm. S5 remained. The same thing happened to me when we toured in front of my tower. Only an A2 remained on my forearm.

We kept walking. As we walked, more and more of the citizens joins us on our tour.

"We were told that the heroes known as *The Instinctsion* would have powers far beyond our own. We were told the story hundreds of times by Jonothan. Well, Jonothan in holographic form. *The final five.* One super with the ability to look into the future and shapeshift. One with the ability to turn invisible and throw things that no one else can see."

"Still need to work on making them *completely* invisible," I said. He continued.

"One with the ability to adapt to survive. One with super strength and the ability to heal even the worst of wounds."

"Lot of good that did him," Stefano said. "And one with every branch of telekinesis."

"I've got most of them. Don't know about all of them."

"These towers are home to people with similar powers." He looked to Stefano. "Your tower is being watched by a telepath who is equipped with just the right branch of telekinesis. He is currently holding the city up." He looked to me. "Similar story with yours. Your watcher is holding a force field around the city. Each tower is protecting our city and giving it he life you see around you. Every morning the watchers input a bit of their power and get it back by night. When Kid wakes up and we are joined by the last of the five, we will have a festival and a ritual."

"Do I want to know what this ritual is?" Stefano asked. "It's a surprise." Jackson said excitedly.

"I've never been a fan of surprises." Stefano said seriously. "You'll enjoy this one. We were worried at first."

"About what?" I said.

"We heard a terrible bang that came from the towers. First it was Kid's tower. Orange particles floated from the tower's top and, when you brought his body here, it fell back inside. With the S3 tower, the bang was followed by an ear-splitting sound. It sounded like rusty metal being dragged across rusty metal."

"What happened after that?" Stefano asked eagerly.

"The particles came in a pair of colors. Red and black circled and spiraled up beyond the clouds. A door moved inside the top of the tower and the watchers of that tower were forced out. Then the particles came back down. They were purple."

"What door?"

"The S3 tower must be run by two people of only similar DNA. Not identical. In our case it was twins. A door moved and blocked them from going any further into the tower. No one has been to the very top anyway."

I looked at the tower marked S3. It had a purple stripe from the ground to the very top. "Why do you keep calling it 'the S3 tower'? That's Scar and Scarlet's."

Jackson looked confused. "Who?" He asked.

Stefano and I looked at each other. How could he not know who they were? A Valkyrie flew down and landed. It was one we hadn't met yet.

"Any new information about the tower?" Jackson asked him.

"No, sir. Everything is silent. I spoke to the seeress and she said that everything will change soon. Shall I search for the final hero?"

"Yes. Take Phoenix and Raven and one of the other nests."

He flapped his massive light brown wings and flew off and was joined by six others with wings. Two of them being Phoenix and Raven.

"That was Sparrow. He takes everything really seri-" "Who is the seeress?" Stefano interrupted.

"She is the watcher of the T1 tower. She can see what we will have to defend against, so she comes down every night to her hut in the middle of the city and we can ask her what she sees. She hasn't come down in a while, but she will be at the festival if you want to speak with her."

I looked up at the sky. Once again, the sun was falling. The moon chased the sun and the stars followed close behind. I yawned.

"I'm afraid the watchers are too busy to leave the towers until the festival. They are setting it up for us and giving a bit of extra power to the city. The T1 watcher is making sure nothing dangerous is heading our way. Until then you are welcome to a couple of our spare houses. They are equipped with all of the living essentials. Stefano, I see that you are wounded."

Stefano checked his shoulder and his leg. Neither than healed. Blood was still dripping from his wounds.

"If you would follow me to the medical wing, we will take care of that right away." "What about when I need to heal on my own?" Stefano asked worriedly.

"I hope it will never come to that but if it does, we have serums in pretty much everything here that will restore your healing factor and telekinesis."

"I'm going to need more than that."

"Consider it done, Sir." Jackson bowed and motioned for Stefano to follow him. "Thank you." Stefano and I yawned in sync.

I went to one of the available houses. It wasn't very roomy, but it was definitely bigger than our shelter in the woods and more comforting than the tube in my old chamber. I took off my muddy shoes and my blue hoodie. I kept on my, once white, T-shirt and jeans to sleep in. I heard a knock at the door. I opened my wooden door and looked down. There was a small group of little girls. They all giggled with excitement.

"It's her!"

"I know."

"Shhh shhh shhh."

"Hi, Aluminum. We...um...brought you clothes for the night." They all giggled. "We will also take your dirty clothes and wash them for you."

"I can control water." Said the girl in the back. She seemed really excited.

I looked at the little girls. I felt bad. They were involved in a project that they didn't understand. They could have been tortured and forced to do things they didn't want to do like we were. But at least in this city, they were away from it all.

I took the clothes they brought for me and traded them with my dirty ones. As they skipped away I said, "Thank you."

"Did you hear that?" One said. "So polite." Said another.

I put on the clean white shirt and jeans and crawled into bed. I stared at the ceiling. I closed my eyes and for the first time, I dreamt.

# CHAPTER 21

# KID

*You still stand with me and are strong enough to make it back again.*

The words echoed in my ears like I was back at Jonothan Industries again. I tried to open my eyes, but they wouldn't open.

"Kid." Said a voice. It sounded deep and distorted. I felt like I recognized it but not in a good way.

I moved around and tried to get up. I felt something heavy jump to my chest. I grabbed at it, but my hands became pinned to my chest.

I kept struggling. My full strength had not returned. "Stop moving!" Screamed the deep dark voice.

"No!" I yelled back. "Get off me!" I kicked and threw my body in every direction. Whoever was holding me down was starting to lose their hold on me.

"If I have to throw you through another wall, I'm not gonna feel bad about it!"

The voice was clearer and sounded more familiar. I stopped moving. I tried to open my eyes. They opened and immediately closed. I tried again, and they were open but everything was blurry. I looked around the room I was in.

The walls had drawings on them. But not with a marker or crayon. They were drawn on with fire. There were no windows with curtains. They were just empty spaces cut into the walls. The doorway didn't have a door, but it had a sign above it with a Red Cross. I looked at the hands that held me down.

The fingernails had dirt under them and the knuckles were bruised and covered in dry blood. The skin was pulled away from the swollen knuckles. The familiar mark on his forearm was just S5. His veins had a slight pink glow to them. His hoodie was a sleeveless t-shirt instead of the hoodie we got from the supply room of MANDS. He obviously tore off the sleeves. His arms were scarred. The scars went up his neck and crossed his jawline and stopped behind his ear. He had dry blood in his nose and some on his lip. I looked at his eyes and saw the familiar left green eye.

"Both a bright orange I see." He said with a smile. I blinked, and everything became clear again.

"There's that normal glow." He said. He removed his hands and fell back into the woven chair that was next to the bed I was in.

"Good to see you, Stefano." I croaked. "Welcome back to the land of the living."

I sat up and threw my legs over the side of the bed. "Where are we?"

"Remember that name we made up? The one you wanted to call our little group." "Yeah?"

"That's what they call this place." "*They?*"

"The citizens of this place. It's a super-city. They call it 'The Instinctsion'." I stood up.

"Take it easy." Stefano warned and tried to push me back.

I sat back down and slowly stood back up. In the chair next to where Stefano was sitting was a folded pile of clothes.

"Your 'fan-base' left that for you." Stefano said with a smile. "Where is my hammer?" I groaned as I stretched my back. "With my staff."

"Where is your staff?"

"Locked in the armory. There's no need for them here. Or so Jackson claims." "Do you believe him?"

Stefano was silent for a while. "Hurry up and get dressed. There's a few people I want you to meet." He got to his feet.

"But I have to-"

"Get dressed." Stefano said again from the doorway. He was excited. He quickly left the medical building.

"-go back. I have to go back." I said to myself.

He was gone so I quickly got dressed. An orange long sleeve shirt was provided along with jeans and my crappy tennis shoes. My hammer and backpack were gone.

I walked out of the medical wing and looked around. Five giant towers were on the outer parts of the city. On the far side of the towers was a massive stone wall. I looked at the ground. A piece of dirt fell, and I could see a lake at least a hundred feet below. The piece of dirt flew back to where it was.

I looked around and tried to find Stefano. He said 'fan-base' so I assumed he had one too. I looked around and saw a crowd of people wearing blue clothing. I ran and made my way to the center of it.

"Oh my god! It's Kid!" The crowd screamed, and more people joined the crowd. I got to the middle and found Aluminum.

"You're okay!" She said excitedly. She hugged me and her fan-base split us and I was dragged away by my own group.

I looked around the group of people wearing orange. Most were wearing the same long sleeve shirt I was. They were silently waiting for me to say something.

"Ummm." I started. They all cheered and then got quiet for the next thing I had to say. "What are your powers?"

They all talked at the same time. Some said they had super strength and others said healing. There were even some powers I didn't recognize. When they were done, they went silent again.

"Do any of you know where Stefano is?" I asked.

Every single one of them pointed to a group of people in green by a giant tower with a green 'S5' on it.

"He's with the other telekinetics." One said.

I made my way through my own group and they followed me to Stefano. I stopped at the edge of his group and called out his name.

"Stefano!"

His group stopped talking and turned around towards me. They made an opening for me to get through to Stefano. Our groups became one. I walked through the path of murmurs and met Stefano. I held out my hand and he grabbed my marked forearm. I grabbed his. We turned to the group. They were silent.

"Oh my god it's Sid!" Yelled one girl. The entire crowd went wild. They jumped in the air and cheered and chanted 'Sid'.

Stefano leaned towards me. "Did they just ship us?" He yelled over the cheering. "I think so." I yelled back.

Stefano raised his arms and got everyone to quiet down. He motioned for Aluminum to join us and her group followed. She met us in the middle of the crowd and the crowd got bigger.

"Where are the ones I wanted to talk to?" Stefano asked the crowd.

Several people stepped forward while the rest of the crowd took a step back. Stefano walked up to them one by one.

"Kid, this is Bella. Not only does she have poison in her fingers, but she is also a forest elemental."

"Why 'Bella'?" I couldn't help but ask.

She took her long blue gloves off and touched a blade of grass on the ground. It immediately turned black and died. "It's actually *Belladonna Nightshade* but having it just 'Bella' makes me feel a little more normal. You know, except for the fact that I kill everything I touch."

"I *destroy* everything I touch." I said.

"Then I guess we have a little something in common." She winked at me.

"This is RedCloud." Stefano said as he guided me to a boy with fire red hair and dark birthmarks on his face. Dark lines went across his cheeks and down his chin.

"I control fire and wind." He said with an Irish accent. "My specialty is fire tornadoes, but no one lets me do those anymore."

"Dude." I said. "Where are you from?" "I used to live in England."

I looked at Stefano. He shrugged and pushed me towards the next person. "This is Nova."

"I have the universe in my hand." She said mysteriously. "What does that mean?" I said confused; shaking my head. "I could put stars anywhere. Like lights."

"But if that doesn't work out?" Stefano asked. His tone suggested that he knew the answer. The huge smile on his face confirmed he knew the answer.

"Stars are fire. I can throw them. If the enemy gets passed those and kills me, I go super nova and kill everyone around me and I'm reborn. If that happens, you'll have to call me Nebula." She said everything with a smile.

"I guess I will. That sounds awesome." I said.

Stefano pushed me to the next person. "Next!" He yelled as he pushed me.

Stefano pushed me a little further into the crowd. "There are families here too. *This* is Luke Warm."

A man stepped forward. He had coal colored spiky hair and a burn mark on one side of his face.

"I'm a fire elemental."

"And this is...I'm sorry, Luke. I forgot your wife's name." Stefano said a little embarrassed. A woman holding a toddler's hand took a step forward.

"Aquarius. My name is Aquarius. I am a water elemental. And this is our son." She had brown hair with dark blue streaks in her hair. Aquarius crouched down next to her toddler and spoke as anyone would to a child. "Tell him your name, sweetie."

"SteamPunk!" Said the little boy with his fingers in his mouth. His hair was a spiky blonde with grey tips.

"No. Not your nickname. Your real name."

"Sizzle!" He said; still with his fingers still in his mouth.

"He's a hybrid super," Aquarius said as she stood up straight again. "Are you looking for my sister?"

"Yeah," Stefano said.

Aquarius reached into the crowd and grabbed at what looked like nothing more than air. "Stop holding your breath, Airrielle." Aquarius said stubbornly.

The clutch of air let out its breath and there was a gust of wind as a woman became visible. Her feet weren't touching the ground.

"This is Airrielle." Stefano said. "The one and only air elemental of The Instinctsion." He praised her and most of The Instinctsion cheered.

Airrielle's cheeks turned red and she floated backwards and then disappeared into the wind. "She's shy," Aquarius said.

"Next!" Stefano said as I met another member of the city.

<T1 A2 S3 K4 S5>

After I had met everyone in the entire city and the basic idea of the city was explained, the sun was going down. We were waiting for the Valkyries to get back with the newcomer and for the festival to start.

We watched the sky, but nothing came. Then all of the sudden we all heard a voice. "Hey! Is anyone up there? Hello?"

We went to the edge of the city and watched Jackson climb the stairs and look over the side.

"State your name, ability, and reason you wish to enter the city," Jackson called out once again in his bored tone.

We looked up and the sky and saw a couple winged creatures fly across the sky. They were carrying something. Or *someone.*

Two Valkyries flew over the wall and crash landed. It was Falcon and Sparrow.

Falcon picked up what he was carrying again. Sparrow leaned over what he was carried and held it to his chest. He rocked back and forth and looked around as a crowd gathered.

Jackson ran down the stairs and over to Sparrow.

"What is that?" He said as he put his hand on Sparrow's shoulder.

Sparrow slowly stood up and pulled away the sheet. "It's Phoenix. He's dead." Silent tears were streaming down his cheeks. He pushed Jackson aside and walked over to Stefano.

"This is *your* fault." He jabbed Stefano's chest with his finger. "For decades we have lived in peace. And now-"

Falcon stood up and pulled Sparrow away. "It's not his fault. You saw what happened." Stefano stepped towards Falcon. "What *did* happen."

"Why don't you see for yourself?" Sparrow said through gritted teeth.

Aluminum, Stefano and I walked over to what Falcon was carrying. It was clearly another body. It was wrapped in the clothing that used to be in the storage room at MANDS.

Stefano knelt down next to it and pulled away the clothing from the face.

It was Raven. Stefano moved her dark hair out of her face. She had bruises and cuts all over her face. Stefano quickly pulled all of the loose clothing away. Her wings were gone.

"Where are they?" Aluminum asked.

"It was MANDS," Sparrow answered. "Jonothan Industries was in view and we chose to fly over MANDS to get there. They equipped themselves with so much more than last time. Guns on the roof and all. They shot most of us down. Raven was hit. She fell right on top of MANDS. They took her inside and tried to get the location of the Instinctsion out of her. Or whatever they could. She didn't say much or anything at all and look at what they did. They took her wings!"

We looked to Falcon who was kneeling next to Raven. "When we broke in and got her and we were flying away," Falcon started. "I looked back and saw that they had attached her wings to flagpoles and flew them above the building. Most of the feathers were plucked away."

Stefano walked away with his hands on his head; breathing deeply. Jackson stepped forward. "Who is that outside of the city?" Jackson said.

"What we were sent to get from JI. *Her* and some chick named Asil." Sparrow said. He nodded to Falcon and Falcon flew back over the wall. Sparrow walked over to Stefano and violently poked at his chest. "If she's anything like *you*, I'll kill you all myself."

"Over my dead body." I interjected. Sparrow chuckled and rose into the sky. He dove straight for where the girl was over the wall.

My group of the city gathered the bodies and took them away. I saw them take Raven to the medical wing, but I couldn't see what they did with Phoenix's body.

Jackson walked over to the three of us. "The festival still goes on. S3 is here." He flashed a smile and walked to the center of the city. "Follow me, you three!" He called over his shoulder. "Please!"

We ran to the center of the city. The citizens made a huge circle with the four of us in the middle. Everyone looked at the sky.

Falcon and Sparrow glided in, each holding the arm of a girl. They dropped her, but she didn't fall. She glided to the ground. The tails of her purple cloak-like hoodie waved in the wind as she made her way to the ground. Jackson stepped forward when she touched down.

"Welcome to the-" Jackson started.

The girl walked towards me and waved Jackson away. A strange force dragged him backward. "Hey, Kid." She said.

The entire city stared at me.

"Umm...hi?" I responded.

"It's good to see you again." She said with a smile. "I thought you were going to be waiting for me at the door though." Her smile faded.

It finally dawned on me who she was. "You're the little girl from the wall." "I have a name."

"I assume it has something to do with the Scar Origins."

She flew into the air and twirled. Purple particles surrounded her and her purple cloak hugged her. "I'm Scarletta." She came back down. "And I'm not little anymore."

"Well, Scarletta. I am going to help Raven and help get the festival going." Jackson said and looked at Stefano. Scarletta glared at Jackson. "Can I get you to show her around?"

"Whatever," Stefano said. He closed his eyes and slowly picked himself up with his telekinesis. He wobbled as he reached a higher altitude and Scarletta joined him in the sky. A few blades of grass and pebbles were following him. They flew around the towers and against the edge of the city. Scarletta quickly took the lead. We all split up to set up for the festival.

<T1 A2 S3 K4 S5>

The tour was over, and the stars were coming out. Even the northern lights came out for the festival. With the full moon as our special guest.

We were collected in the center of the city once again. The towers all emitted their own colored particles. T1 with yellow, A2 with blue, S3 with purple, K4 with orange and S5 with green.

The particles collected in the sky and formed a spherical shield around the city. We could feel the city descend above the lake. And then into the lake.

We watched the water climb the transparent sphere. We were sinking. We finally hit the bottom of the lake and were all still staring at the sky.

The stars and moon were distorted under the water. The colored particles in the shield detached and hovered above the houses and towers. All of the particles cast their own bit of colored light. They dimmed just enough for the northern lights to join in.

The particles stopped coming out of the tower tops. The doors to each tower opened and the watchers stepped out. Each silhouetted against their colored backlights.

The festival had started.

# CHAPTER 22

# SCARLETTA

I walked around the festival. The watchers came out of their towers and everyone was having the time of their lives.

I made my way to the other three 'prophets'. I felt like an outsider, so I only listened in and watched their conversations. First, I listened to Aluminum's conversation with her watcher. She and her watcher were by a fire just outside the A2 tower.

"How long have you guys been here?" Aluminum asked.

"The Instinctsion has been here for more than 50 years. I'm only 15 but I've been here for about 32 years. My turn to ask a question. Can you fly?" Said the excited doppelgänger in the matching blue long sleeve shirt.

"I don't think so." "I can."

"You *can*?"

"Yup. I can teach you."

"It would be an honor to learn from you." "No, ma'am. The honor is all mine."

"You know you don't have to keep calling me ma'am, right?" "What should I call you then, ma'am?"

"Call me Aluminum."

The girl hopped excitedly. "Yes, ma'am. I mean…Aluminum."

I walked over to where Kid and his watcher were under the K4 tower. "Why didn't you like Harry?" Asked the young watcher.

"He left me in the dark. I can't really blame him now."

"Especially since he saved your life." The watcher said.

"Several times now. Hey, is there any special quality of that wall?"

"The entire city is alive in a sort of way. The wall is the skin. It 'heals' rather quickly." "Wanna see who can break through it first."

"Absolutely, sir."

"It's Kid. You watchers are so weird."

They ran off to the closest part of the wall and took turns destroying the wall and watching it rebuild itself. The wall rebuilding itself looked like it was rewinding to when it was intact.

I walked over to the S5 tower and expected Stefano to be there with his watcher. Instead, he was with Jackson. They were by the biggest fire pit in the center of the city.

Jackson sat on the log that was meant to be a quick means for a bench while Stefano leaned against it. His watcher sat adjacent him and stared into the fire. They all had a mason jar of glowing liquid in their hands. Jackson's behavior gave potential evidence that the liquid in the jars was a sort of alcohol.

"Listen, Stefano. I know you're not a hundred percent set on staying with us but just give it until the end of the festival." Jackson tried to negotiate. "In the very middle of the festival we've got these wonderful games. And in those games, we-"

"What? What games?" Stefano asked. He looked at his watcher. His almost identical watcher only shrugged his shoulders.

"Huh. Jonothan really didn't tell you anything, did he?"

"No. Not a thing." Stefano took a drink from his jar. He screwed up his face and shivered.

"That's all right. Anyways, the games-"

"How do you know you can trust Jonothan?" "What?"

"Jonothan. How do you know you can trust him?"

Jackson scoffed. "He-he gave us life. If that's not worth a person's trust, I don't know what is." Stefano pulled himself up on the log. He let go of his drink and it hovered around him. "He may have given your life but you guys are basically prisoners."

"*Prisoners?* We're not prisoners. We're free." "You're not free, Jackson. You're living in fear here."

"We're not living in fear. Even ask your watcher." Jackson pointed to Stefano's watcher. The watcher only shrugged his shoulders.

"He's lived in a tower all his life. A tower located in a city that is suspended above a lake encased in a shield to prevent any kind of attack and then another shield to prevent anyone who isn't like us from seeing us. *That* is living in fear."

Jackson stood up and looked down at what he thought was his hero. "It is for the safety of our people. We live amongst our own species and-"

Stefano got to his feet. "Your species is in the real city! Not this *joke!*" His watcher slowly got to his feet and watched the two go back and forth. Both jars hovered as Stefano argued with his hands and his watcher awkwardly stood with his hands in the pockets of his jeans.

"*Joke*?! This is our life! We have done this for decades!"

"Jackson." Said Stefano a bit calmer. "This is a joke. One set up by Charles and Jonothan as a distraction, so they aren't just waiting for what you call the final five."

"Who the hell is Charles?!" Said Jackson; throwing his hands in the air. Some of his drink spilled.

"Charles is the twin brother of your psychotic 'creator'. If one is evil you better believe that the other is too. You have been misled, Jackson."

"We have been guided," Jackson said defensively.

"You have been *misguided*!" There was a silence. The groups of citizens who had once been playing around in festival games were now quiet. Kid and his watcher stopped punching the wall and Aluminum and *her* watcher had joined the circle that had formed around Stefano, his watcher, and Jackson. "This city is a joke," Stefano said again. "The *Instinctsion* is a joke!" His jar of glowing liquid fell and shattered on the log he leaned against. People in the growing circle winced at Stefano's offensive insult.

"YOU *ARE* THE *INSTINCTSION!*" Jackson shot back. Silence fell again. "Now you understand," Stefano said slowly.

"Say what you want, Stefano. I'm not gonna give up on you. I don't know what you're trying to do but I'm not going to give up. I will continue to believe in the prophecy I was told the moment Jonothan gave me my ability."

"Yeah." Said some of the crowd.

"I will continue to believe in the Instinctsion." Jackson continued.

"Long live The Instinctsion!" Said a member of the crowd. Everyone shouted in agreement. "I will continue to believe in *you*." Jackson finished. The crowd cheered.

"As will this entire city. And *I* among them will follow you and the other prophets into battle. I believe in you," Jackson yelled over the roar.

"That makes one of us," Stefano said. The crowd fell silent. "Actually, that makes *five hundred* and one of us."

Stefano left the crowd and his watcher followed. They went to the S5 tower.

"How do you get inside," Stefano asked his watcher.

"This console." His watcher pointed at the hand-scanner next to the door and then returned his hand to his pocket. Stefano put his hand on the scanner. The scanner made an electronic sound of rejection.

"Watcher, why can't I get in?"

"Because only a watcher can get in, sir." "Then open it, *watcher*."

"I can't." "Why not?"

"Because *you* have to do it, sir."

Stefano slammed his hand against the scanner. It made another sound of electronic rejection. He slammed it again. And then again and again. He slowed and slid down the side of the building.

"I don't belong here, watcher," Stefano said into his arm which was just below the scanner panel.

"You can't lose faith in this place, sir." Said the watcher. "You lose faith, sir, and things fall apart."

"Stefano." "What?"

"My name is Stefano." "I know."

"What is your name, watcher."

"I don't have one." He sat down in front of their fire and stared into the embers. Stefano joined him. He hovered two jars of the strange liquid over for him and his watcher. I stopped watching them when I felt two taps on my shoulder.

I turned around and held my hand up. Two girls were held above the ground surrounded in a purple field.

"Please don't kill us yet." One pleaded. "What did you just say?" I asked.

"Can you put us down?" The other asked.

I set them down. "How does someone get into the towers?" "You must be a watcher." Said one.

"There can only be one." Said the other.

"Unless you're talking about *our* tower." The first one said. "Then there's *two*." They said in unison.

"But not after tonight." The second one said. "Then it's *you*." They said in unison again.

I looked from one to the other. They looked pretty close to Scar and Scarlet. I had seen pictures of them, but these were complete strangers. They weren't clones either. They were actual twins.

"I'm going to resist the urge to punch you both in the face if you tell me what that means." "You see. At the fest-" They started in unison.

"One!" I pointed to the one in the red long sleeve shirt. "You. Speak." "At the end of the festival..." She looked to her twin.

"Speak." I edged.

"You have to kill your watcher." Said the second. "*Watchers* in our case." The first one added.

"I don't want to kill you." "No." Said one.

"Of course, you don't." Said the other.

"You just want to punch us in the faces." They said in unison. "What are you two supposed to be doing right now."

"Well, we're *supposed* to be enjoying the festival."

"But if you look around, all the watchers are following their replacements." "We've waited so long to meet you."

I looked around. That's exactly what the watchers were doing. In the center of the city, Jackson had the telekinetics move the entire fire pit and had the strong group drag in a ton of rope and four massive logs.

"What's the order of events for the festival?" I asked; staring at the strong group as they pounded the logs into the ground like posts and wrapped a rope around them.

"First it's socialization." Said one.

"We are passed that part." Said the other. "Then it's feasting." Said the first one.

"But no one cares about that so that part is over with." Said the second. "Now it's the games." They both said.

I tore my eyes away. "What are the games?"

They looked at each other and then back at me. They each grabbed one of my arms. "Time for you to find out."

I was dragged and then pushed into another circle. It was in the same spot as it was before but wider. I ended up on the inner edge of the circle. I looked around. Stefano, Kid, and Aluminum were all pushed to the inner edge of the circle by their watchers as well.

Jackson was in the center of the circle. The strong group left what they were doing. They made a ring. A ring big enough to be an arena.

Jackson looked around. "Where is Little Boom?" A little boy walked forward. He put his hands together and struggled to pull them apart. He then collapsed his hands again and pulled a small orb from his palm. He put it in Jackson's mouth.

Jackson walked to the edge of the arena and climbed a ladder with a short platform at the top. Almost like a diving board.

"Welcome!" His voice was like a sonic boom. The orb that he put in his mouth glowing white in the back of his throat. I could see the sound waves travel and hit the force field and cause the lake water to ripple. "To the Games!"

The crowd cheered. I turned around and saw the strong group push hand-made stadiums to the arena. Everyone got to their seats. Us 'prophets' somehow managed to sit together.

"These games are....TO THE DEATH!"

Part of the crowd cheered. Another part winced. The rest stayed quiet and processed. "Now because I love each and every one of you...I gave those with a healing ability their serums and now they can reverse death of more than themselves!"

The entire crowd cheered.

"It's to the death but the death isn't real. It may look and feel real but, trust me, it isn't!" The crowd still cheered.

"First battle! Bolt! Versus! Amy!"

More cheers. Kid leaned over to Stefano and yelled over the cheering. "Why do they call her Amy?"

"It's like 'any' if you change one of the letters. She can be anywhere. She is a teleporter." All four of us nodded.

"Can Amy get Bolt to finally shut up? Let's find out!" Boomed Jackson.

A guy with dark blonde hair sped into the arena. He waved to the crowd. A girl with dark blonde hair appeared in the arena and blew a strand of hair out of her eyes.

"Fight!"

The crowd was silent as they waited for the first punch.

"Hey, Amy," Said Bolt. "Lookin' good. Don't want to mess up your hair so I guess I'll go easy on you."

Amy got into her fighting stance.

"And in exchange," Bolt continued. "You can have my number."

Amy put a disgusted look on her face and then disappeared. She reappeared behind Bolt and kicked him where no guy should ever be kicked. She walked away, and the fight was over. The crowd cheered over Amy's victory.

Bolt got on his knees. He stood up and tried to speed out of the arena. He got a few feet before collapsing. He got back up and did it again. He kept doing it until he was completely out of the arena. He wasn't dead, but the fight was already won.

"That's a way to make short work of things!" Jackson boomed. "Next fight! Asil! Versus! Ra-" The crowd cheered.

"Sorry folks. She can't fight. She-"

"Speak for yourself, Jackson!" Raven walked into the middle of the arena. She still had a few cuts and bruises on her face, but they were mostly healed and hidden with a smile.

The crowd cheered again.

The other girl known as Asil walked into the arena. Jackson and Stefano stared at her. The crowd didn't notice what Jackson and Stefano did.

"What is it?" I yelled to Stefano.

"Nothing. Don't worry about it." He waved me away. "Fight," Jackson said instead of yelling.

Asil jumped into the air and tried to kick Raven in the face. Raven bent backward and Asil went right over her. Asil tumbled on the ground. Raven straighten up and then jumped into the air. She landed; having forgotten she didn't have her wings. She slowly turned around. Asil quickly walked up to her. She grabbed her throat with one hand and punched her repeatedly in the face with the other.

The crowd booed.

"In any other case" Jackson bellowed. "I would let this continue. But due to Raven's condition, this is where this round ends. Victor! Asil!"

Asil pulled her fist away and it was difficult to determine who's blood covered Asil's swollen knuckles. Raven fell, unconscious, to the ground.

The crowd clapped out of respect. Asil strutted out of the arena and Raven was unwillingly escorted out by Sparrow and Falcon who wrapped her in their wings.

A couple of rows in front of me I heard a few people talking as they respectively clapped for Asil. They leaned towards each other and talked quietly over the clapping. "What kind of super fights without using her powers?"

"I think she's a human. I'm going to kill her." Said one. "Me too." Said another.

Another leaned towards the conversation. "We all can."

Stefano flicked two fingers towards him and the one who had suggested killing Asil hovered towards him and froze in front of Stefano's face.

"No one touches her as long as I'm still breathing," Stefano said. "But she-"

He pinched his fingers together and the super was starting to have a hard time breathing. "Got it?"

The super nodded painfully and then was hovered back in his seat. The group leaned in closer and talked. I couldn't hear much but I did hear 'Asil' a few times.

"Why are you protecting her?" I asked Stefano.

"There are some things I want to learn. Like how many other humans have been here and why they are hated so much now."

"Final fight! Nova! Versus! And I may regret this one but, RedCloud!" Half of the crowd cheered, and the other half groaned.

The two stepped into the arena.

"Isn't that the guy that does the fire tornadoes?" Kid asked. "Yup." Aluminum answered.

"Okay! To add a bit more control over you-know-who, this will be a team battle! Ladies and gentlemen give it up for Belladonna! And! Falcon!"

More cheering.

I looked over the edge of the stadium where Raven, Falcon, and

Sparrow were right below me. "You're playing the games *too*?" Sparrow complained.

Falcon put his hand on Sparrow's shoulder. "Have a bit of fun. We could use some." He opened his massive wings. He looked at Raven. He used one of his wings to push Raven under Sparrow's arm. "Just like old times." He nodded and with one flap of his massive wings, he was in the sky.

He violently landed next to RedCloud. He barely caught himself. "Try not to burn down the entire stadium this time, yeah?" He took off his white jacket, so he could stretch his wings to their full lengths.

"Don't tempt me, brother." Said RedCloud as he took off his leather armor; exposing his dark-colored birthmarks.

"Still not your brother."

Bella walked out next to Nova.

"I like your new gloves," Nova said to Bella.

"I hate them." Said Bella. She slid off her blue gloves and dropped them on the ground. Her fingertips had tiny purple thorns in them.

"Better?" Nova asked. "So much."

RedCloud pulled a battle ax from his leather belt.

I leaned over towards Aluminum and Stefano. "I thought you said he was Irish." "He is." Said Aluminum.

Stefano leaned over. "He's from England, with an Irish accent, with Native American birthmarks and a Scottish warrior background."

I said nothing. Jackson said it all for me. "Fight!"

RedCloud spun and sent a fire tornado towards the girls at the same time Falcon took to the air. The fire burned some of Falcon's feathers and falcon spiraled to the ground. He lifted himself up and shook his head. Dirt fell from his windblown hair.

The girls jumped out of the way of the flaming tornado in opposite directions and right where RedCloud wanted them. He threw his ax at Bella. She ducked just in time, but the blade of the ax cut her collarbone.

Nova put a hand to her lips and blew a kiss at RedCloud. Stars came out of her hand and added to the already floating particles in the sky. The entire crowd awed at them.

RedCloud was no longer in a fighting stance. Instead, he looked around at the beautiful stars with his mouth open.

Bella walked up to him. He looked at her. She put a hand on his cheek. RedCloud fell to the ground and screamed out in pain. His veins bulged and turned purple. Tiny purple thorns expanded in his veins.

Falcon finally got up and ran at the two girls. Nova threw her arms out and a burst of stars shot in every direction. People in the front rows of the stadium protected their faces from the small bits of bright fire.

Falcon fell backward but quickly got up. He took two flaps to get into the sky and dive-bombed Belladonna. He pulled up as he was right over her head and flapped his wings. Dirt got in her eyes.

He flew to Nova and picked her up. He flew to the highest part of the shield over the city and then dropped her. She hit the ground and crumpled in a terrifying sound of breaking bones.

Falcon picked up the ax RedCloud had thrown as he flew over Bella and landed. He slowly straightened up and looked over to Bella. She had mud in the corners of her eyes.

They ran at each other. Falcon swung the ax at Bella and Bella had her hands in front of her. They both died. Falcon lay on the ground as his veins housed purple thorns that grew through them. Bella bled out at the neck.

The crowd cheered as the four bodies were dragged out of the arena and to medical where the healers were waiting for them.

"Final fight!" Jackson boomed.

The crowd was silent. They waited for the final contestants. "Stefano and his watcher!"

The entire stadium joined Aluminum, Kid and I as we stared at Stefano and his watcher in the row in front of him.

"Did you guys put my name in a box or something?" He asked us. We all shook our heads. "Kid and his watcher!" Jackson announced.

Everyone looked to Kid. The crowd cheered for Kid and not Stefano.

"Scarletta and her watchers!" More eyes. More cheers. "Aluminum and her watcher!"

The little girls in the row behind us leaped out of their seats and launched themselves at Aluminum. Some were in tears. They others patted her on the shoulders. "Versus!"

The crowd turned toward Jackson. The silence was uncomfortably loud.

Jackson's voice was quieter. Almost like he was whispering. "She has asked to not be called by her name until the end."

Everyone looked as a girl in a gold cloak stepped forward into the arena. She stepped in the middle and kept her hood up.

The watchers nudged each other and whispered. They knew something we didn't. Jackson went back to his booming voice. "The HYDRA!"

The crowd cheered.

We were held above the crowd and passed to the arena. We all stood in separate corners. To my left, I could see Aluminum. Kid was to my right and in the opposite corner was Stefano. In the very center was the girl.

The crowd stood and cheered as a massive tail launched out of the cloaked girl. Her arms became solid muscle boulders thicker than the city's wall. Her body grew, and wings shot out bigger than any Valkyries'. Her head cracked open and unleashed seven dragon-like heads. Each with their own razor-sharp teeth. The heads each found a target. The ones that didn't have a target were planning and clicking sparks in their mouths.

Stefano looked at Aluminum. "I told you the hydra was real!"

I looked at what everyone else was doing. The crowd stopped cheering and talking, and it sounded like they stopped breathing too. Stefano and his watcher had their staffs in thier hands. They paced back and forth and spun their staffs as they waited for the first move. The watcher clicked his staff open into a bow.

Kid had a heavy war hammer. He clinked his hammer with his watcher's hammer. They laughed.

Aluminum's watcher leaned toward Aluminum. She whispered something and then they both made shields. The bubble-like shields began to hover. They hovered in their shields with their machetes at the ready.

My watchers stood in front of me and handed me a small dagger with a purple jewel I had never seen before. They nodded to each other and then hovered in front of me. I unsheathed my dagger and looked up at the hydra.

My finger was comfortable over the jewel. When my finger touched the jewel, the dagger suddenly expanded and became a sword. One similar to the ones Romans fought with. One of the hydra's heads looked at me and grimaced. I fixed my stance.

"Fight!" Boomed Jackson and one of the heads lunged at me.

<T1 A2 S3 K4 S5>

We all struggled to catch our breaths. Stefano limped around the mangled corpse of the hydra. He leaned on his staff with every step. He pulled a tooth from his left thigh.

"Every damn time." He said through gritted teeth. Blood trailed down the side of his face.

His watcher sat at the end of the line of wounded watchers. He was covered in blood and lay his broken bow over his knees.

Kid's watcher sat with his legs crossed. He was cleaning his hammer while Kid paced back and forth in front of the hydra's severed heads. He waited for more heads to take their places even if he had to assist in making room for more of the hydra's heads.

My watchers were taking in what had just happened. They stared at the godly creature's corpse; unblinking. I stood and watched everyone. Their emotions. Their expressions. They all fought hard. The only one who didn't show anything was Aluminum.

Her watcher looked like she was dying. She lay on the far-left end of the line of watchers. She held her stomach where razor teeth pierced, and talons ripped through. Aluminum knelt down next to her watcher.

The crowd was done cheering. They saw our expressions and how we handled everything and that none of us were having any fun.

Not anymore.

# CHAPTER 23

# STEFANO

"What a wonderful spectacle!" Boomed Jackson as the hydra was dragged to the side of the arena.

Yellow particles formed a band that wrapped around the hydra. It turned back into a girl. Her cloak appeared some feet above her and gracefully floated down onto her motionless body.

"They did fight hard! Let's give our heroes a hand, shall we?" Jackson said and started to clap. The stadium held their fists in the air and then dropped them. They took their seats and waited for the final part of the festival.

"Right. Now for the Change Over Ceremony!"

Our watchers stood us in a line. Aluminum on the far left and I was on the far right. The watchers stood in front of us and stared into our eyes. It felt like looking in a mirror but everything in the mirror was different.

"Now the watchers must choose. Battle for their right over the tower! Or! Accept their fate." I looked at Aluminum and her watcher. Her watcher weakly lifted the blade of Aluminum's machete and gently placed it on her neck. She tilted her head and flashed a bloody smile.

I looked at Scarletta and her watchers. They knelt and took out two daggers. One ruby red and the other was black as night. They put their daggers in each of Scarletta's hands and bowed their heads.

I looked at Kid and his watcher. His watcher stepped forward and put his hammer into Kid's hands. He stepped back and smiled. Then he bowed.

My watcher pressed the button on his broken bow. His final arrow, still in perfect shape,

slowly came out of the side. He took it and put it in my hand. He went back to his spot, flashed me a smile, and then turned around.

Everyone else pulled back their weapons. I pressed the button at the top of my staff and it opened into a bow. I pulled the bowstring all the way to my cheek. The back of the arrow was resting under my eye. The feathers were waiting in a crushed tear. I was doing it again. I was crying. Why was I crying? I didn't know this person. I let go of the arrow and watched the arrow pierce my watcher's back; straight through his heart.

I heard a few winces from the crowd and the others standing next to me. I ignored them all. I lowered my bow and it collapsed itself into a staff. I turned around and saw the girl's body. Who was she?

All of the sudden she stood up. No blood. No bruises. No scratches. Nothing. She pulled back her hood. I couldn't believe it. Everyone else turned around. "Tressa?!" We all said in sync.

"Brave, Stefano." Said a voice behind me. I turned back around. "Long live The Instinctsion, right? As long as it dies by Stefano's hand only."

It was my watcher. He had blood dripping out of his mouth and around where the arrow pierced his heart. He put his hands on my shoulders and pulled my chest to his. Piercing me with the same arrow that had pierced him.

I shot out of bed and put myself in the corner of my room, so I could see all of my room. I looked around the room I was in. There was a broken bow mounted on the wall next to the arrow that killed my watcher. They were above a desk. I got out of bed and walked over to my desk. I pushed all of the towers of paper into the trash can.

I went to my window and looked over the city. It was on the top floor. Everything was back to normal. The kids were playing, the Valkyries were flying, Sparrow constantly flew around my building and threatened my life, the sky no longer looked distorted, and the sun was shining.

The sun hit my window and I saw my reflection. There was not a single scar for evidence of what I had to do to get to where I was. Both my eyes were green. I refused to take any more serums, but the tower gave back more power than it took.

I walked to the silver console in the middle of my room and put my hand in it. Green particles fled from my veins and onto the console. I removed my hand and the console held a constant green glow.

I went back to my window and opened it. I took a breath of fresh air and then I fell. I caught myself with my telekinesis and flew over to Aluminum's tower. I was getting better at flying. It was the stopping part that was getting to me.

I tried to slow down but ended up face-planting into the window. The blinds parted, and I saw Aluminum's once again irritated face. She opened the window.

"You know I have a door, right?"

"Yeah," I said. "But where's the fun in that? You need to practice it again anyways."

She groaned and closed the window. She walked over to her desk on the opposite wall and turned towards me. She started running at the window. Before she hit it, she phased through it and caught herself in a blue bubble shield.

"Happy?" She asked. She sounded like she was talking into a fan. "Getting better. Let's go inside."

"Not yet." She said. She was looking in my general direction but not *at* me. I turned around to see what she was looking at. It was Sparrow. He noticed I wasn't in my tower and headed straight for me.

I looked back to Aluminum. She was no longer hovering in a bubble anymore. She was inside. "Open the window!" I said; panicked. Sparrow blamed me for everything that happened to the city. Even the small things like rain. Everything made him want to kill me more than he already did.

Aluminum rolled her eyes and opened the window. I threw myself inside and slide across the floor.

"Stop doing that," I said. "Start using the front door."

"Where's the fun in having the ability to fly if you have to use a door?"

Aluminum sat on her bed. Her blue covers were neatly made and carefully laid over her pillows.

"Tressa said you wanted to see me," I said as I got to my feet. "Her name isn't Tressa."

"But she looks exactly like her."

"She's not *her* though. She's a watcher that has been here for a long time and won't get replaced."

"What's her name anyway?" "Definitely not *'watcher'*." "What is it then?"

"She told me not to tell you."

"Whatever." I walked over to her desk. She had leaning towers of paper. One of them was full of sketches. I pulled a paper off of the pile. It was a sketch of MANDS. I picked up another pile. It was a list of sentences.

"What are these?" I asked. I levitated a few papers over to her. She snatched them from the air and studied them. Then she looked up to me.

"Can you hear Tressa? Like she's talking in your ear?"

"She did when we were escaping. I can't hear her anymore."

"She spoke to me a few times." Her eyes lowered. "At least I think it's her." I looked through the giant pile. "Maybe more than a few times."

"I heard her before we got here. I have a theory that we carried a bit of her here. And now she is with Titanium."

"Her name is Titanium?" "Um-"

"That's awesome." "I guess so."

I looked at the other piles on her desk. "That's not why you called me here. Why *did* you call me here?"

She stood up and joined me at her desk. "There's no other way to say this. I'm going back to MANDS."

I dropped the paper. "Why?"

"To kill President. I made a poison that I'm going to use on my machete so that President suffers as much as we have. Maybe Fabian too."

"Fabian ages as fast as we do. By now he's got to be like 32 or something." "I want you and your group to come with me."

"The telekinetics?" I sighed. "You are so determined to kill my Greenies. Any other extreme requests?"

"And the remaining Valkyries."

"He's gonna try to kill me but, okay. When do we leave?"

"As soon as possible. While people are just starting to wake up. Because there's...something else."

"What is it?"

She walked to her door and made sure it was locked. She went to the window, closed it, locked it and then closed the blinds.

"I'm going to hit Jonothan Industries too." She said in a hushed whisper.

"I'm in. I'll go get my group and see if there are any others. How will we get there?"

"Take your greenies and others who can fly and go over the mountain. I'll put a shield around those who can't fly and phase them through the mountain. I will arrive first, so they will be concentrated on breaking the shield and killing everyone inside. That's when you reveal yourselves and swoop down and take out as many as possible. I will deal with President while you find Fabian. Distract him for as long as possible and then I will try to help you kill him."

I stood there for a while. She thought about it since the day we left. She actually had a plan. I nodded and opened the blinds and the window. I jumped out and caught myself. "Long live The Instinctsion, right?" I flew and told everyone who could fly to join me in the sky.

"No! I know what you are doing, and I say no! Get back on the ground!" Jackson yelled.

Many of the citizens were too afraid to go against Jackson. They all probably knew what was going to happen.

Half of my greenies joined me. Falcon flew to my side. "Are we going to battle?" Falcon asked.

"Yup," I said.

Sparrow flew to my other side. "Perfect opportunity to kill you." "I'd appreciate it if you could wait until the end."

"What's the end?" Falcon asked.

"When the Jonothan Industries tower crushes MANDS."

I stopped flying and turned around to see who joined me. It was mostly my group but there were a few of Aluminum's followers, some shape-shifters who shifted into birds, and air elementals.

I looked down by Aluminum's tower to see how many she had gathered. I saw a few orange shirts, a couple purple, a few green, and a lot of blue. I hovered a little lower to identify who all was with us. I recognized Bolt, Amy, RedCloud, Asil, Luke and his wife and even Raven.

Jackson was gathering those who still followed him. That was the rest of my Greenies and all of Kid's and Scarletta's group. He quickly walked over to Aluminum and her army.

"What is the meaning of this?" He said through gritted teeth.

I violently landed between Aluminum and Jackson and barely caught myself. "They are still threats, Jackson. Even if they can't see us, they *will* find us."

He looked from me to Aluminum and then back to me. "You plan on killing our creator? You and Aluminum?"

"Kid stands with us as well." Aluminum pushed forward.

Kid jumped out of his tower window. I did not realize we were so close to his tower. He landed at my feet.

"I stand *against* you if you are going to kill the one who told you how to bring me back. Why are you attacking them anyway?"

I looked him in his glowing orange eyes. "He brought us here, so we could never leave. Either we attack, or we wait for him to attack the spot he put all of his mistakes. His brother tortured us."

"I am against what President did but he is not bothering us here."

There was a huge explosion that came from a building against the wall. The armory. RedCloud walked towards us holding several weapons in one hand and getting the feel back for his ax in the other.

He saw us watching and held out my staff. I held out my hand and my staff returned to my hand.

I opened my staff into a bow and got into a fighting stance. "You're beginning to sound a lot like Jackson, Kid."

Kid held his hand out and one of his orange-shirted followers put his hammer into his hand. The weapons were distributed and soon the entire city had their weapons.

Aluminum put separate shields around Kid and I. "Scarletta stands with us then. Her army as well."

Scarletta hovered in and gently landed. "You are all the family I know, other than Jonothan. I do not agree with him hiding me in a wall for who knows how long so in return I will give you until sundown before I hunt you down with Kid and our armies." Purple particles radiated from her. She held out her dagger. "Now!"

She put her finger on the purple gem in the handle of the dagger and it opened into a sword. The tip of the blade was pressed against Aluminum's throat.

Aluminum got rid of the shields and headed for the side of the wall nearest the shore. I jumped into the sky and began to fly.

As I caught myself, Kid jumped and grabbed my legs; forcing me to the ground. I face-planted into the grass. I got to my feet and tried to figure out what happened.

Kid was getting back on his feet. "I will not let you do this."

"I wasn't asking for your permission." I ran at him. He picked me up and threw me into my tower. I broke straight through the thick metal side and landed in one of the empty rooms on the lower level.

I looked through the hole I had made and saw Kid. Sparrow swooped down and tried to attack Kid. Aluminum threw her arm up and trapped Sparrow in a shield. She forced him to the ground. "This is between them." She called out.

I gathered as much telekinetic power as I could. I flew at Kid and was bringing my entire tower with me. I wasn't going to come back so I wasn't going to need it.

I gripped the top of the tower with my mind and tipped it over. I watched as the tower's shadow engulfed Kid. I threw myself to the side just in time.

The tower crushed Kid. I hit the ground and rolled away from the sea of dirt and scrap. The entire city watched in awe. Some watched, horrified at what I had done. I got to my feet and walked over to the tower where Kid had stood.

His head was mostly visible under bent pieces of steel. A massive shard of glass trapped his head in a box of steel and glass. He tried to free himself, but he couldn't find the strength.

"Then leave!" He yelled. A small pool of blood had started to fill in his mouth.

I took to the sky again and watched as Aluminum gathered her army in a bubble shield and glided over the wall and onto solid ground that didn't have a lake under it.

I flew above the clouds. My army copied my actions. Everyone with their weapons.

"You okay?" Falcon asked. He flapped his massive brown wings once and continued gliding. "I'm fine." I lied.

Jonothan Industries was rapidly coming into view. We looked for MANDS but couldn't find it. We landed on the top of the mountain and looked at the top of JI. Aluminum and her group walked out into the open right where MANDS should have been.

Falcon walked forward. He squinted his huge owl-like eyes. "Hey, Spar? You see what I see?" Sparrow walked next to falcon and squinted. "What are you...oh no."

"What?" I demanded.

"It's a trap!" Falcon and Sparrow flew towards Aluminum. The entire air army followed. We hovered above Aluminum.

"Run! It's a trap!" We all called from the sky. My group landed where Aluminum's group was and tried to pull them out of the way.

All of the sudden, the entire MANDS tower shot out of the ground. It was a giant tower. We were all pinned on top of each other and to the roof as it rapidly grew from the ground. The force of the building rising out of the ground held us in place.

The building reached its maximum height and froze for a while. We all go to our feet. Then, the roof sloped, and we slid off of the roof. We grabbed as many people as we could before we all hit the ground.

I grabbed Aluminum's arm and tried to hover, but we were all falling too fast. We hit the ground but with reduced force. Not all of us were so lucky.

The entire building slid to the side several yards. I looked up. MANDS put JI in its shadow. We all got back to our feet and looked at the top of the tower.

A bright white light shone through the windows on all four sides and traveled down towards the ground like an elevator. When it reached the bottom, a door on every side of the massive tower opened. The bright light silhouetted a giant dark block.

Then, the block began to break apart. They were soldiers. Not guards. Their grey and white armor was blinding white now. It wasn't a thick plastic. It was a new form of metal that was a mix of tungsten and titanium. And stronger than both. They weren't carrying dart guns anymore. They had fully functioning guns. Some even had flamethrowers.

They met on the side of the building that we were all on.

They formed 9 massive legions. They positioned themselves in a giant square that was 3 legions by 3 legions. Every legion held roughly 6,000 men.

We were in a jumbled line; shoulder to shoulder (as best we could anyway). Fabian flew down out of nowhere and landed in the middle.

"Stefano. Aluminum. How wonderful it is to see you. We were actually just coming to see you. Though it is a fantastic thing for you to have saved us the trouble. I really wish you would have given us a little more time. I would have cleaned up a little more. Maybe move the tower to the right instead of the left." Fabian said. He wasn't the same age he was when we last saw him, but he wasn't much older either. I would have guessed he was 21.

"What do you want?" Asked Aluminum.

"Well, you're the one who came here. I would like to ask you the same thing." "I kind of really want to kill you," I answered.

"I would love for a good old-fashioned brawl but let's not waste any more of that wonderful blood that we share. Hm? How about you all lay down your weapons and we can go back to the way things were. You and all your friends." H pointed to one of the young fire elementals Aluminum had brought. "*That* one has a fire in his eyes. I love it."

I looked at Aluminum. "Do you trust me?"

"I'm here, aren't I? I'm here for the same thing you are." She said. "How many people are in one section?"

"There's 6,000 in one. There are nine sections, so we are up against about 54,000. Maybe more."

"How many people do *we* have?" "248."

"Add me and you," I said as I studied the pale army.

Aluminum looked at me. "*248.*"

I looked at RedCloud. "You can go back. Jackson will forgive you for leaving and keep you safe."

He swung his ax and flicked a piece of dirt off of it. "I'd rather fight." He looked up to me. "By your side. Brother."

I looked back to the space between the two sides where Fabian was. I flung open my bow and nocked an arrow. I pulled the arrow to my cheek and let it fly.

It was flying straight for Fabian's head. In between his gray irises. He quickly caught it before the arrow pierced his skin. He threw arrow away and put two fingers to his head. He pulled them away to find a single drop of blood. "If that's the way you want to play, then-"

"Oh, misty eye of the mountain below!" Sang one girl on our side. "Keep careful watch of my brother's soul! "She was joined by more people. "And should the sky be filled with, fire and smoke!" More and more people joined in. I even joined in. "Keep watching over Durin's sons."

Soon the entire line of willing Instinctsion was singing.

# CHAPTER 24

# PRESIDENT

"If this is to end in fire, then we should all burn together! Watch the flames climb high, into the night! Calling out father oh! Stand by and we will, watch the flames burn auburn on the mountain side! And if we should die tonight, then we should all die together. Raise a glass of wine, for the last time!" They sang loud and proud.

I watched them through the high-tech window Jonothan made for me. I zoomed in on each and every one of their faces as they sang and swayed together. They all had one thing in common: a lack of fear.

"Gardo!" I yelled.

Gardo quickly ran to my desk from outside of the door. "Yes, President?"

"Why are they singing?"

"I'm pretty sure it's because they aren't afraid, President."

I swiveled around to face Gardo. "I can see that. But *why* aren't they afraid." I swiveled back around. "We gathered 6,000 men and cloned them. There are 54,000 soldiers down there. There must be no more than 250 of those kids. So why aren't they afraid?"

"Maybe because they don't know what we can do?"

He was right. As dumb as the big lug could be, he certainly had his moments. "Computer!" I yelled to the window.

A digital face appeared. An AI of my own making. "I do have a name, you know?" He said in his British accent.

"And I don't care. Send a message to every individual guard. We are going to play a little game."

"Might I suggest checkers, sir?"

"I was thinking a little more along the lines of chess. Except we are taking only two prisoners and destroying the rest."

"The word 'prisoner' has reactivated a memory in my database. What would you like done with the traitor known as *Jason?*"

"Keep him caged. For now, we play another game."

The kids kept singing. "Now I see fire! Inside the mountain! I see fire! Burning the trees! And I see fire! Hollowing souls! I see fire! Blood in the breeze! And I hope that you remember me! "Scan and find someone who is either made of the forest element or can control it." "Scanning now."

"Oh, should my people fall! Then surely, I'll do the same! Confined in mountain halls! We got too close to the flame!" They echoed.

"Scanning complete. There is one with thorns in her fingertips and in her blood. Shall I send two flamethrowers forward?"

"Is she the only one?"

"My scanners have also picked out a face matching one in the MANDS database." "Who is it?"

"First name: Lisa. Last name: Blight. She currently goes as: Asil. What are your orders?" "Send the two flamethrowers forward. Conner and John. Let's finish what we started.

# CHAPTER 25

# ALUMINUM

It was amazing, and I was hoping they would respect our courage and call off the war. They certainly had numbers, but we had the heart.

Their 54,000 stood ready against our diminished 248. We would have had 248 if we hadn't lost so many when President threw us off of his roof. The soldiers stood in legions while we stood, shoulder to shoulder, in a sloppy line.

I stood on Stefano's left side. It was mostly blues on my left but on the end was orange, yellow and purple. Sadly, there were also the little girls who gave me my clothes when I had first arrived at The Instinctsion. I hoped they wouldn't come. As far as I knew, one of them could turn into a chickadee and that was it.

On Stefano's right was a long line of greens with very little blues, yellows, and purples. There were one or two orange shirts and then the ones he introduced to Kid. RedCloud, Asil, and the Valkyries were right next to Stefano.

There were quite a few who didn't belong to any of our groups. Belladonna wore dark blue, but her power was her own. It was unique. RedCloud wore no shirt. He said that it got in the way. Asil wore tan cargo pants with a tucked in black long sleeve shirt. She looked ready for a mission assigned by a guy on a Kimmunicator. The Valkyries wore loose black letterman jackets with white sleeves from a nearby high school over their massive wings. The Valkyries didn't belong to a group. To them, they belonged in that moment in that war.

Fabian walked to the left side of us with his back against MANDS. He stayed in between us and stood by the door of MANDS. Two guards with giant tanks on their backs walked to where he stood.

"What do we do?" I asked Stefano.

"Nothing yet. They aren't doing anything." Stefano said as he studied the current situation. We watched impatiently to see what they would do. I looked around to see what everyone was waiting for.

I looked straight up and saw a beautiful orange color. I looked to the west and saw the sun. It was quickly dropping behind the mountain we had come down. I looked back at the soldiers. I could see a flash coming from inside one of their helmets.

"They are waiting for the sun to go. They are waiting for dark, so we can't see. They have high tech helmets. Stronger tech than before."

Stefano stepped backward. "Nova!" Nova stepped backward from the line and it was just Stefano and Nova visible. "On my command!" Nova nodded and disappeared back into line.

The rest of the soldiers marched up to the two with flamethrowers as one unit. Their unified steps echoed in the valley. Their final step was loud.

The Instinctsion twisted and rotated their weapons in thier, cold, clammy hands.

I looked back at the sun. It had completely fallen and was dragging the orange bands of light with it.

I looked at Stefano to see how he was preparing himself for the battle. He stared at Fabian. I looked over to Fabian and I couldn't believe what I saw. Scarletta and Kid were leaning against MANDS with Fabian. "I'm going to kill him," Stefano said with a stone expression. "Fabian or Kid?"

"Yes," Stefano responded. He turned around to see how much light was left. The long rusty-colored arms of the sun were almost gone.

A little boy stepped out of line. I remembered him from my profiles I took on every citizen. His power was the beast ability. He could grow into an energized and hopefully unstoppable creature. He walked over to Stefano.

"Stefano, sir?" He said; looking up at his hero.

"What is it?" Stefano said without taking his eyes away from Fabian and Kid. "I'm scared." The boy said with no hesitation.

Stefano looked down at the frightened little boy. He looked around to fully process the situation. He looked at the giant mass of soldiers and then to our slightly diminished line of nervous warriors.

He took a few steps in front of The Instinctsion and turned around to face us. He studied us. "Listen!" He started loud yet calm to get everyone's attention. "I know you're scared! I'm scared too! Okay? But the thought of stopping *them* and saving future people like us keeps me going! They said that I was special because of some *garbage* in my blood! They were wrong! Because I see something special in all of *you*! It has nothing to do with your blood. It's something that I don't have! I came here because I don't belong, and I have nothing to lose! You all have something to lose! You young children! You men and women! You fathers and mother, aunts and uncles, brothers and sisters! You are so very brave! And right now, they can see that! Just by singing we have scared them and showed them that we are not going home until we are done! We have showed them that we are not giving up! They are afraid! Show no fear, Instinctsion! Show them our weapons! Show them our fangs and claws! Show them our fire and ice! Spread your wings and perfect imperfections. Show them the things they gave you and show them what we turn on them tonight! They are undoubtedly going to try and kill us tonight. Kill them! Long! Live! The Instinctsion!"

The line cheered. Stefano's eyes were fixed on the sky behind me. I turned around to find that the arms of the sun had finally lost their grip in the night and disappeared into the darkness.

"Nova!" Stefano yelled.

"On it." She replied. We looked over to Nova and tried as best we could to see her in the pitch black.

We saw a spiraling column of stardust reach several feet into the air. She stopped and pulled her arms in. Then, she threw her arms out and stars flew all over the valley. High and low, small and large. We had light.

In the little light that we had, I could see a few star-struck soldiers gazing at the little lights. I could see their looks of awe through their bulletproof, tinted, high tech visors.

Nova gently touched back on the ground. Then came a new form of particles we had never seen before. White particles individually fell and touched the ground.

"Is this Fabian?" Stefano asked. He reached his hand out and caught the particles in his palm.

I reached my hand out and watched one particle settle into my hand before turning clear and then into a liquid. "Hey, Nova. I think your stars are broken."

I looked up at the multiplying particles. One landed on my nose. I felt how cold it was before it turned into a liquid and dripped off of my nose.

"Stefano!"

I looked to see who had called his name. In the light of the levitating lanterns, Kid walked to what was now the middle of the battlefield.

"What do you want, you traitor?!" Stefano asked.

"We can talk about this! There's so much you guys don't understand! Please don't do this! No one else has to die!"

They were both silent for a while. Stefano stepped forward. "You're right!" He said; staring at his staff. "No one else has to die." His staff clicked open into a bow and automatically nocked an arrow. Stefano looked up at Kid. "Just *you*!" He let the arrow fly and it missed Kid

"You missed!" Kid taunted.

"I only miss once! And besides, I wasn't aiming for *you*!"

Kid turned around to see that one of the soldiers with the flamethrower had an arrow sticking out of the gas tank on his back. The invisible fuel for the flamethrower was pouring down the soldier's back.

"So be it." Kid walked towards MANDS where Fabian and Scarletta were. "You tried," Scarletta told him. They both looked at Fabian.

"Fire!" Fabian yelled.

The two guards with flamethrowers stepped forward again. They lit their flamethrowers and aimed at Belladonna. The soldier with an arrow in his fuel tank pulled the trigger on his flamethrower.

He spontaneously burst into flames in a fiery explosion and ran in circles as his flesh burned inside of his metal armor. He stopped and fell to his knees and then fell forward onto his face. Smoke emitted from his armor.

The legions stayed strong and ignored the burning corpse, but one soldier tried to take a step, and another put his arm out to stop him. "Connor." The held back soldier grunted.

The remaining flamethrower began shooting flames at Belladonna. Her screams filled the night, but she didn't die. She ran forward into the 9 legions. It was the perfect time to start fighting and Stefano saw this.

"Charge!" Stefano yelled. We formed an arrow with Stefano leading the line and ran straight into the middle of the formation. The formation was being torn in two. Before we broke into the formation, the last Valkyries with wings took to the sky.

One of the little girls tugged on my shirt as we ran. "Wanna see what I can do?" She said with a smile.

"Show me what you got," I replied.

The little girl ran in from of me and then I front of Belladonna. She jumped on a soldier and blue started sprouting from her body. She had the power of beast. Blue hair covered her body and she resembled a small ape. A very *angry* and very *aggressive* small ape. She tore the armor away from the soldier and used him to jump to the next after sinking her yellow fangs into his throat. Belladonna put her hands out and her thorns made contact with the thinner armor of the exposed soldiers. He fell to the ground and thrashed around. He quickly stopped Belladonna knelt down. The fire was out but she was burnt bad. Her head fell, and she looked at the green ground slowly turning white with every particle. Her chest stopped moving.

Stefano was loosing every arrow he had. He rapidly went through them all and collapsed his bow back into a staff. He swung it at every soldier that came near him.

He tripped one soldier and hit another in the head. Then he swung his staff and plunged the end of it in the small space between the bottom of the helmet and the top of the body armor of the soldier he tripped; crushing the soldier's windpipe.

We formed our sloppy formation on the inside of MANDS' formation. Stefano was making his way toward Kid and Scarletta and leaving everyone else to defend him and themselves as he moved. I decided to head to MANDS since I was already heading that way thanks to Stefano. I was determined to kill President.

The soldiers kept coming. I fought with everything I had. I put myself in a shield and tried to cut through the mass but the soldiers either held me, so I couldn't move or got sucked into the shield with me.

I threw a disc and completely decapitated a soldier. The protected head fell to the ground and rolled away. I watched it. It rolled over to RedCloud.

RedCloud was making fire tornadoes. The soldiers were keeping their distance. He managed to get a few and cook a few of them alive inside of their metal armor.

One managed to get close enough and hit RedCloud in the back of the head with the butt of his weapon. RedCloud fell to his hands and knees. He was hit again. He rolled over to continue to try and fight.

The guard aimed his rifle at RedCloud. "Do you know who I am?" He screamed.

"You and a few other thousand soldiers are wearing the exact same thing. What do *you* think?"

The soldier removed his helmet. Dark blonde hair fell almost into his blue eyes. "Skylar?"

"I loved you, Reed. And you hurt me. Now I'm going to hurt *you*."

RedCloud/Reed readied himself to die. He only made himself look like he was giving up though. He was *really* subtly pulling his ax closer to him.

Skylar couldn't do it. He dropped his gun and started to walk away.

From that moment I could see that humans and supers probably lived together at one point and something must have come up to tear them a part. Maybe Jonothan was getting nervous with Charles' actions and suddenly pulled every super away and put them into a super city. Humans can't see the super city. The supers were never seen again.

Another soldier walked over to him and aimed at RedCloud's/Reed's chest. RedCloud/Reed planted his ax into the soldier's chest. The soldier's coughed and tried to grab the ax to pull it out. RedCloud/Reed threw a fire tornado and he followed in its wake. He directed it to the edge of the formation that was trapping The Instinctsion. Then he jumped into it and went passed Jonothan industries; the opposite direction of the super-city.

I spun my head around to where the rest of the Instinctsion was. The first thing I saw was the few people who talked about killing Asil. They passed on a message as they fought. A circle began forming. They pulled soldiers into the circle and used their powers on them. In the very center of the circle was a very confused Asil.

Stefano was on the very edge of the battlefield where he couldn't save her. The circle grew wider and wider. Then, one by one, the Instinctsion took turns using their powers on Asil. The first one was a telekinetic. He raised her high above the ground and then turned around and let her fall 15 feet.

Asil tried to get to her feet. The next Instinctsion had lasers that shot out of her eyes. She shot Asil in the shoulder. Asil fell to the ground again from the force.

Another with teleportation, Amy, appeared next to Asil. "Stefano isn't here to protect you now." She said as she kicked Asil in the stomach. Asil flew a few feet from the force of Amy's kick. "How dare you, a *human*, come into our camp and almost kill our wounded." She kicked her again. And again. And again, and then teleported to her spot in the circle.

I saw people who didn't even want to hurt Asil. They were a part of the circle watching what the others were doing and becoming more and more influenced by what was happening around them. It wasn't long before they joined in on the fun.

I couldn't watch anymore. I knew where it was going. I looked around for someone who hadn't been corrupted. I saw Nova. Her stars were shinning bright around the battle. She dragged a few from the sky after kicking a soldier's helmet off and exploded a star in his face.

Her power was absolutely mesmerizing, but it wasn't enough. The soldiers formed a circle of their own and fired every bullet they had at her. Nova pulled her arms and legs in. The soldiers fired as they closed the circle in on her. She was glowing, and some stars were beginning to come back to her. The soldiers were so close to her, they were practically firing at their feet. Then, there was a massive explosion. The blast was horizontal and left the soldiers that were shooting her in a never-ending slumber.

Nova stood up. She looked different. She had long black hair but, as she snapped her head in every which way to figure out what was going on, her black hair parted and revealed rainbow colors underneath. She threw more stars into the sky and ran out of the battle. The cold white particles were building up and making it harder for us to fight. We were freezing.

I pushed the soldiers out of my way and flew to the edge of the battlefield. I ran inside and went up what felt like hundreds of flights of stairs. I made it to the top and caught my breath.

The first room had President written all over it. I gripped my poisoned machete and slowly stepped inside. President was in his big office chair and was moving the view his window had, without touching it.

I looked over his shoulder for a better view of the window.

Kid and Fabian had decided to join the battle and Stefano was heading straight for them. They were clearing out all that stood in their way. A blur sped in front of Stefano.

"Bolt! No!" Stefano yelled.

Bolt stopped directly in front of Fabian. He flashed a smile and ran in circles around Fabian. Fabian was losing air. It was being taken from his lungs as a column of trapped air began to form. Fabian took a deep breath and thrusted his hand into the blur.

He caught Bolt by the throat. He held him above the ground and Bolt's legs kicked uselessly.

He crushed his windpipe and threw him into the MANDS tower. I felt the building shake as Bolt crashed through one side and tumbled out through to the other.

Kid watched in horror.

President zoomed in one of the families. Luke and Aquarius fought back to back in a circle of soldiers.

Aquarius' water power was amplified in the worsening blizzard. The rapidly dropping temperatures took the moisture out of the air and put it in the white particles on the ground. She gathered the particles into a giant sphere and dropped it on a growing section of soldiers. Then she spun around to help Luke.

Luke's power was weaker. We were able to scorch a few soldiers, but a few fireballs were no tornado.

A soldier managed to shoot Luke in the shoulder just close enough to his heart. He fell to the ground at the bullet's impact.

Aquarius dropped next to him and made an ice shield around them. Bullets hit the ice shield and cracked it but never punctured it. Luke was hit in an artery and was bleeding fast. He smiled and put his warm hand on his wife's cheek. I could see his eyes glaze over from where I stood. Aquarius let the thick ice shield fall and screamed in agony. The particles that blanketed the ground around them turned into Ice and spread like a deadly ripple of spires. The spires of ice impaled hundreds of soldiers around them.

Those who didn't get impaled, took their aim and shot at the two.

I could see the circle of Instinctsion growing smaller and a motionless Asil lying in the center. Her skin was scorched, melted, pulled away from her bones, her bones were broken, and she was peppered with bullet holes. I wouldn't say she was *missing* limbs because they were broken up and scattered around her.

Beyond her I could see several blue monkey-like creatures jumped from soldier to soldier. Below us, Stefano finally made it to Kid.

Kid twisted his hammer in his hands. "Jonothan Industries is good." "You're standing in front of *MANDS,* you idiot!"

Fabian walked up next to Kid. He held his hand out and a thick ice staff formed in his hand.

Kid stared at Stefano with determination in his eyes. "Trust me."

All of the sudden the other half of the Instinctsion came into view over the mountain. They were being led by Jackson. Jackson had a sickle sword in each hand and wore a long white silk robe. He ran the group of Instinctsion straight into the remaining legions and wrapped around the legion as best as he could.

He said that his only power was being able to sense where other supers were located in the city. He led the Instinctsion to the MANDS formation on a light bridge he had created. He jumped 50 feet into the air and landed in the very center of the MANDS formation. The nine legions were becoming a jumbled mass inside of the thin circle of Instinctsion.

Jackson spun and flew and even breathed fire. He swung his swords and cut every soldier that got close enough. Jackson was more than he said he was. And so was everyone who followed him. Their powers were what they said they were, but they were stronger than any of us could have anticipated.

I looked back at Kid and Stefano. Kid swung his hammer and hit Fabian. Fabian flew backwards into the building.

"Run!" Kid warned.

"I'm not running." Stefano replied.

They both smiled. Stefano's smile faded when a spear was suddenly thrusted through Kid's chest. Kid looked down at the bloody ice spear. He poked the bloody tip.

"Ow." He groaned and fell over. Fabian was standing behind him.

"Pity." He said as he pulled the spear from Kid's back. He turned it over in his hand and it melted down into a small dagger. "I liked that kid. Now *you*." He pointed the dagger at Stefano. "I don't like you."

"That's good. Means I won't have to bring flowers to your funeral." Stefano swung his staff and broke Fabian's dagger. Fabian generated an ax of ice and kicked Stefano's chest and Stefano fell onto his back. Stefano thrusted his staff forward and broke off the twin blades of the ax.

The blades fell and nearly cut him.

Fabian put the remaining part of the axe in the ground. White particles climbed it and formed a spiked ball hanging by an ice chain attached to the top of the staff. Fabian pulled it from the ground and started to swing the flail.

"Oh, come on." Said Stefano. "That's hardly fair."

"*Fair?* I want to kill you, not play a game." He swung the flail and Stefano dodged it and twirled his staff and separated the ice chain.

Fabian used the staff and broke it against Stefano's head. Stefano collapsed but quickly turned himself over. Fabian took the two pieces of the staff and stabbed them into Stefano's shoulders and pinned him to the icy ground.

Fabian held out his hand again and an ice spear formed in it. He held it high above his head. "I feel like we've been here before." He laughed a short laugh.

Just as Fabian was bringing down the spear, Scarletta came up behind him and opened her dagger. A sword went through his chest almost in the exact same place as the spear that went through Kid's chest.

The sword went back into dagger-form and Fabian collapsed. He wasn't dead, but he was slowed down for a while. Scarletta sheathed her dagger and searched Fabian's body for something.

"If anyone's going to kill you, it'll be me." She gave up her search and pulled the staff halves from Stefano's shoulders.

Stefano rolled his shoulders and I could see his wounds close up. He tapped Kid with his staff. "You okay?"

"Give me a minute." Kid groaned. After an acceptable answer, Stefano and Scarletta ran into the battle with the rest of the Instinctsion.

Scarletta was heading for Raven who was getting hit with multiple rifles. She was on the ground and the soldiers were kicking her.

Raven held out her hand. "Stop!" She yelled. The soldiers began to float. Raven looked up at the small group of soldiers that were levitating off of the ground and high above her head.

She dropped her hand and the soldiers were forced to the ground. Another soldier saw what had happened and aimed at Raven. "Witch! Witch! Witch!" He called to his comrades.

Raven put her hand back up and purple particles surrounded the soldiers and tore them apart. Raven turned around to see Scarletta holding her hand out. They both smiled.

"This is going to hurt a little bit, okay?" Scarletta said as she put her hand on Raven's shoulder. Raven nodded.

"Close your eyes," Scarletta said. Raven closed her eyes. The wings that were flying on the flagpole shriveled up and fell off of the pole. Thin bones slid from Raven's back about six feet in opposite directions. Raven whimpered in pain as the thin bones thickened. Skin stretched from her back and covered the bones and then stretched more. Feathers slid through the skin that hung off of the bone wings. Feathers quickly covered the entirety of her wings. Each feather reached six inches. "Open."

Raven opened her eyes and her wings followed. She stretched them, and, in the small star lights, the feathers had purple highlights in them. Raven flew into the night sky alongside two other silhouettes. All three of them dive-bombed a group and took three soldiers high into the sky and dropped them. Raven quickly took the lead.

"Hands up and drop the weapon or I'll spray your brains all over the fancy little window." President swiveled around. "Put the gun down, Gardo. We aren't savages." President motioned to the lone chair in front of his desk. "Please. Take a seat."

I fixed the grip I had on my machete.

"He said *sit.* "Gardo kicked the back of my knee and I was forced to the ground. I pulled myself into the chair.

"Your friends really are great fighters. Why weren't you down there?"

"I *was* down there, genius."

"Not for very long."

"I had some business to take care of." "I don't think you got it done."

"Not yet." I pulled my machete above the table and thrust it forward at President's chest with my right hand.

Gardo kneed my elbow in the opposite direction it was meant to bend. My machete fell out of my hand and Gardo thrust a dagger into my open palm. The tip of the machete went through President's tie and no further.

"Gah!" I screamed at the blade that pinned my hand to the desk.

I moved my left hand over to my right, so it looked like I was going to pulled the dagger out of my hand. I was trying switch the hand the machete was in. Gardo saw my plan.

Another knife came out and went through my left palm. I screamed again. "You don't learn, do you?" Gardo said irritably.

I stared at the knives in my hands. They looked like Scar's knives. They had no cross-guards on them like regular knives would have. The knives in my hands were throwing knives. The machete handle was between my hands and just out of reach.

President got out of his seat after motioning for his bodyguard to leave.

President picked up my machete and walked behind the chair that I sat in. "This is a beautiful blade. Where did you get this?"

I remained silent. I could hear President twirling the machete around in his hands looking for the answer. He stopped twirling it.

"*Jonothan industries*. The supply closet." He sat back down in his seat and set the machete down in front of me. The blade was facing me. "Did you know, you weren't supposed to go on that mountain with weapons? You were meant to go up there with just...well, just instinct. The moment you found *this* you failed the test. Now I have to start all over again. And not just that but Asil left to search for your precious clones. She was looking for more than just the clones, you know? She was looking for her mother. That was Jonothan's fault. He started the Scar Origins without checking to see if she had a daughter." He swiveled his chair around and watched a little more of the battle.

I took a deep breath and slowly lifted my hands up. The knives painfully slid through my hands. My breathing increased but President didn't notice.

"They fight like each and every one of them is possessed. They fight like they want to live. They fight off of true instinct. *Remarkable.*" President said in awe. I glanced through the window and saw a purple blur float to the top of JI tower.

My hands were free, but I couldn't wrap them around the handle of the machete, so I improvised. When President swiveled around I leaned back in the chair and kicked the blade of the machete.

The machete flipped, and the blade only cut President's hand before he could completely catch it by the blade. He turned the machete around, so he was holding it by the handle and pointed the tip at my throat. He put the side of the blade against my head and pushed my head to one side.

President rested the machete on my neck and then pulled the machete back and held it high above his head. Then, his entire body stiffened, and he froze. He coughed, and blood dripped down his chin. "What did you do?" He choked. I backed against the door and watched the blood pour from his mouth. He collapsed onto his hands and knees.

"Fabian!" He called.

Suddenly Fabian appeared in front of me in a loud poof of smoke. He could *teleport*?

He knelt down next to President and put his hand on President's back. Fabian's irises were glowing bright white like they were flashlights, but I knew he wasn't trying to add light. HE was healing President. Blood stopped dripping from President's nose and mouth but by the look on Fabian's face, the blood was all he could stop.

He slowly turned his head to me. "What did you do?" He asked quietly and weak. "What did you *do*?!" He screamed as he sped at me.

He was a blur. He put his forearm up and hit me in the sternum. I flew out of the window. The wind whirled passed me as the world went black.

## CHAPTER 26

# KID

The battle of MANDS was brutally gruesome and didn't slow down until the sun had returned to us place in the sky. By then, it was over. The outcome matched that of The Games except the losses were real and the body count was unimaginably high. I paced back and forth between two towering piles of bodies and waited for another heavily armed soldier to try crawling away or reach for his weapon. I was on edge.

The building that once had MANDS at its top was smashed on the ground and its rubble was scattered among the two hills it had once rested between. MANDS was no more. We had destroyed MANDS and any chance of it experimenting on children ever again.

Nothing moved except what was left of The Instinctsion. We won but with how many were left, we were the real losers.

They searched for the bodies of supers. Most were mutilated beyond recognition. I distracted myself with the return of my favorite color to the sky. The long orange arms of the sun were reaching passed the mountain and gripping the mountain, so it could pull itself back up.

Jackson made his way across the field and was heading for Stefano. "You fought well," Stefano said. "I never knew you could-"

Jackson punched Stefano and Stefano flew to his right from the force Jackson used.

"Do you have any idea what you've done?! We had over 500 citizens! Now we don't even have a *hundred*!"

"You think this is *my* fault?" Stefano said with a hand on his jaw.

Jackson grabbed him by the shirt and lifted his face to his. "It is! And if you say it isn't, you better go talk to Sizzle!" Jackson threw Stefano down.

"*Steampunk*? What's wrong? Where is he?"

Sizzle made his way through the sea of glowing white armor and trails of blood and to Stefano. He was older than the last time we had seen him.

"Steampunk. You're...you're..."

"I know. I'm older." Said Sizzle in a deep, calm, voice. "Where are my parents?" "...Steampunk-"

"Where are they?!" Sizzle shouted. He knew the answer. He just wanted to hear it from Stefano's mouth.

"They're dead," Stefano said under his breath. I could hear the guilt in his voice.

Sizzle's hands began to sizzle. He gathered a cloud of steam and held it above his head.

A soldier groaned, and Sizzle threw the cloud inside of the soldier's armor. The soldier cried out and even after the cries stopped, Sizzle held the cloud there.

He let the cloud fade away. His eyes were red, and his jaw was clenched. He walked over to Jackson with his head down. "Just...do it." He said with sorrow in *his* voice.

Jackson walked over to Stefano. "There will be a trial when we get back to the island." He said. He motioned for one of my strong team to come over. He knocked Stefano out and threw him over his shoulder.

<T1 A2 S3 K4 S5>

We took the route I had first taken when I ran away from MANDS. No one said anything as we hiked the mountain. I was near the front of the massive line of injured Instinctsion.

Behind me was Stefano who was put in strange cuffs I recognized from the MANDS lunch hall. Behind him was Aluminum. She was walking but she stared at the holes in her hands. They weren't healing. Something was wrong.

We made it to a clearing and stopped for a break. It was the shelter where Fabian and the clones found Stefano and Aluminum.

"We stop here for a little while." Sizzle commanded. Jackson nodded. Sizzle was in his teenage years, so it was strange to see someone as old as Jackson take orders from him.

Everyone fanned out and caught their breaths. Stefano was thrown to the side. His hands were cuffed behind his back and his legs were bounded together. He lay on the ground. Not blinking; just breathing. Sizzle walked over to the shelter.

The shelter was torn to pieces and part of it was burned. Sizzle stepped inside and sat down on what was left of one of the make-shift beds. He pulled his knees to his chest. The tips of his spiked hair turned gray and steam emitted from his hair and collected above his head. He began to cry.

I walked over to the shelter and watched him. What was I supposed to say?

*Just go talk to him.*

The voice was back. I knew it wasn't Tressa. I knew it was Titanium. But it felt like Tressa. It felt good to believe it was sometimes.

I knocked on the broken trunk of a tree that was made to form a doorframe.

Sizzle collected the tears on his face and quickly put them in the cloud and then hid the cloud. He quickly stood up. "What do you want?"

I sat on what was left of the adjacent bed. He calmed and sat down across from me. "Are they going to kill him?" Sizzle asked. A few tears were returning to his eyes.

"I hope not." It was the first time I had spoken in a while. My voice was deeper. "I don't think it was him who came up with the plan to leave. And it definitely wasn't him who killed...I'm sorry, Sizzle."

"It's fine, sir."

"You don't have to call me that. Quick question." "Yeah?"

"Do I look older to you?"

"The city helps us live longer. It stunts aging and growth. If we leave the city, a few years catch up with us. It feels weird to go from 4 to 17. You were in the city long enough for it take effect on *you*."

"I was 12 when I came to the city." "Your voice is deeper and you're taller." "Same with you."

"Can I tell you something, sir?" "Just 'Kid'."

"Sorry."

"It's fine. What is it?"

"I don't want him to die."

"What *do* you want to happen, Sizzle?"

Sizzle looked me dead in the eyes. His tears were gone again, and his face was cold and hard. "I want him to suffer."

"Let's get moving again!" Jackson called from outside.

We left the shelter and the group started moving again. Sizzle walked by my side, but we didn't say anything to each other. We helped each other over logs and jumping creeks all without a word.

Finally, we made it back to the city, but the city was gone. Everyone crowded up against the edge of the lake.

One of my members stepped up to the very edge of the lake. He held Stefano. He effortlessly raised Stefano high above his head and threw him into the lake.

Less than half of the remaining Instinctsion gasped and leaned so far over the side, they nearly fell in. I was one of them. Then, Jackson jumped into the lake. Everyone looked around and backed away from the edge. We looked for what to do next. Then an idea came.

The Instinctsion took turns whooping and jumping into the lake.

Pretty soon I was the only one not in the water. I took a deep breath and threw myself into the lake.

I straightened my body and cut through the water and ended up falling through the Instinctsion's force field. I landed on my feet in the Instinctsion.

I straightened up and looked around. The towers were no longer towers. They weren't vertically tall anymore. They were horizontally tall. The entire city was a giant pentagon.

The towers lay on their sides. The green tower was dark and the glowing green S5 was faded.

It touched the bottom corner of the Seeress' tower which was the T1 tower. Her tower held its bright yellow glow and touched Aluminum's tower. Her tower was bright blue and touched Scarletta's tower which glowed bright purple which touched mine which was bright orange.

I looked at the gap between Stefano's tower and my own. Even the

Instinctsion could see that we were growing apart. He saved me the first time we left MANDS. I had to make it up.

I looked around the pentagon. There was a fire pit in the very middle. Against the horizontal towers were the same stadium seats. There was a podium with cuffs behind the fire and a massive chair in front of it. To the right of the chair was a smaller chair. The entire thing looked like a strange sort of courtroom.

I watched as one-by-one the Instinctsion found their seats. Raven came in under Sparrow's arm. Raven looked like she had been crying. Her eyes were red and swollen and her face was wet.

"Where's Fal?" I asked them. They kept their heads down and kept walking.

*Come take a seat.*

I searched the diminished crowd for the Seeress. I found her and joined her.

"I saw something while you were all away." She said as she nudged my arm. Her droopy yellow cloak swayed around her arms.

"Is it good?" I asked. "Is it what we talked about before I left?" "You'll see. We just need to wait for Scarletta."

"Why does she need to be here?"

"She plays the greatest role." She looked at me. "She does?"

Her eyes became fixed on Stefano being cuffed to the podium behind the fire. "More than you know."

Jackson sat in the giant throne-like chair. It was a trial.

CHAPTER 27

# SCARLETTA

I flew straight up towards the window and smashed through. Jonothan had been looking through it and my sudden presence caused him to stumble back into his chair.

"Scarletta? What are you doing here?"

"They said they were going to kill you. I'm here to make sure that doesn't happen." "Why aren't you helping your friends?"

"I already talked to Titanium about the outcome. And besides, I don't want to play a game I know I can win."

"That's my girl." He said as he straightened up in his chair. "Why else are you here, Scarletta?" "They can't remember anything. I can't either. Something tells me that you had something to do with that."

"Smart girl. Charles collected pieces of your memory every time he brainwashed you and your friends. He has them in vials in his building."

I walked over to his window and watched numbers on both sides of the war start to diminish. "I'll collect it from the rubble." I noticed how hard Jonothan studies the war below him.

"Why are you fighting? Why are you just watching the war? They said they are going to destroy you and your building." I said.

"I don't play games I create. I put them in a place where they were safe and hidden. They left and are being slaughtered. They won't attack me. I'm stronger than Charles. I'm stronger than MANDS. I made it all anyways."

I said nothing.

"You think that your people will *win?*" He joined me at the window. "You'd be surprised."

"Fabian has what you're looking for."

<T1 A2 S3 K4 S5>

The war was over and the Instinctsion was going back home. I glided out of the top floor of Jonothan industries and gently touched down among the rubble of MANDS.

My bare feet were beginning to hurt on the broken pieces of reinforced concrete, so I hovered over the rubble.

A pile began to shake. The concrete joined together, and a giant golem stood up. The eyes glowed bright white.

"Scarletta!" It roared and stomped towards me but with every step, concrete fell. By the time the creature got to me, the concrete was all gone. It was Fabian. He fell and knelt at my feet. His head fell, and he began to cry.

"Fabian?"

His head slowly lifted and the bright white in his eyes faded back to gray. "He's dying."

"I know. What am I supposed to do about it, Fabian?" Fabian was like my brother. Jonothan said he was my cousin but I held him closer than that. I knew little about him except that he killed my predecessors and refused to hurt me.

"Help me." He said in his broken voice. Tears began collecting in his gray eyes. "You've both done terrible things."

He got to his feet and sniffled as he wiped away his tears. "I have something that you want. That you *all* want."

"The memories," I said under my breath.

He reached into the pocket of his no longer white hoodie and pulled out five small vials with their own glowing colors. Yellow, blue, orange, and green. They were slightly drained.

I held my hand out and waited for him to put the vials in my hand.

"Not until you help my father." He said as he put the vials back into

199

the pocket of his hoodie. The spectrum of colors shone through the many holes in his hoodie I looked around. "Where the hell is he then?!"

Fabian started walking away. He walked over to the biggest pile of rubble and held out his arms. He rotated his palms and as he did, a giant piece of concrete began floating. A door was revealed under the concrete.

"The bunker survived. Even though your friends dropped the rest of the building on it." He dropped the piece of concrete to the right of the door and the other piles of concrete shifted.

He walked inside of the bunker. President was sitting in a wheelchair. "Father! I told you not to move!"

His hair was gone and the bags under his eyes were a dark purple. He was still in his suit and tie. One hand was completely black in color.

"I'm *dying.* I'm not dead yet."

"What am I supposed to do to help?" I finally asked as President struggled to get comfortable in his wheelchair.

"*Help?* Is that what he told you?" "Yeah. He told me that-"

"We've made our peace, *witch.*" He chuckled.

"We just wanted you to watch and then send a message," Fabian said with a sinister smile on his fallen head.

"...watch what?"

Fabian moved President's bed and revealed a trap door. He went through a trap door and it was just me and President in the room.

"Kneel and this will be so much easier for you." "Why would I kneel to *you?*"

"I'm going to count to five." President groaned. "I'm going to count to *three.*" I retorted.

"Very well then." President pulled a thin silver remote from the inner pocket of his suit. He pressed the only button on it and I was pulled to the wall with the door by an invisible force. My hands were far apart from each other and my feet were bound together against the wall.

I quickly freed myself and unsheathed my dagger. I clicked it open and pointed the sword's tip against President's throat.

President spun the button clock-wise and pressed it again.

The same force came from behind me and pinned me to the wall again. It was stronger though. And purple. I was being held to the wall with a power that was my power but stronger.

Fabian crawled up from the trap door with the ends of two ropes in his hand. He got to his feet and yanked the ropes. Two men groaned beneath our feet.

They climbed the latter. The first through the trap door was Jason. He had two black eyes with one of them very swollen. His jaw was swollen, and he had gashes all over his face. His gums were bloody. His hands were tied together in front of him and his wrists had rope-burns.

Next was Harry. He had matching gashes and bruises. I knew he was a super but for some reason, he wasn't healed. He stood next to Jason; facing me.

"Kneel!" Fabian threw a force at the back of their knees and they fell to their knees.

President pulled out two pistols and handed them to Fabian. Fabian took them with a sinister smile and looked at me.

"Take them." He said and levitated the pistols in front of me.

"No," I said. I recognized the two men. I didn't know enough about them, so I couldn't just kill them. I didn't know what they did. All I knew was that they were against MANDS. Fabian's smile disappeared, and he used his telekinesis and forced me to take the pistols.

"Aim at them."

I tried to keep my fingers off of the triggers using my own power. That was all I could do against him.

"Pull the trigger."

Harry and Jason closed their eyes and prepared themselves. There was nothing they could do to get out if it and they knew it.

My finger kept going around the trigger guard. It didn't take long for Fabian to lose his patience and use his power to force the pins in the guns to hit the primers of the bullets.

Jason and Harry simultaneously fell to the ground with blood dripping from the bullet holes between their eyes.

Fabian let me fall to my knees in front of Harry and Jason. A tape flew from the darkness into Fabian's hand and a solid red light appeared.

He knelt down and held the tape in front of me. "You take this tape to The Instinctsion and bring me the other three. Tell them that if I don't have those three that I will kill again and again until they are the only ones left."

I took the tape.

"Give them to her," President commanded Fabian.

Fabian put his hand in his hoodie pocket and took his hand out. Five vials levitated in a set path to his hand. He tilted his fingers forward and the vials flew to me.

"It's her choice whether or not she wants them to remember," President said.

I took the vials and was encased in small pieces of concrete. I couldn't see as I was lifted up and thrown. I hit the ground and the concrete fell off of me. I was on the top of the mountain again. There was a beaten down trail I could only guess was left by The Instinctsion. I followed the trail to the lake where the city had once floated. Except, the city wasn't there.

I threw the tape into the lake and watched it sink curiously fast. I closed my eyes and fell forward into the lake.

I was only in the water for about five seconds before I was falling through the air. I opened my eyes before I hit the ground and instinctively bent a knee and held a hand in front of me.

I straightened up and looked around. I was in the city again. I should have known that after such a war, they would protect what little they have left.

The city was rearranged. The force field was its normal dome shape, but the towers were on their sides. The five towers formed a pentagon that was open between Kid's tower and the extremely damaged tower that once belonged to Stefano.

The tape was right next to me, so I picked it up and put it in my purple hoodie pocket. I was outside of the pentagon, so I walked inside. Stadiums were against the five towers and in front of one was a judge-like bench where Jackson sat. The entire city was gathered in the area.

There was a fire pit in the middle of the pentagon. Stefano was cuffed to a podium behind the fire.

Jackson got to his feet.

"Scarletta. We weren't going to start without you." "What is going on?"

"Stefano, the former *hero* of The Instinctsion, former member of the Final Five, and rescuer of the five, is being charged with betrayal of The Instinctsion and the murder of Luke and Aquarius Warm." He sat back down in the throne-like chair. "Our first witness will have their say and the accused with remain silent." He looked into Stefano's eyes from the other end of the fire pit. "I will tell you this now, Stefano: the outcome does not look good for you."

I took my seat in the stadium against my tower and my followers. There were very few.

Stefano stared at the cuffs that held his arms to the podium and made it, so he couldn't use his powers. He didn't say a word.

First to the witness stand was Sparrow. He stretched his wings out before taking a seat in the smaller chair next to Jackson. Raven leaned forward in her seat and rested her arms on her knees.

She was in my stadium. Her face was hard and calm, but I could see the fire in her eyes.

"I followed Stefano into the war. I admit I was wrong in that. But because of Stefano's decision to leave, there are only two of my kind now. He wouldn't let us leave the battle. Falcon would still be alive if he would have let us leave!"

The cuffs made a loud screeching sound.

"Gah!" Stefano screamed. "He's-" His jaw was clenched, and his face showed the incredible amount of pain he was in. "He's lying!"

The entire pentagon roared in denial. I knew the truth. I knew the truth. Those who followed Stefano could have left at any moment. It was Aluminum's decision to leave and her method of getting people to the battlefield was basically trapping them.

"Silence!" Jackson boomed. Silence fell on the crowd. "Next witness." Kid took Sparrow's place.

"With everything that is against Stefano, I know the outcome isn't good. He has to pay though. I wouldn't have gone down there if he hadn't said he was going to attack Jonothan. None of us would."

Jackson turned toward Kid. "Right now, his sentence is execution."

I took the tape out of my pocket and rotated it in my hands. I put a hand in my pocket to make sure the vials were all there and unbroken. One felt lighter than the rest.

"I understand that, but he *is* a hero. He deserves a more civil punishment."

Jackson leaned over the arm of his chair and glared into Kid's eyes. "Next witnessssssss." Kid went back to his seat in front my tower.

Sizzle took the chair next to Jackson. Sizzle stared at Stefano's distorted image through the top of the bonfire.

"Sizzle? Your statement."

"Stefano is responsible for the death of my parents. As Kid stated, none of us would have gone down there if Stefano hadn't said he was attacking Jonothan. I want him to suffer but I don't want him to die."

"What do you suggest as an alternative?"

Sizzle finally stopped staring at Stefano. He turned his head toward Jackson. "I want him to play The Games."

"Stefano is not the only one being accused. Aluminum! Please step forward." Aluminum walked to Stefano's side. Her hands were bandaged, and blood was seeping through the bandages.

"I would have your punishment as The Games but because The Games are now Stefano's punishment, I have a better ruling for you." Jackson grabbed one of his sickle swords and walked up to Aluminum. He grabbed the blade and held the handle towards Aluminum. "Take the sword. If you can grip it, I will let *you* decide your fate. If not, the city decides for you."

Aluminum reached out and put her open hand on the handle. She slowly wrapped her fingers around the handle and slid the sword from Jackson's hand. She struggled to hold it and the sword fell to the ground almost as soon as she had taken it.

One of Aluminum's followers ran from the stadium and grabbed the sword. She picked it up for Aluminum and held the handle towards Aluminum. Aluminum tried to grab the sword, but the sword fell again. Jackson used telekinesis and the girl was pulled away from Aluminum.

"The Instinctsion will decide!" Jackson held his arms out and waited for a reply of some sort. Everyone blurted out the same answers.

"Let her live!" "Freedom!"

"Let her rule!" "Let her stay!"

"Enough!" Jackson boomed. It was like recapturing silence and control was another one of his powers. "She stays." The crowd cheered. "But she won't fight." The crowd still cheered. As Jackson started walking back over to Stefano, silence fell again.

"As for you, Stefano. You will participate in The Games. If you win, you die. If you lose-"

"I know." He looked up and turned his head to Jackson. "I die." His head fell. "Let's just get this over with then.

The cuffs holding Stefano's hands together and to the podium separated from the podium. He was escorted out of the pentagon area. Everyone followed.

I looked through the gap between the two towers and saw a different scene than the one we entered from. We walked across an earthen bridge into a cave. I never saw a cave when I first arrived in the city.

Everyone filed into the cave. Inside the cave was another world. The edges of the cave were covered in green grass and moss despite the weather outside. The cave ceiling dripped, and water soothingly ran in the corners. Against the walls were stadium seats. It was like these people enjoyed watching each other die.

Jackson got into the lone throne-like chair made of rock that was carved into the wall opposite the entrance. The Seeress ran up to me before I made my way to my seat.

"Two things need to happen." She said

"What are you talking about?"

"That tape and those vials that you're trying so hard to conceal, you need to do something with them. Either destroy them or show him. I don't think it matters what happens to the tape. The tape isn't what's bothering me. You are making me nervous the way you just watch everything go down, Scarletta."

"How am I making you nervous?" I said a bit loud. A few heads turned towards us.

"Shhhh!" She leaned closer. "I know what needs to happen in order to save Stefano. You do too. It is getting so close for it to happen and you haven't done anything. Do *something*."

"I don't even know who you are other than a fortune teller." "I'm Titanium. I'm the best shot at saving you five."

"There's only four of us."

"Go sit down."

She ran off to the right side of the cave. I went to the left. Kid sat by me and Aluminum sat by Titanium. Stefano was escorted to the middle of the cave and released from his cuffs. He cracked his knuckles and looked around. There was enough room for an arena.

"I want to say something!" Stefano yelled. His voice bounced around the walls of the cave.

"I think we've had enough of your speeches," Jackson said as he waved his hand. "There will be three fights. If those three do not kill him, then there will be another. And then another." Jackson turned to address Stefano. "I will have every man, woman, and child in this cave fight you until you join our dead and stop breathing."

Stefano looked at his hands. He slowly made his dirty hands into fists. He looked around for the first contestant. No one stepped forward.

"If there will be no fight then I might as well execute him right n-"

"No!" Kid quickly got to his feet. "I will fight!" He ran down the stone steps. "I will fight!" He stood in front of Stefano and stared at Jackson. His back was to Stefano. "I will fight." He said again.

Kid turned around and looked into Stefano's faded green eyes. I could see the glow from my seat. One eye was glowing normally and in the other was brown sown into the faded green.

"Kid. You have to kill me." Stefano said quietly.

"Shut up and let me think of way to get you out of this." Kid hissed as he searched the audience from over Stefano's shoulder.

"Kid-"

Kid spun around. "Weapons?"

Jackson waved his hand and Kid's mighty war-hammer flew into Kid's hand. Stefano's hand was empty.

"What about *his?*" Asked Kid.

"He does not fight with a weapon."

"If he doesn't fight with a weapon, then I don't fight." "You don't fight, and I execute him now."

Kid held his weapon with two hands and faced Stefano again. Stefano let his clenched fists open. He stood in a welcoming stance and readied himself.

Kid looked up at me. He turned his head to Titanium. I followed his eyes and looked into her pale blue eyes with yellow slivers.

She nodded, and Kid looked back into Stefano's eyes.

# CHAPTER 28

# STEFANO

I looked into Kid's eyes. His orange eyes were less orange than when he woke up in the city. I looked at Aluminum. Her eyes were a dark blue and the injuries she earned from Charles were no better.

I could feel my power diminishing as I stood in front of Kid. "You're all getting weaker." I said to Kid.

"Shut up." He whispered; rotating his hammer in his hands.

"The only way to go back to your full power and beyond is to go back." "Shut up, Stefano." Kid said a bit louder.

"You were right. Jonothan has the answers. He has what it takes to bring you all back to your full power. The only way you can do that is if you kill me. Jackson isn't going to let me leave but if you kill me you can-"

"Shut up!" Kid pulled his hammer behind his head and swung it, with as much power as he could muster, into my rib cage.

I was picked up off of my feet and spun in the air. I hit the rocky ground and looked up to Kid as he stomped towards me. Each step he took forced little spurts of dirt up through the ground of the cave. The cave floor was layered.

I flipped my first two fingers up and the chunk of rock that Kid stood on was quickly raised into the air towards the cave stalactites. If I wanted to kill him, I wouldn't have to try. I didn't want to kill him, and he was purposely making it hard. I shifted the path of the chunk of rock and a couple of stalactites pierced his left thigh and the right side of his abdomen. I let the rock gently fall back in place. He was dragged away from the arena floor. I followed his gaze towards Titanium. She nodded her head.

I wiped my upper lip. Blood that had poured from my nose had stained my hand. I got to my feet and tried to pop my back by rotating my torso. A sharp pain shot through the bottom right of my ribcage. My blood-stained hand flew to my ribs. I could feel a few pieces of bone shift around under my skin. My ribs were broken.

"Next fight!" Jackson commanded. No one stepped forward. They only looked around. Jackson let out a heavy sigh and stood up from his chair and drew his sickle swords.

Titanium stood up and ran down the stadium to Stefano. Jackson sat back down. "Fight!" He said as he waved his hand.

I knew Jackson was going to kill me soon. I brought my hands up in a fighting position and balled them up into fists. My plan was to make it look like I was actually trying to win and just let Titanium do her worst.

"Don't hold back," I told her.

"Trust me." She said. "I have a plan. Not completely sure if it goes down the path I saw but it's a plan."

"What?"

She brought her fists up and began circling me. I knew she didn't have a weapon, but it made no sense for her to not use her powers. Her powers weren't diminished like the rest of us.

She threw the first punch and hit me in my broken ribs. It hurt but if she was actually trying then my plan was going to work better than I thought. I threw my first punch towards her head. I wasn't *trying* to hit her or as hard as I did but she moved in the way.

I was taking too long on my second strike, so I threw another one by her head. She moved at the exact moment I threw the punch and I landed it. She fell backward.

It seemed like she was *trying* to get hit. I needed to test it. I kicked above her head and she kicked her legs, so her face made contact with my unprotected foot. She wasn't trying to fight me at all.

I encased her in a telekinetic field and raised her above the ground. Every time I used my telekinesis, I could feel it diminish. Just holding her above the ground was getting harder and harder. I roared as I used all of whatever power I had left to force her into the ground. There was a ripple of Earth that dispersed away from her as she hit the ground. There was a snap as her body hit the ground and she stopped moving.

The crowd was silent. I looked at what I had done. Tressa sacrificed herself when we ran away. Now the new version, almost a reincarnation of Tressa, did the same thing. I killed her.

"Oh shi-"

"Next fight!" Jackson interrupted me.

I was snapped out of it. Titanium was dragged out of the arena. At the last second, before I lost view of her, I saw her open her eyes and then quickly close them.

Scarletta didn't hesitate or wait for someone else to come down. She certainly wasn't going to wait for Jackson to threaten me again.

She stopped in front of me with one hand in her pocket and the other on her dagger. "Fight!" Jackson boomed.

"I have a plan." She said.

"I'm sick of plans. Just fight." I got into another fighting stance and brought my fists to my face. Scarletta turned around and tried to pull something out of her pocket. I quickly punched her in the back of the head.

"Ow!" She cried out. She turned around. "Why?" She asked rhetorically. She used her power and pushed me into the back wall by the cave entrance. I was trapped by a purple force. She turned back towards Jackson. "I was given something by Fabian and President." She pulled out a tape.

Jackson stood up and walked down to the arena with his hands out. The tape flew to his hands and he just stared at it. He looked up at Scarletta. "What is this?"

"It's a tape. People in the human city used to have these in every home. It is a recording of Fabian forcing me to kill Jason, a man who helped the heroes escape, and Harry, a man who gave Stefano the answers to escape."

Jackson processed it and let his arms fall. "He gave you something else, didn't he?"

I saw Scarletta shift something in her pocket and her pocket looked flat. "No." She responded. "Fabian warned that he would continue to kill us until he gets the final three. That's Stefano, Kid and Aluminum."

"What's in your pocket?" Jackson asked again. He held out his hand. Scarletta took a step back. "Nothing."

"I'm not going to ask you again."

"End this nonsense, Jackson. We are done with The games. Make your judgment on Stefano and I'll consider showing you what else was given to me."

"Fine," Jackson said with a harshness in his voice. He walked away from Scarletta. "My ruling for this *traitor* is..." He walked up to me. "Banishment! "Jackson walked back to his chair and sat down. "If I ever see you again, Stefano, I will kill you. Mercilessly,". Two people from the strong group grabbed my arms and escorted me outside of the cave. They threw me onto the ground. At least it was grass I landed on.

I stood up and brushed myself off. "Wait!" I heard from behind me.

I turned around to see Kid and Scarletta running towards me. Kid was healed but I could see gnarly scars through the holes in his jeans and hoodie caused by the stalactites.

"You'll need this." Scarletta handed me a vial with a neon green liquid glowing inside of it. "What is this?" I tapped the vial. The liquid didn't move but small dark green particles swam around the strange liquid.

"It's your memories. I do have to warn you though, it could be a lot to take in so take a little bit at a time."

She handed Kid his vial of neon orange.

"And you too, Aluminum." Scarletta held the vial towards me. I turned around and Aluminum appeared behind me. The vial of neon blue was placed into Aluminum's open hand. Scarletta knelt down by a dandelion. "You too." The flower morphed into Titanium.

"This isn't mine. It can't be." Said Titanium. "You're a rapid-reincarnation. You'll remember."

We all took small sips from our vials. The memory tasted sour and sweet at the same time but it was so much to take in that it was spicy as well. We all had a curiously disgusted look on our faces except for Scarletta.

"Where's yours?" I asked.

She reached into her pocket to reveal an empty vial. "You already drank it?" Kid asked; surprised.

"There was never anything to drink. I need to find out who drained it."

"Who do you think did it?" Aluminum asked with a sour look on her face. "Either Fabian or Jonothan."

I threw an I-told-you-so look at Kid. He got the idea.

"You will need this too, Stefano." Said Aluminum. She rolled my backpack off of her shoulder and it fell at my feet. She tried to pick it up for me, but I held my hand out to stop her from trying.

"My bag," I said in surprise. "How?"

"There's a lot of perks to being able to turn invisible. I couldn't find any others."

I opened my bag and there were two things in it: my staff that was pocket sized and the map to the human city. I took out the small staff and held it in my hand.

A vertical opening on the side of the staff began to glow green and it opened into its full size. I threw it forward in my hand and it opened into a bow. I threw it forward again and it collapsed back into a staff. I twirled it around my fingers and it went back to a pocket-size.

"Where will everyone go?" I asked as I threw the bag over my shoulder. "I kind of have to stay here." Said Titanium. "Not much of a choice."

"There's always a choice." Said Aluminum.

"I'm going to Jonothan Industries. Hopefully, I can get some answers and maybe some history lessons. Feel free to stop by." Said Scarletta.

"I'm not staying here while Jackson is in charge. It wasn't cool what he did to you, Stefano." Kid said.

"Yeah." Said Scarletta. "You both commit the same crime and one of you gets praised while the other gets beaten and banished."

"You don't have to leave, Kid. I'm gonna do something about Jackson's place in that chair." "Are you going to kill him? "Kid asked.

"I'll imprison him."

"But you won't kill him so I'm not staying." Kid looked at me. "I'm going to the city to find something to help me start this new life with. The *right* way. And you?" Kid looked to me.

I shrugged my shoulders. "I'm going to the only place I can."

"I'll go with you for a while then." Kid said. I smiled. I didn't know if I wanted him to come along or not.

We split up. Scarletta flew in the opposite direction of us, Aluminum and Titanium went back inside the cave with a look of determination and Kid and I walked straight for the human city.

I didn't know if he was going all the way back with me, but it was nice to think that way.

# CHAPTER 29

# ALUMINUM

Titanium and I walked back into the cave. Jackson was sitting in the chair carved into the cave wall.

"You're sitting in my chair." I said.

"As if I'd ever let you rule this city. You don't have what it takes."

I put shields under my feet and floated in front of Jackson. "I'm taking the city." I whispered to him.

"Never." Jackson stood up and drew his sickle swords.

At the same time, the entire city got to their feet and readied their weapons and powers. The Valkyries had their wings pointed straight up like they were going to take flight at any moment. Spears and swords and tridents were in everyone's hands.

I touched back down and started walking out of the cave. The Instinctsion was at my back. "Over my dead body!" Jackson yelled as he ran at me.

I quickly put a shield around him. I kept him in a bubble shield and he watched as I rebuilt the city.

A few remaining telekinetics raised the city out of the water and everyone gathered on it. First, we floated to a mountain with an extremely steep side that fell into a ravine. I put a shield around the city and phased partway through it. The giant chunk of earth was attached to the rocky mountainside.

I had all of the towers restored and put on the mountain in order. The side of each tower that was facing out was metal with the normal marks at the top. The backside was stone and carved into the mountain. The lights were on in three towers in case Scarletta, Kid and/or Stefano came back.

We stood back and admired our work. The green chunk of earth stuck out of the mountain and clearly didn't belong. But then again, neither did we. It was a perfect fit. The five towers stood against the mountain. In front of the towers was many houses. Everyone built their houses with their powers in favor of their powers. Weapons were permitted in the city and allowed to be in every house.

In the center of the earthen chunk was a special place for Jackson. I lowered the bubble through the dirt and rock and stopped in the middle. It was all compacted enough to where it wouldn't collapse on him.

Titanium took another swig from her memory vial and nudged my arm. "I'll be back." She said. She jumped off of the edge and turned into a raven.

I released the shield on the city and Jackson. Jackson was quiet, but everyone cheered as the mountain welcomed our new home. A waterfall spilled out of the mountain and split around the chunk of earth we had attached to it. We were home.

# CHAPTER 30

# PRESIDENT

I lay in the uncomfortable bed too weak to move or eat. I was only on day three or four of being sick. Maybe even day five.

I couldn't open my eyes, but I could feel everything around me. It hurt to feel. I wanted to let go but I could feel that Fabian wasn't ready. He was crushing my hand in his and tears were soaking my hand.

I opened my mouth, but no words came out. Only a groan. I tried again. "Fabian?" I groaned.

"Yes? I'm here." He said. He sniffled. "You need to do something for me." "Anything."

"Restart the program."

"But what about the funding." "Go. See. Jonothan."

"I will."

He wasn't leaving. I could feel myself slipping but I didn't want him to see me go. I gathered as much strength as I had left. "Now!" I yelled. I could hear him get to his feet and open the thick steel door.

He left it open. I could smell the air. There was no blizzard or any snow at all. The crisp smell of winter was gone. In its place was the smell of fresh grass and pine trees.

Birds were chirping, and squirrels were chattering. I finally opened my eyes and turned my head towards the open door. I saw all the green grass and trees. I could see a trail heading up the mountain I had created. Trees grew 100 feet tall and the mountain wore a thick coat of grass and moss. I looked to the side of the mountain where I had once seen caribou. A brown animal was coming towards me. It was a small bear with cinnamon fur. It slowly made a beeline for me in my exposed bunker.

The bear sniffed me. It didn't want to hurt me.

Then, I looked into the bear's eyes. They were a pale blue with yellow slits. Then the beast spoke.

"Remember me?" It growled in Tressa's voice. The bear raised her paw and slashed at my throat.

Blood was spilling onto the bed and pooling on the floor. Fabian came back in. "Father?" He ran towards me.

The bear jumped into the air and turned into a raven and flew over Fabian's head and out the door. Fabian's image was fading. Quickly, he became nothing but a blur that disappeared into the darkness.

# CHAPTER 31

# TITANIUM

***18 Months later...***

I stayed mostly in my tower and kept to myself. After the first couple of months, I felt like I wasn't needed and that I didn't belong. There was nothing to stop me from feeling this way. I drank all of the memory vial and, after each gulp, I felt more like Tressa and less like myself. I felt less like Titanium. My eyes were pale, but I wasn't blind. Even so, I could feel that my vision was beginning to fail me.

I heard a knock on my door.

"Who is it?" I said as cheerfully as I could. "Aluminum."

"Come in," I responded as cheerfully as I could manage.

The door opened, and Aluminum came in wearing a blue dress with dark blue bars on her shoulders and around her waist.

"Do you wanna go for a flight? Or maybe a walk?" Aluminum asked me.

"Don't you have a city to rule?" I asked. I didn't mean to sound rude but, after the words left my mouth and Aluminum's feelings were unaffected, I didn't care.

"They are responsible and all of them have been working hard. We all deserve a day or two off, don't you think? Especially you, Titanium. You have scouted and looked ahead at the wellbeing of the city. You've told us about threats whether they are natural or supernatural. And all while... you deserve a break, T."

"All right. I guess."

I got up and put on my yellow jumpsuit with black bars on the shoulders, knees, elbows and around the waist.

We jumped out of my yellow-trimmed window and flew to the top of the mountain where the waterfall started. I flew as a hawk and Aluminum floated up in one of her bubble shields. Trees were full of green and clumped so close together that we had to stay on the very edge of the mountain.

We sat and listened to the rushing water for a while.

"So, Tressa is coming back?" Aluminum asked me out of nowhere over the roar of rushing water.

I looked at Aluminum. "Is that the only reason you wanted to talk to me? Yes. She's coming back. Each day that passes I can feel more and more of her inside my head. It feels like something is wedged between the lobes of my brain and it's just sitting there; growing there. She will kill me before she takes control. And do you know why that is, Aluminum?"

"No."

"When Scar killed Tressa, Tressa latched onto the only living thing in the room at the time which was Scar. Scar went to Scarlet to get weapons and clothing and Tressa latched onto Scarlet. When everyone escaped the building completely, Scarlet ran with you and Tressa latched onto you. Then you and Stefano built a shelter and she latched onto him until you both came to The Instinctsion. From there, she latched onto what closely resembled where she started. That's me. She will most likely kill me when she fully takes over. Is that what you want to hear?"

"No. I miss her, but you mean so much more to me. You've helped me rebuild the city. Together, you and I have built something. This is a safe haven for every super alive because of the two of us, T."

I stood up. "Is that all?"

"No." She got to her feet. "During Stefano's trial, you told Scarletta that you were trying to save us *five*. She told you that there were only four of us. What did you mean?"

I let out a sigh. "I didn't know about the memories, so Tressa wasn't on my list. I wanted to save you, Scarletta, Kid, Stefano and..."

"Yeah?"

"And Fabian. He's not a bad guy, Aly. He's just a kid who was given a lot of power and not taught the responsibilities of the power."

"He killed a lot of people though."

"I saw it in a prophecy when you, Stefano, and Kid first came to the city." Aluminum thought about it. "Can I get the details to this 'prophecy'?"

"No, because you will know about it and be careful with every decision you make. It will alter the prophecy. I can only tell you that it's best that everyone is split up right now."

"Do you want to go back to The Instinctsion?"

I sat back down and admired the view for just a little longer. "Not yet." The mountain looked over a ravine hundreds of feet wide and thousands of feet deep. The waterfall that flowed around the city's platform turned to mist long before it reached the bottom of the ravine.

"Alright." Aluminum said as she sat back down next to me. "A little longer.

CHAPTER 32

# ALUMINUM

Running The Instinctsion was getting more and more stressful every day that went by. Everyone needed and wanted *something*. The hardest part was helping them decide which was more important. A need or a want.

That and I had noticed Titanium cutting herself off from everyone else. She felt the same way Stefano did when Jackson was in charge. She felt like she didn't belong.

She kept herself locked away because she was starting to hear Tressa's voice in her head. Tressa was coming back, and I didn't know if I completely wanted her to or not. She was gone, and the only thing left of her was her voice. We all heard it. We carried her straight to The Instinctsion when she died. Stefano, Kid, and I brought her back.

"Aluminum! Aluminum!" Cried a fire elemental girl as she ran into the main room of my tower. "Yes, Winter?" I sighed heavily.

"There's a person climbing the mountain!"

"What? That's impossible. We're thousands of feet up and in the center of a few hundred foot ravine."

"He's *really* strong!" "Fabian."

I phased through my tower window and safely glided to the ground and gathered everyone in the center of the city.

"I didn't think he would come. I need every super with super strength at the edge. If he climbs over the edge, knock him back over. I need water and ice together behind them. If he gets up, soak him, freeze him, and throw him over."

"He's getting closer!" "Weapons! Set up a blockage!"

Everyone stood in a formation with their weapons and powers at the ready.

Fabian climbed the edge and fought off the strong group. He was stronger than I had thought. He wore a gray cloak with an orange bit of fabric tied around his left bicep and a green bit of fabric on his right bicep.

His hood was covering his eyes even as he spun in the air and kicked the first line of defense. He quickly made it through them and was drenched in water.

Scorn, a water elemental, used her power and froze Fabian in place. I walked up to his frozen image. I motioned for the last of the fire elementals to come to me.

The girl, Winter, used her flame power and thawed out his head. I pulled back his hood and he gasped for air.

"Even though I got passed my group, I still say that they did the best." Kid said. He wriggled around and broke through the ice prison. Everyone hugged him. "If I say that I love you guys, will you continue to give me body heat?" Everyone laughed and hugged him harder.

"Where have you been?" I asked.

"Well I was trying to stop by The Instinctsion but for some reason, it wasn't where I had last left it."

"How did you find it?"

"It may have been over a year and a half ago but there's still a very heavy dirt trail leading here." Everyone looked around with worry. "Don't worry, guys. I covered the tracks." There were collective sighs of relief.

"Do you have any stories for us?" Asked one of the younger kids.

"Of course, I have stories. Later tonight I'll tell you all stories of my travels and how everyone is doing. Maybe even how my life as a scavenger is going. I'll tell it around the fire."

I watched him walk away with the city at his heels. They started to set up the fire area as the sun began to fall.

# CHAPTER 33

# KID

The sky had darkened, and the only light was that which was created by the girl with the ironic name. She lit the fire in the middle of the circle. Only faces were illuminated by its light.

"My journey started with my return to the rubble of MANDS." I waved my hands around for added effect. "Fabian searched for something that was deep inside the rubble. He had originally become a scavenger like me. I buried myself in the rubble and watched him frantically search; throwing *massive* chunks of concrete and metal like they were nothing.

"What was he looking for, Mr. Kid?"

"I thought he was looking for something to help his decreasing powers. But I was wrong. He was looking for a file. A file he was sent to find and return to Jonothan Industries. Stefano would say 'I told you so' but I think Jonothan Industries is against us. Whether it is or isn't, Scarletta is there. Jonothan holds her as his prized possession and he lets her boss people around. A *lot*. She's got a new power and it's gone to her head. Anyways, I snuck in and I took a few techs from JI for my new group and larger pieces of concrete from MANDS for temporary shelters."

"New group?"

"Yeah. Some of the people from the war weren't dead. Some were just unconscious, and some were in comas. I gathered them up and took them with me as I moved around. I've been out of the state and to the lower 48.

From there I went across the seas and to other continents. My scavenger group was too used to the cold that this state provides so we kept moving forward and eventually met back up here.

"Where else did you and your group go before you left Alaska?"

"My next journey was to the city. It took me a few months to find it and couple more months to find him."

"Find who?"

"Stefano of course. He is working in a warehouse taking out the trash and constantly sweeping. He's got a fake name. At first, I just hung around and studied his patterns. He's a lot more cautious than Fabian and Scarletta. More cautious than even you guys. When I finally had it down, and he attacked me, we spoke for a while and a portion of my group and I stayed with him in his apartment. Turns out he didn't want to destroy MANDS. He was trying to gather as much telekinetic power as he could so he could lift it and put it in the middle of the city, so he could expose MANDS. MANDS just ended up being bigger than any of us anticipated."

"And then where did you go?"

"Man. You guys want to skip all of the good parts, don't you? I left and then came back to see how things were going. I didn't know that Aluminum was in charge until I started climbing and heard battle commands being given."

Everyone laughed and started telling their own stories of the 'Attack on Kid' and didn't notice me sneak off. I walked over to Aluminum who was admiring the finally distracted Instinctsion.

"Did you finish your memories?" I asked her.

She reached into her pocket and revealed the remaining liquid. "Fifth of this disgusting stuff to go."

I reached into my pocket and revealed the same amount. "How much did Stefano drink?"

I looked away from the fire. I noticed that I was finally taller than Aluminum. "He didn't say."

"How's he doing now?" "He's being hunted." "By who?"

"JI."

# CHAPTER 34

# STEFANO

The warehouse door opened, and the black company van backed up. The van's back doors opened, and my boss stomped into the warehouse.

"Sean Wildee! Get this crap out of the van and put it away! You have 30 minutes!" He walked away and left me to unload the packed van.

I grabbed the first box (full of forks for some reason) and put it with the utensils that definitely didn't belong to us. I looked around for anyone that might be spying on me. I didn't see anyone.

I ran over to the television shelf and levitated the televisions from the van to the shelf. "Wildee!" I heard from outside of the warehouse.

I ran to the television and flew it into my arms. I dropped it into my arms and sidestepped to the television shelves.

"What did I tell you about visitors?!" My boss said with his arms crossed.

"That I can't have them until I get the job done, Sir," I replied as I heaved the television onto the shelf.

"Then who the hell is the kid in the office?" "No idea, Sir. Permission to go find out?"

"Granted. But you make it short and then get your ass back here and finish this!"

"Yes, Sir!" I ran out of the warehouse and ran to the office.

I opened the door and saw someone in a glowing white hoodie. He turned around and revealed his gray irises with white specs.

"I need you to come back with me." Said Fabian.

"You are so lucky that we are in the office of the place I work, or I would drop this building on your head faster than you can move into your stone form."

"It would be much better for you to do that than not coming with me."

He didn't sound like he was threatening me. Instead, he sounded scared. "Why?" "Scarletta."

"Oh. She finally got around to kicking you in the head? Good." "She's stronger than you think, Stefano-"

"Don't use that name!" I hissed quietly.

"She reminds me of it every chance she gets." "What are you even talking about?"

"She is second in command at Jonothan Industries and acts like she's some sort of queen."

"You're not making any sense."

"She beats the people who don't do as they are told or fail her. She beats them with her powers. She enjoys cutting off my limbs and watching them grow back. She enjoys watching people in pain and hearing them scream. She is a *witch* and she is hunting you guys."

"Why is she hunting *us?*"

"When she killed Jason and Harry-" "*You* made her do that!"

"When I made her kill them, something in her snapped. Ever since she has been hurting people and even killing them. Jonothan convinced her of something that my father said. Don't get me wrong, I still support my father. But she isn't the Scarletta you knew. She wants to kill The Instinctsion."

"Then it's your fault, Fabian! I don't know what I'm supposed to do about it!" I sighed and thought for a minute. "What happens if I do follow you?"

"I'm kind of hoping that you will take down Scarletta or at least *try.*" "And if I don't?"

"Then she will try to kill me, and I will fight back. If I lose, she's coming after you no matter what. If I succeed, I'm going to kill you. *Slowly.*"

"I'll get back to you on that one. You don't scare me, Fabian."

Fabian put his hood up and walked out of the building. I turned around to head back to the warehouse when the bell above the entrance door rang. I walked behind the counter and set up the high-tech register.

I looked up and saw a curly head of brown bouncing hair exploring the aisles of advanced technology. I found myself walking around the counter and walking down the same aisle as the customer. She was a woman with olive skin and bouncy brown curls. She wore a long coat that was dark green and leggings. She turned her head and looked at me. As she turned her head, her beautiful brown curls bounced off of her shoulders. One eye was blue and the other was brown. I had been studying her appearance for so long that I didn't notice she had asked me a question.

"What?" I asked. I could feel the blood rushing to my face.

"I said, Mr. Brown-eye-green-eye, do you think I should get this?" She held out a microchip in a plastic package. I could see her start to blush.

"You shouldn't get that one." I looked at the shelf of chips that allow a single individual to access their bank account, car and house with the chip that would be surgically inserted into their hand. "Actually, don't get the chip at all. It's painful to get inserted and it's always inserted below too much skin and the signal gets blocked. Not to mention the malfunction where it shocks the user."

"Then what would *you* get, brown-eye-green-eye?" She asked playfully and took a step closer. Her mismatched eyes sparkled.

"Your number," I said without thinking. What did I just say? She looked down and giggled. I figured I would just keep going with it. "What do you say, brown-eye-blue-eye?" She giggled again and took a step closer to me. She reached into my back pocket and pulled out my phone. She opened my contacts application and added herself.

"I say that you should pick me up when you get off." She slid the phone back into my pocket. We laughed.

"So, brown-eye-blue-eye, what do you want to get?" I asked to clear out the sudden silence that had moved in while we stared into each other's mismatched eyes.

"It's Wendy. And I don't really want to get anything. I just thought you were cute and wanted to talk to you." She spun around and started walking out the door. "Don't forget about me."

I went back behind the counter and rested my arms on the counter with a stupid smile on my face. I rolled up my sleeves and looked at my glowing veins. She was making me so nervous that I had started to rely on adrenaline and instinct. I reached into my pocket and pulled out the memory vial that I had been carrying around. Maybe if I drank it, I could remember something important about Scarletta that I had forgotten. Maybe if I drank it, it would allow me to remember everything I would need to remember about Wendy. In the future, I wouldn't want to forget about her.

There was only a sip taken out of the vial. I took another swig of it. The sour taste burned my tongue and then I remembered something that wouldn't help me, but I thought I would never remember...

My name.

# CHAPTER 35

# SCARLETTA

Fabian took a while to conform to my ways. To bend to my will. To do as I say. It took 6 months for him to listen. It took a full year for him to perform to my standard.

Fabian worked with Jonothan Industries underneath me. I stayed under Jonothan.

Jonothan Industries had taken a break from trying to make humans better. Jonothan gave up his brother's 50-year-old dream and stuck to evolving his technology. We put 'Better Tech in Every Step'. A motto that Jonothan had tried his best to live by. We made phones, shoes, hoodies, lights, security systems, smart house technology, computers, and so much more. But I didn't want to keep doing it.

Every day I could feel my powers growing stronger. I could feel a dangerous and painful urge to use them to their maximum potential. Fabian made for a perfect practice dummy, but it wasn't enough. Not for me.

A knock came from the office door and Jonothan walked into his office and sat in his leather across from me. He opened a file that he came in with and read the report to me.

"You've done great, Scarletta. We've sold 500 phones, 300 pairs of anti-gravity shoes, 610 television networks-"

"Why can't I get into the vault?" I asked.

"What do you mean?"

"The vault. I can't get in. What's in it?"

"There's very delicate things in there, Scarletta dear. You're not ready for it." "I'm not ready? I'm not *ready*?"

Fabian knocked and opened the door to the office. "Scarletta, I wish to report-" I turned around. "Where is he?"

"That's what I wanted to tell you. He-"

I stood up and opened my dagger into a sword and swung it as fast as I could. Fabian's hand fell to the floor. I used a gust of telekinesis and pushed Fabian as hard as I could out of the office. He flew into the corner of the hallway. The thick metal infused concrete broke as his body hit it. He fell to the ground. I turned back towards Jonothan.

"Does *that* look like I'm not ready?" I walked over to Jonothan with my sword pointed towards him. "There's still a lot you haven't told me. I saw the file with a big 'S' on it. I saw the journal in your desk. I saw how you watched the war. I want answers."

We were both standing and circling his desk. We kept the same distance and soon I ended up where Jonothan had sat. "What do you want to know?" Jonothan asked.

I thought of the question that had been bother me for 18 months. "What happened to my memory vial?"

Jonothan sat back down but in the chair opposite his leather one. "You never told me that you got it. Well, Fabian had a sip from all the vials. Then I poured out a third and gave what was left, the juicy stuff, to the one who I thought needed it the most. The one who has gone 50 years with nothing more than what we told her. I gave it to S. She drank some and poured out the rest."

"Who is S?"

"The Scar Origins needed to start *somewhere*. She actually has an ability. Extraordinary things that others can't do. More than a simple magician. She's a witch."

I couldn't think of anything else to say.

"Anything else you would like to know?" Jonothan asked.

"No but there is a power I want that I don't have." I said quietly and calmly. "And what power is that?"

"Jonothan Industries." I slowly pushed my sword through Jonothan's chest. He didn't scream or cry out. He just smiled and closed his eyes. His head fell, and a tear escaped from the corner of his eye.

<T1 A2 S3 K4 S5>

The chair was facing the high-tech window that looked over the rubble of the old MANDS tower. The rubble was being corrupted by moss and grass and few vines. Fabian walked into the office and sat down in the chair in front of the desk. "Jonothan?"

"Yes?" Came Jonothan's voice.

"Scarletta is out of control and I know you won't agree." "Agree with what?"

"I want to fight her. Not just me. I want to bring MANDS back to its feet and stand against her. I'm sick of being kicked around by her."

"What are you asking, Fabian?" "Uncle...I'm not asking for much." "What *are* you asking for then?" "All I'm asking for is a quarter."

"Oh, Fabian." Said Jonothan's voice. The chair swiveled around. "You are so much like your father." Jonothan's voice got higher until it returned back my voice.

"...Scarletta?"

## About the Author:

Stefan G. Johnson was born October 8th of 1998 and raised in Anchorage, Alaska where he attended Dimond High School up until 2017 when he joined the U.S. Army and left for BCT. After BCT and AIT he continued his six-year-old dream to finish the first book of his carefully planned trilogy. He built the characters with his sister and two cousins. Their plan six years ago was to make a movie of Instincts.

## SUMMARY

The government has activated a company called MANDS; a company that plans to replace all armies with genetically engineered children. The plan is to start immediately after they pass the test. But what if they never get that far? And what happens if that was intended?

Printed in the United States
By Bookmasters